WEAVING WHISPERED SECRETS

THE ERASEHER SERIES BOOK FOUR

SARA NICHOL QUINCY

First published by Milcann Hunnee 2022

This novel is entirely a work of fiction. The names, characters and incidents portrayed in it are the work of the author's imagination. Any resemblance to actual persons, living or dead, events or localities is entirely coincidental.

Sara Nichol Quincy asserts the moral right to be identified as the author of this work.

Sara Nichol Quincy has no responsibility for the persistence or accuracy of URLs for external or third-party Internet Websites referred to in this publication and does not guarantee that any content on such Websites is, or will remain, accurate or appropriate.

ISBN: 978-1-957719-06-1 (Epub)

ISBN: 978-1-957719–07-8 (Paperback)

ISBN: 978-1-957719-13-9 (Hardcover)

SaraNicholQuincy.com

MILCANN HUNNEE
PUBLISHING COMPANY

For Phoenix

The scared little girl that I locked up in a dark place in my mind for so many years because I thought I hated you and that you would never be good enough. I was wrong; you've achieved more than I could have ever imagined and I'm sorry. You are enough; you have always been. This is for you beautiful, be free. I'm proud of you!

CONTENTS

I

SHALLOW PROMISES

"Jacob Adrian Miles, Jacob Adrian Miles, Jacob Adrian Miles… Jacob Adrian Miles…"

"Eva?" a man's voice called from outside the room I was in. "You awake?"

Jacob Adrian Miles, nothing else matters. Don't forget that name! "Jacob Adrian Miles," I continued, chanting it to myself quietly.

"Oh hey, you *are* awake," Reagan opened the door, peeked his head in then walked into the room. "You're looking pretty good for being asleep for so long. What do you remember?"

"Nothing…"

"Okay, Eva, I'm not stupid… I know you remember more than that." He wasn't so easily convinced. "I gave you the antidote shot as soon as we got here. It's been over half an hour now. You're telling me it hasn't started to work at all yet?"

"I'm telling you the truth. The only things I know are what you told me when I first woke up. That's it."

"Eva, I'm on your side… Stop lying to me."

"What did you say my name was again?" The name didn't sound familiar. It should sound familiar if it really was my name.

He sat on a table next to the door and sighed then leaned back against the wall, figuring we'd be talking for a while. "It's Eva… Well, that's one of them… Is that your problem? Did I not give you the name that went with your first memory of me? This antidote part is a bit tricky, I'll admit, but still… you have to remember more than you're letting on."

"What are the others?"

"You're telling me you don't remember any of your names?"

"Reagan, you cooperate, I'll cooperate."

He smiled as he squinted his eyes, "Hmm… I think I've underestimated you, Eva… I haven't seen you in a few years, and honestly I think I forgot how conniving you really were. You remember everything don't you?"

"I know what you want from me. I'm not dumb either. So… if you want me to talk, you're going to talk first. List my names, now!"

He seemed more relaxed than I suspected he should. "Forgive me if I act a bit confused, but… I mean, I've never been through this process… from your side, that is. So… ah, if you remember everything, why do you need me to tell you who you are?" He shifted himself a little on the table to get more comfortable.

"You're right. I don't need anything from you. You need something from me… and we both know what that means… You're going to answer any question I give you to my satisfaction. Then and only then will we discuss Marcus and the intel."

"Hmm," He grinned as he squinted one eye and tilted his head, "I don't get where you're coming from but fine… I don't guess it'd hurt anything. Elliceva, Jordan Ellice Eva and Jayde." He listed them slowly but not like he didn't remember.

"Who called me Jayde?" I could remember the others but I was still having trouble with that one.

"No one… Marcus and I were the only two who knew that was your real name." He said, looking genuinely confused by what I was doing.

I couldn't remember as much as I wanted, but knew he wouldn't tell me the truth to fill in the blanks if he saw that was the case. I had to make him believe I remembered it all, and the questions were solely to corroborate his side with my memories.

"Go on…" I wanted him to tell me as much as he could.

"Going into the espionage program, you made an alias just like we all did. So of course in the system you have your technical name," he used air quotes when he said it, "which was Jordan Ellice Eva. Then you had your exfil name. You know, the one you use if you're caught and in danger and you need help—Elliceva. Then your real one—Jayde. You only told us because we were all close. I promised I wouldn't tell anyone and I know Marcus wouldn't ever either. You never gave us your real last name though, so…" He ended it with a shrug.

"Exfil name… that's how you found me…" As more memories rushed in, more things began to make sense.

"Yeah, I was honestly pretty shocked. I mean it's been almost 5 years that we've been looking for you. So… you should have seen my face when your exfil name actually popped up in the system. I know I made fun of you when you first told me what it was. I thought it sounded… well, weird. But I'm not too proud to admit you were right. You said the weirder the better, for an exfil name anyway."

"I did." I was agreeing, although I really had no recollection of the event yet.

"How many times have you been erased?" He asked, assuming it was his turn, but it wasn't.

"I'm not done." He smiled and rolled his eyes after I said it. I went on, "Marcus… What do you know about Marcus?"

He suddenly lost his smile and started to look away, but quickly brought his eyes back to mine. "You're telling me you don't remember Marcus?" He sounded like that would be a hard one for him to accept.

"No, I never said that. Answer the question." I actually did remember Marcus and what I did to him but I wanted to know if he knew what I had done. It was hard for me to ask about him, but I knew I couldn't show any of the emotions I was feeling.

"Ok, well… I don't know what you remember but he was my younger brother." He smiled as he began to reminisce. "He was a pain in the ass, you know… That's why I thought it was great that he initially paired up with you. You two were made for each other." His smile disappeared again as he went on. "But honestly, Eva, that's one of the reasons I wanted to find you so badly. His tracking signal went out around the same time yours did. We haven't been able to track him… I was hoping you could help me find him."

As soon as he said it, more memories of the two of them came flooding in. They were more than brothers; they were best friends, cohorts… 'In it 'til the end,' they would always say. I didn't know what to tell him. I knew where Marcus was but I knew giving him that information wouldn't benefit me. There was no waffling on what I should do. I needed to lie. "I'm sorry, I don't know where he's at."

He stared at me for a second, gauging if I was lying then silently nodded as he looked down. "You know what will happen to you if you're lying, right?" His friendly demeanor quickly went sour for a moment.

"Why do you feel like you have to threaten me, Reagan? You know I loved him more than anything else in life. I want to find him, too." I said, furrowing my brows.

"Loved? You don't now?" His face looked suspicious. "You told me you loved that Coddy that I shot in New York too. You're making yourself look awfully suspicious… How do I know you're not a double agent?"

"You're an idiot if you believe that shit." I was surprised at how easy it was for me to deflect. Having my full memory of Eva returning was quite useful. "For one thing, that's insulting to Marcus if you think I could hide being a double from him the entire time we were together. He's a brilliant man. He'd have caught that shit early on and had me hung, whether he loved me or not and you know it! Secondly, if I *was* a double, you can bet your ass that you would have never been able to find me in New York. That wouldn't even make sense, Reagan, and you know it." I was getting a bit heated as I said it, but didn't stop myself. I knew the passion in my voice would help convince him that I was telling the truth even though I wasn't.

His face changed to look solemn, accepting the scolding and

willing to move on. "Fine. You make a fair point. The way he loved you… You're right, he'd have known."

"Good… We're in agreement then. We look for him… together. That's what I want too! But first you have more questions to answer."

"You know that's not the way this is supposed to work, right? I'm supposed to be the one interrogating you."

"Reagan, do you want my help or not?"

He didn't say anything, he just nodded.

"About six or seven months ago, when my tracker came back online, who sent the two agents to retrieve me?"

"Parker…" He said it matter-of-factly, not trying to hide anything. "Your tracker came back on when you were at a Coldier base, mind you. So naturally, she assumed you were a double… you can't be mad at her." He said, then leaned forward, resting his elbows on his thighs. "Now, you want to tell me what you were doing at that base… and better yet, what happened to those men?"

I didn't change my face when he asked; I left it without expression. "I killed them…" I said it unapologetically.

"What?" He scoffed, surprised, though I suspected it was at my honesty, not the fact that I could do such a thing.

"They said they suspected I was a double… then like idiots they tied me up and started beating me and told me they brought serum to erase me… That was the first I had ever heard of the Sicari having a serum, so I had no idea it wasn't like the Coldiers'. I had to kill them. I thought they were about to erase my memory. I couldn't allow it. You know Marcus would have done the same!"

"I'd love to believe you, Eva, but things don't line up." He said, leaning back again. "If you want my help when you report to Parker on where you've been the last five years, you're going to have to start being honest with me."

"Is Parker who sent you to find me in New York?" I started scanning the room after I asked. Just in case he got any ideas and thought he needed to detain me, I wanted to be aware of my surroundings.

"She is…"

"Well, does she still suspect I'm a double?"

"She does…"

"Then why haven't you detained me yet?"

"Parker sent me with her orders. She said I was to bring you back to report. She wants the intel, that's obvious. But… to be honest, I don't give a shit about the intel. I need you to help me find Marcus. She won't let me do any searches unless his tracker comes back online like yours did."

"Interesting…" It was all beginning to click. "Well, how am I supposed to prove to her that I'm not a double? 'Cause you realize, if I can't do that, then I won't be able to help you find *anybody* if they decommission me."

"They won't decommission you even if you are."

"What?" That didn't sound right, but he didn't look like he was lying either.

"You're the last Gypsyin, Eva. Your whole unit has either been decommissioned or lost. That's why I told you that you were of more value than the intel. Parker might suspect you're a double but she doesn't really want to believe it. She has plans for you… once you give her the intel she already told me of two other missions she wants to send us on."

"Us?" It'd been a long time since I'd been on a mission. I had too much running around in my head at that point to think of doing anything for anybody except myself.

"Right, with Marcus missing, I'm your superior now."

"But you're not gonna take me on her mission, are you?" I was beginning to figure it out. "You're gonna take me back to the last place I saw Marcus."

He nodded, keeping his face serious. I think he knew what he was admitting to was beyond mutinous. "Now… you want to tell me where that was?"

"Don't insult me, Reagan, you know I'm not that dumb." That information was leverage, something I wasn't about to give up without being free again.

"Eva… If we're going to have a working relationship, you're going to need to obey orders."

"Ha…" I laughed, "You can say you're my superior all you want but I've been free long enough. I don't really feel like working anymore. Get me?"

He looked confused, "It doesn't work like that… You're an agent… You signed up, you do the job, you follow orders. That's the deal. There's no such thing as a free agent."

"That's nice, but see this right here?" I lifted my arm and pulled up my sleeve so he could see it didn't have a tag. "This right here says I'm a Gypsyin, not a Sicari… So…" I shrugged, "I'm pretty sure Gypsyins are free people."

"Do you even realize what you're saying?" He acted perturbed that I would even suggest such a thing.

"Oh, shut up, Reagan. You can't act all high and mighty when you just said you plan on disobeying our commanding officer's orders. Look, you want what you want, and I want what I want. We can both have it if we work together. Deal?"

He didn't say anything he just stared at me, thinking, then slowly let his eyes drift away and down toward the floor. After a moment, he finally brought them back and began to speak. "I can't agree to anything if I can't trust you. How do I know you're the same Eva that I knew five years ago? That's a long time, a lot of things could have changed. Plus, you haven't told me anything yet about how you got erased, then un-erased, then erased again. It doesn't make any sense."

I remembered everything at that point, but knew I couldn't mention anything about Jake to him. If he knew I was with another man, there would be no way to convince him that Marcus was still alive and find-able. "I understand, but how am I supposed to believe anything that you're telling *me*?"

He nodded like I made a valid point. "Okay… then promise me."

Oh shit, I thought. He remembered I didn't make promises I can't keep. The idea of changing that suddenly crossed my mind, but it was a difficult one considering I hadn't broken one yet that I knew of. "Promise what?" I asked, hoping it would be something vague and easy to keep.

"Promise me that you really do still love him and that when we find him, he's who you intend to be with."

"Reagan…" It wasn't hard, considering I knew that wasn't going to happen. "I promise, I love him. He was the only Sicari I've ever been with and the only Sicari, Gypsyin, whatever… I ever would want to be with. The day we find him will be the best day of my life. Wherever he's been and whatever he's been doing, if he will still have me, I will be with him and no one else. Is that what you wanted to hear? Is that enough?"

He nodded with a hopeful smile, "He loved you, Eva." He said with a sincere look. I could tell he felt emotional. His voice sounded like it was higher. "I don't think you even knew how much he loved you. The last time I saw him, he was considering running away with you. He told me he thought you were pregnant…" He paused as he started to tear up, "I just want to find him… you know?"

I started to tear up as well the more he talked. I could feel the pain in his voice, the sorrow he was carrying not knowing what happened. "I know…" I whispered as a tear rolled down my cheek. Even though I knew the truth, the tears were real. "I miss him too, Reagan. I promise you I do." I paused and thought about if I should address the pregnancy. I knew what had happened, but I didn't know if I wanted to mention it to him or not. "I thought I was pregnant, but I wasn't sure, you know?… If I was, I lost it. When we got split up, it was too much…" I was still crying, but I didn't say any more. I didn't want to lie to him any more than I had to.

"Okay…" He said sliding off the table then looking down at me. "I'll leave you alone now, I guess. First thing tomorrow morning you see Parker, so for right now you should try to rest. Get some sleep. Since I'm your superior now, I'll be in the room with you when you report to her, so I'll try to help things go in your favor but I can't make any promises."

I nodded. I didn't need any promises from him though, since I realized I could take care of myself just fine. "Is she still as sweet and patient as she was five years ago?" I asked, being sarcastic.

"You know it…" He said, half-smiling as he looked down. "Oh, I should warn you about one thing, though. Since Marcus is missing and she knows you're the only one with knowledge of the intel, she said she plans to extract it from you tomorrow. She doesn't want anything to happen and possibly lose it again."

"Extract it? What the hell is that supposed to mean?"

"Well, I don't want to scare you but they developed a new serum a few months ago. Apparently, it's been in the works for a while. She said she would use it on you if she needed to."

I didn't know if he was being serious or if he was making shit up to throw me off. "What does it do?" I hoped if he was serious, then he would give me as much information about it as he had so I knew what I was up against.

"Ha... Well, it's supposed to be a truth serum but..." he shrugged, "they only used it once before and that guy died... They went back to the drawing bored after that and have tweaked it a little, maybe it works now... but honestly, I don't know."

"Oh, really?" I still wasn't sure if I should be suspicious or not. "I thought you said I was valuable since I was the last Gypsyin?"

"I meant it, but you know Parker well enough to remember she's kinda crazy, too. I'm pretty sure she's Bipolar... One minute she wants you, the next, the intel is more important. I don't know... and to be honest, it's only gotten worse the last five years. But... like I said, I'll do whatever I can to spot ya in there, k?" He probably thought that was more comforting than it actually was.

"Yeah, whatever..." I was over him and liked the idea of him leaving like he said he would.

"I'll wake you in the morning." He walked over to the door and flipped the light out, then turned to shut the door behind him.

"Not if I have anything to do with it," I whispered to myself as I lay back down on the cot. Resting was actually the last thing I planned on doing. Now that I had a head full of useful memories, I planned on doing whatever I needed to devise a plan to escape as soon as I got a chance. I knew Jake wouldn't be able to find me and it'd be dangerous if he even tried so I needed to get back to him before he had a chance to get to me.

2

LAND OF THE PEASANTS

"Why are you doing this... Jacob... Answer me!" I didn't know if I should fight him or relent. If he wasn't actually on my side, I had nothing to live for so I might as well give up and let him take me.

"Don't fight me, Jayde, please... Just let me cuff you." His voice had no remorse.

"Have you been planning this... Is this what you wanted with me this whole time?" I didn't fight him. I gave in and let him cuff me.

"It's a long game, *Eva*, you know that! That's why you lied to me about who you really were the entire time you had your memory back."

"I didn't lie to you... You knew I was a Sicari... and I did love you. I still do..."

"I can't believe anything you say... if you're willing to kill the man you loved to keep the intel safe, then do you really expect me to believe you wouldn't pretend to love me for the same reason?" He spun me around to look at him when he finished with the cuffs.

'It's a long game...' I thought about what he had said. "So you never loved me... It *was* all just so you could get the intel from me to give to Miller..." I was talking out loud more to myself than him. It started to sink in... It *was* all a big game of chess and now he'd finally

won. I had let my guard down just like Miller had planned and let myself believe in love again and it finally came back to stab me in the back.

"That's correct. When Miller told me who you really were, it was an easy decision. I'm loyal to him, not your father." Jake said, taking a hold of my arm with one hand and pushing against my shoulder with his other, forcing me to sit on the ground next to his truck.

"Who I really am?" I said it under my breath. "So you knew? This whole time you knew?" I asked, looking up at him.

"Of course I knew… Miller told me you were Jayde Prescott when he sent me out to capture you."

I didn't respond. I was done talking to him. I'd never felt that kind of pain before. Not only was it like my heart was shattered but it was also an extreme anger with myself. I knew I was better than that. I knew I shouldn't trust anyone, especially any Coldier that wasn't my family. The feeling that I had let my father down was hard as well. That's the last thing I wanted to do.

"I just have one question for you, Jayde…" He didn't even look at me as he asked it, he just continued doing something in the backseat of the truck. "Did Marcus really ask you to kill him or did you just do it so you'd have the intel all to yourself and not have to share it with the Sicari?"

"You don't know anything, Jacob…" I said, disgusted with him. I knew the truth, and I didn't need to answer shit for him. I only did what I did to Marcus because I really loved him and he asked me to.

"I know enough, *Jayde*… You know that's the problem with playing both sides… if you're loyal to one, you're a traitor to the other… you can't have both!"

"Go to hell!" I never thought I could say those words to him before and actually mean it.

"Well, we should be in Nashville by morning… when I hand your ass over to Miller, you can tell me later what hell feels like. Now get in!"

. . .

I woke from the dream hyperventilating. It didn't help that I had part of the blanket shoved in my mouth just in case Reagan decided to listen for me to talk in my sleep. I realized it must have been early since the lights were still out and Reagan hadn't come to wake me yet. I took a few deep breaths to get myself to calm down as I lay back down against my pillow. The dream felt so real, I could feel a buzz from the adrenaline rush.

"Holy shit... Who am I?" I lay there and thought about the dream and the memories from my past that had returned. I was trying to piece it all together; trying to remember what I had done, who I actually was, what I really felt about who, and what they likely felt back.

"Am I... No... Oh my gosh..." Even though I had all the memories, without sifting through them I hadn't realized yet who I really was and what I was doing. I was loyal, but I wasn't as well. I was honest, but I had also lied so many times.

There was love for Jake, a real love that I felt. That wasn't a lie. The dream, though... it felt so real. I couldn't help but wonder how realistic it was. *Could he really have been lying to me this entire time? Was he really in with Miller?*

"Mustache man... Oh my gosh. Miller is Mustache man." I whispered to myself.

Just because I had my memories back didn't mean everything all-of-a-sudden made sense. I still needed time. I needed to piece everything together to really know what had happened. It was like every time I was erased I had lost pieces of my puzzle, but now having them back didn't mean I saw the bigger picture, it just meant I had a pile of puzzle pieces. I still needed to put all those pieces back where they went. Only then would I understand it, see it, and know what to do with it.

I hadn't been laying there for very long when I saw shadows in the light under the door. I quickly closed my eyes and decided I would pretend to still be asleep. I needed to see how well I could trust Reagan. To do that, I needed to find out how well he trusted me first. I heard the door open, but it wasn't loud. I didn't see any light coming through my eyelids so I got the idea he didn't turn it on. Then I heard the door click like he had closed it again. *What is he doing?*

I let my eyelids raise just enough to peek through my lashes. I could see he'd walked over to the cot and was standing over me. At that moment, I realized he didn't have the same good intentions that he had led me to believe he had the night before. I didn't care what his plans were anymore; I wasn't going to allow myself to be at his mercy. I didn't hesitate to act.

In one fluid, lightening-fast movement, I rolled out of the cot and onto my feet, then spun around him, putting me at his back. I took him so completely off guard that he was still staring at the empty cot when I attacked.

"Eva!" He'd caught on finally but it was too late. I wrapped one arm around his neck. Putting one knee in his back, I bent him backward and locked my other arm, creating a choke hold. I had him and we both knew it. He tried to tap on my arms but I wasn't going to release him, not that soon.

"What do you think you're doing, Reagan? Think you can sneak up on me?" I said, pulling him over toward the door. He tried to spin out of it but each time he tried to turn, I dug in harder, making it more difficult for him to breathe. He tapped on my arm again, requesting a release.

"I'll let you go if you promise not to pull this shit again!" I felt superior for once and I liked it.

He tapped again, but in a sequence that I understood was yes. I let go as I kept myself facing him, but reached behind me to feel for the switch to flip the lights on.

"Eva... you..." it was hard for him to speak. I must have had him tighter than I realized. "You little shit... what... ugh... What the hell was that for?" He was bent over with one hand on his knee, now rubbing his neck with his other hand. He slowly stood upright and moved backward as he looked at me, then sat down on the cot.

"That felt good..." I couldn't help but grin. It was nice having my full memory of fighting back as well. I liked that I could defend myself and didn't need anyone's help anymore.

"I can't believe you," he said, sounding horse.

"Bullshit, nice try making me the bad guy. You should have announced yourself. What did you expect sneaking in here and standing over me in the dark? You think I'm just gonna let you—"

"What?" He interrupted me, "What do you think I was going to do to you?"

"I don't know… I can't read your perverted little mind. You men… I swear you're all the same." I didn't know why I said it but it felt right. I suspected all my memories of what the different random men had done to me were joining forces. So many times they took me and used me, abused me, and I was over it. I'd decided I wouldn't have any more of it, starting now.

"Look, I don't know what's happened to you the last five years, but you're wrong…" His voice sounded like it was coming back. "I wasn't going to do anything to you, gosh… I just didn't want to wake you with the light. I thought it would be a hard on your eyes."

I squinted at him like I was suspicious of what he was saying. That sounded too kind of him. *That's not the Reagan I remember*. I wasn't buying it. "Yeah, okay… whatever."

"Well, this wasn't pleasant, but at least I can say I think the real Eva is back. Whoever that person in New York was trying to save a Coddy wasn't the Eva I knew at all. That alone was enough for me to see you'd been erased." He said as he stretched his neck to one side, then the other, before standing back up.

I squinted again as I thought about what he had said while trying to find the memories to support his statement. The more I thought about it the more I saw he was right. I did hate Coddy's, or so I had made people believe, anyway. I knew the truth; it was an act, one that I apparently got pretty good at.

"You're right," I said, thinking it would be best to return myself to the same character he had previously known as Eva. "They brainwashed me… that's what they do though. They take them as slaves… filthy Coddy bastards." I meant it mostly. I hated what they were doing with Gypsyins. It wasn't right. Deep down though, I knew it wasn't every Coldier that was that way. There was still Jake and

Lane; they were different. I hoped my father was too, but I didn't know.

"Eva?" He said looking at me. He'd caught that I started to stare off. "You okay?"

"Yeah, I'm fine… Why?"

"Look, I know we've had a rocky past. Honestly, you never really acted like you liked me, and I can understand that. But we're gonna have to work together now, so… you need to trust me."

"Nice speech, Reagan, but you get what you earn. You want my trust? Get me through the report with Parker without her extracting shit, and I'll think about it. How's that sound?"

He smiled, "Yep… same Eva…" He moved past me to open the door. "Come on, let's go. She's waiting."

I followed him through the door and down a hall. As we walked out of the room, I recognized where we were. I'd been there many times before. We were inside the Praetorium. It was the main headquarters of the Sicari, the only place that strategic operations were conducted from. Such operations were the only kind that my Gypsyin unit was involved in.

If things hadn't changed, it was the only place the Sicari had electricity. Unlike the Coldiers who were able to keep themselves sustained nicely, most of the Sicari towns couldn't. Because of that, most had resorted to living like people did two hundred years ago. They rode horses to go from place to place, used candles for light, outhouses as their bathrooms, and so many other things I couldn't list them all. Essentially, living in New York with Jake had made me feel like I was royalty and now being back with the Sicari was like returning to the land of the peasants.

I knew where Reagan was taking me. Parker had a detainment room she liked to pretend was a report room, but she was smart and knew to think ahead in case agents didn't want to cooperate. I'd been in there many times with Marcus. After each mission, we would sit and tell her where we'd been, what we'd done, who we'd talked to, and so forth.

The last time I was there was after I told Marcus I wanted to run away with him. I remember being nervous and hoping he didn't report me for making the suggestion that we become deserters. I did love him but that wasn't why I suggested he leave with me. I was compromised. I wasn't supposed to fall in love with him. Our relationship started as a ruse and in the beginning was perfect for my deep cover but it backfired, and I got in too deep.

I knew we were going to have the intel within that week, and I didn't want it. Once I had the intel, my real mission started; get it back to my father. I loved Marcus too much, though. I didn't want to do it anymore. I knew the intel would break us, and it did, worse than I had even imagined it could.

"Eva!" Parker was standing at the end of the hall outside her office. "I'm happy you're back. Reagan has done a great job retrieving you," she said, looking from me back to him as she smiled. Her demeanor was oddly much more friendly than I remember it ever being. She looked the same as I remembered her, though. She was short and stout, quite muscular for a woman. Her hair was still short, black, coarse, and tightly coiled, her signature look. It blended in nicely with her smooth, ebony skin. She was wearing the same uniform all Sicari wore— whatever they wanted.

"Nice to see you too, Parker." I wasn't exactly enthused, and I'm sure they could both hear it in my voice.

With a forced smile still on her face, she walked inside the room with me and Reagan both following right behind her. "Please, have a seat." She said as she pointed to one of the two chairs across a table opposite hers. "I know it's been a while and you have a ton you need to tell me, so I brought in breakfast for you." She smiled again as she referred to a couple of dainty dishes sitting on the table. One had a piece of cooked meat with a little loaf of some sort of bread and the other had a hard-boiled egg with the same bread.

"You're too kind." I was already in a shitty mood and wasn't really feeling like being there. Not to mention, I wasn't happy with my predicament as far as the intel was concerned and her fake smiles weren't helping things, either. Plus, whatever she considered breakfast didn't look appetizing or filling.

"No orange juice?" Reagan joked as he sat down next to me and took the plate with the egg.

"Not today, sorry." She half-smiled, then pulled a thick file out from her desk drawer and set it down in front of her. It was bigger than I remembered it had been. "All right, Eva… Let's get started."

I thought it was cute that she expected me to go right back into agent mode after I was brought back in. That wasn't my plan nor my intention, however. "I have to pee." I really meant it, but thought it would be a perfect opportunity to stall as well.

She frowned, then brought the end of her pen down and started gently tapping it against the table while she thought. "Fine," she said finally. "Follow her, Reagan."

"What?" I acted upset that she would even suggest that I needed an escort. "Why? Gosh, Parker, I'm not going to try to escape…"

She smirked and looked at me, tilting her head down a little like she knew I was full of shit. "You heard me," she said, taking the pen and waving it toward the door for both of us to proceed as she agreed.

"I won't watch. Let's go, Eva…" Reagan said as he got up out of his chair and walked toward the door.

I rolled my eyes, then followed him until we were out in the hall. I remembered the bathroom was down the hall at the end to the left so I quickly walked past Reagan toward it. "Don't try anything, Eva. This can go smoothly if you just let it." He said, stopping short of the door as I opened it.

"You're right, Reagan, because if you want what you want, you're gonna be the one to do all the talking." I smirked. "Now, if you're not sure how you're gonna do it, I'll give you a good five minutes while I'm in here for you to figure it out." I turned and went into the bathroom then shut the door behind me.

If they thought I was going to try to escape, they were both idiots. I knew better than to attempt such a feat from the Praetorium, mid morning no less. If it was anything like I remembered, it was on heavy guard 24-7, so trying to leave on my own would be just as stupid as if someone tried to break in.

My plan was simple: make Reagan do all the hard work and ride his coattails. I meant it when I said Marcus was brilliant, but Reagan was just as brilliant. I knew if he wanted what he did as bad as he said he did, then he would come up with a plan to get us both out and in the field in no time.

It only took me three years, but I learned how to mentally out maneuver both him and Marcus. I slowly learned what each of them wanted and held dearest. Then that is what I used against them. For Marcus, it was my love and loyalty, which honestly was to my own downfall. That wasn't the case with Reagan. He didn't need the same things Marcus did. What Reagan needed was to be the best. He didn't care to have a family, a spouse, affection, love, or anything you'd think a man would want. He was the ultimate sportsman. Everything was a challenge for him, but he took it to almost obsessive levels when his opponent was Marcus.

Without his brother, he was nothing, and I'm sure his life was miserable now. Everything was always a challenge between them; who was best at what. Who completed more missions, who shot more of the enemy, who would be promoted higher than the other. I think that's why he didn't want me that day at the academy hall. He didn't see me as an asset. He saw my mouth as a stumbling block, a liability… a sabotage he would happily hand over to his brother so he could get ahead. The more I thought about it, the more I figured maybe he was right after all… because he was still standing here, alive and well and Marcus wasn't.

3
WHO'S A DOUBLE?

My plan went better than I had ever expected it would. Reagan must have taken me seriously because when we returned to Parker's office, he didn't hesitate to jump right in with a series of lies he'd fabricated for me all on his own.

"That's it, that's all?" If Parker's face was showing any emotion, it was suspicion, sheer suspicion. She didn't believe him, and it was obvious.

I thought it was funny and was eager to see what else Reagan came up with. I never saw Marcus try to lie like that, and definitely didn't remember Reagan being the type—quite the opposite, really. Both of them would about throw their mother in front of a bus before they would resort to something so atrocious as lying to a commanding officer.

"You know I wouldn't lie to you, Parker. I'm vouching for her because I believe everything she's told me. She never had the intel. Marcus did, and that's why you need to send us both out to retrieve him. She knows where he was last. The last thing you want is for that intel to get into the hands of the Coldiers..." The way he spoke sounded fluid and sincere even though I knew he wasn't. I took a mental note at that moment of how good he was at being believable, even when I knew he was lying straight to her face. If he was that good at manipulating her, I couldn't trust him. He'd do the same to me in a heartbeat, I was sure of it.

He's not who he's pretending to be. He's not this nice of a guy. I reminded myself. *He'll manipulate me to get what he wants, too. I doubt he's changed. I'm sure he's still the same asshole he was five years ago.*

Parker looked away from him to me, "What was your relationship with Marcus, Eva?" she asked bluntly, not even pretending to hold her cards. "He asked to keep you assigned to him three separate times… except the last time… The last time you were here he told me he didn't want you assigned to him anymore. Why was that?"

I wasn't sure if she was bluffing or if she was being honest. I had no idea what she was talking about, but was having trouble not letting the shock show on my face. I knew we'd had an argument the day before our last report prior to us leaving for Knoxville, but I'd have never thought he wouldn't have wanted me to be reassigned to him again. "I… um…" I felt so blind-sided I didn't know what to say. I didn't know if I should tell her what we really were to each other, even though it was against the rules, or to just keep lying like we'd been doing.

"They made the best espionage team I've ever seen," Reagan jumped in to help me. "I can assure you, that's all they were. Marcus was nothing but professional; he knew better than to have a relationship with a fellow agent."

Parker leaned back against her chair like she'd heard enough as she looked at him, then me, then back to him. "Well… this isn't what I was expecting to hear today… I'm disappointed…"

"I can't tell you want I don't know." I said apologetically. All I could really think of though, was how fast I could get out of that room and as far away from the Praetorium as possible.

"Fine… Reagan, I'm sure this will make you happy. Your next mission is to go and find your brother. As for you Eva, I'm going to partner you with—"

"She's not going with me?" Reagan interrupted her. He didn't seem happy. It was quite bold of him to question our CO like that.

"If you were in my shoes, Reagan, do you think it would be smart to send Marcus' brother and his ex-girlfriend both after the man that *they* claim is the only one with the intel? Or… since I don't trust Eva one cent yet, do you think it might be better to pair her with someone I know will keep better track of her? You know… just in case you're both lying to me." She crinkled her face up after she said it. Apparently, she wasn't as gullible as Reagan thought she was.

"I'm not his ex-girlfriend." Hearing her call me that hurt. Even if he was dead and we weren't technically still together, the fact that she didn't know that and still insinuated that I was an ex meant something. Not only had she strongly suspected that we were together but then now she had a reason to suspect he'd broken up with me before he died. *Why would she think he'd broken up with me?*

"Eva, please," Reagan stopped me from saying anything else. He probably knew it wouldn't be helpful for me to go on, either. "Parker, I'm begging you. She's the only one who knows him as well as I do. Plus, she can take me back to the exact location where they got split up… If you want your intel, I don't think it's a good idea to not let me take her to look for him."

"Have you thought about what if she does have the intel and Marcus is actually dead? What then, Reagan?" She was talking about me like I wasn't even in the room and it was beginning to tick me off, even if she was right.

"I don't!" I said vehemently. "If I had the intel, you'd know it. I would have given it to you already. There's no reason I would have held onto it this whole time for nothing. *And* if it's as amazing as you said it is, if I already gave it to the Coldiers, wouldn't you see the effects of it by now? Besides, what kind of intel is good after five years, anyway?"

I forgot how good I was at lying. I must have come on stronger than I realized. Both Parker and Reagan were now looking at me with amazement. "Forgive her, Parker, she's probably forgotten the consequences of speaking to a senior commanding officer like that."

Reagan was doing whatever he could to keep our plan afloat even though my mouth was close to sinking it.

"Fine..." Parker sighed like whatever I said made her believe me. "You're right, Eva. If you did know the intel and already handed it over to the enemy, we'd have seen a major Coldier offensive by now. At Fort Knox, there is a massive weapons and armor cache left over from the US military from before the collapse. Since manufacturing is still on the ropes and mass production of weapons and armor is no longer happening, weapons and ammunition are becoming more scarce. We know neither side has the resources to overcome the other, so the weapons cache would be everything we need to supply us with enough firepower to finally stand toe-to-toe with the Coldiers and win, if not dominate the rest of the eastern United States again. The intel is the access code, a numeric sequence that opens the vault to the armory... Only one man knew it and we sent our best agents to retrieve it from him." She gave me a sour look after she said it. "So... now, Eva, you see why after five years it *is* still important."

"Why did you tell me all of that?" I knew what the intel was. I knew the code. I remembered it better than I remembered my mother's name; but I didn't understand why she would tell me when she was suspicious of me already.

"For two reasons," she said, tapping her pen against the desk again. "One... to see your face when I said it, to see if you knew what I was talking about..." She stopped to stare at me. I furrowed my brows like I was confused but I wasn't. I knew what she was doing now. "The second reason is for Reagan. If you two are going to go find Marcus, who potentially is a double, I might add, you should know what I told him before he left here five years ago. Retrieving and carrying the intel is dangerous. It's the most dangerous mission you'll ever be on in your entire lives. Reagan, if you find your brother and he *is* a double, are you willing to take proper action?"

Reagan swallowed. I could tell the new mission he'd begged for us to be on was now a lot more troublesome than he'd previously thought. "Yes, Ma'am... I understand the severity. When we find him, if..." He sounded like it was hard for him to say it but he was willing. "If...

he… um…" He cleared his throat and tried again. "Yes, if I find out that he is working for anyone but the Sicari, then yes, I am willing to detain him and decommission him myself if necessary."

Knowing how close he and Marcus were, I didn't believe him but I didn't care if he was lying; it didn't affect me. I knew the truth, and I knew nothing either of them was saying really mattered. The intel *was* dangerous, just like Parker had said, and because of that I needed to think long and hard about whether I would ever tell it to anyone. Even though my original mission was to get it back to my father for the Coldiers, now I didn't feel like anyone on either side should have it.

The rest of the report went without a hitch. Reagan did more sucking up—I knew better than to say anything else—and Parker acted like she was no longer suspicious of either of us and was willing to let us search for Marcus.

I could tell after we left the room and went back to Reagan's office, he wasn't acting the same as he had before the report. I figured he didn't have any idea what the intel actually was and the importance of it when I had talked to him the night before. The moment he told me Parker was more interested in me being the last Gypsyin than she was finding the intel, I realized he must not have known what it was.

"Are you okay?" I asked as I sat down on a large swivel chair behind his desk.

"No…" He said, being frank as usual. "Did Marcus tell you what the intel was about before you met with the contact? Did you know it was a code, or anything else she said?"

"No," I was actually telling him the truth for once. I didn't know anything about the intel until the moment we spoke to the contact and he gave us the code. "Marcus met with the contact alone," I said, now lying. "I saw Marcus kill him, though. Before he returned to me, I saw him shoot him point blank. We actually had a fight about it later. I didn't understand why he would kill him. It didn't make sense. If he told Marcus the wrong code, we'd never be able to get the right one from him. "

Reagan didn't look at me. He just nodded, taking in the information. "Did you know he didn't want you reassigned to him?"

"No," I said quietly as I thought about it. "I don't understand why he would have done that. Did he tell you why?" I asked, hoping he had some insight for me.

"No…" He said, thinking about it, trying to piece the puzzle together as well. "I don't understand why she would refer to you as his ex-girlfriend either…" He caught onto the same thing I had earlier. "Unless… no… he wouldn't."

"What?" I suspected what he had concluded, but I wanted to hear it from him.

"Eva, did Marcus ever make you suspect he was a double agent?"

"Reagan…" I said it with a small gasp, like how could he.

"I'm serious, Eva… I meant it when I told her I would investigate it. If he was… is… then he'll have to face the consequences. I'm sorry, I know you love him but—"

"I never promised her that." I interrupted him. "I do love him, and I don't think he could do such a thing." It wasn't hard to act. I meant everything I said. "What would I even look for? I don't know how a double is supposed to act?"

"Eva, I know he loved you. He did. It was real, but for him to ask for you to be reassigned doesn't make any sense. Not unless he was afraid he was going to get caught and didn't want you going down with him." He began to sift through a few papers on his desk as he continued. "The other thing that bothers me is that he didn't share with you how dangerous the intel was. I don't understand why he would have been okay putting you in that kind of danger. That doesn't sound like the Marcus I knew, the brother I loved."

"Reagan, stop." I put my hand on top of his to get him to pay attention to me for a second and not sift through papers anymore. "Your brother is a good man. He's not a double agent! He was proud of being a Sicari. His position was his life… I know he loved me but honestly, I believe he loved it more. He was loyal, Reagan. I'm sure he still is!"

He half-smiled as if he wanted to believe me, but was having a hard time with the idea. "All right, I guess we will see when we find him." He said, pulling his hand away and turning around to walk over and sit in another chair. "Now that we've been cleared to go after him, we need to make a plan. Where were you when you lost him? Tell me everything you can remember, every detail."

It wasn't hard to remember what happened; I felt like every detail was seared into my brain. How the serum was powerful enough to remove that memory was beyond me. I knew I had to twist it, though. I couldn't tell him how it went exactly. I had to lie again. "Nashville…"

The moment I said it something else hit me. It was like a chain of memories lined up in place, waiting for me to filter through them. Nashville was where I killed Marcus. Marcus asked me to kill him because he was shot. He was shot because Miller knew where we would be. Miller knew where we would be because he had the letter I sent to my father. My father was supposed to have men capture us, not kill anyone. Marcus was supposed to be released, not shot.

Miller! I couldn't help but think of all the things that happened that weren't supposed to, all the evil things he did to me… Then the things that I did to Marcus that weren't supposed to happen, only because I had no choice. Everything was Miller's fault. Erasing myself in the cave had made me forget how badly I wanted to find Miller and kill him.

"Eva?" Reagan caught me staring off, thinking. "What else?"

"We need to go to Nashville. We need to find Miller first…" I said still zoning out.

"What? Who's Miller?" Reagan asked, confused.

"The Coldier that captured us… me and Marcus." I snapped out of it to look at him again. "He'll know where Marcus is. He interrogated us separately after we were caught at the byway lines. He did things to me that I'm still trying to forget. I have no idea what horrible things he might have done to your brother." I let the emotion that I was feeling show on my face. If it was genuine, I didn't want to hide it, it could only help my believability.

"Oh my gosh, Eva… Why didn't you tell me this earlier?" He sounded distraught.

"I don't know." I was trying to stop myself from crying, which I was sure he could see.

"Would they have killed him?" It seemed hard for him to ask.

"I'm not dead, so I don't know. After torturing me to get the intel I didn't have, they just erased me and released me back outside the city." That wasn't even close to the extent of the real story, but I couldn't really tell him just how bad it actually was or how I was eventually released.

"No, you're not dead but you're not the same Eva I remember either." He said, looking at me. It was the first time he'd ever looked like he actually cared about me. "If you were erased with their serum, then how do you remember what you do right now?"

"Ming," I smiled as I thought of her. "I was taken in by an older woman that had a special herbal soup. I don't even know if she realized what she had, but it worked similar to the Sicari's antidote serum. I don't think it brought everything back, but it did enough. That was only last year though, likely what brought my signal back online."

He acted like he believed me even though again my facts were slightly skewed. "So they erased you, then threw you out in the wild to live on your own?"

"Yes... I was just a Gypsyin to them, though. Maybe that's why. Maybe they didn't see me as a threat. But if they saw Marcus' tag, I don't know, Reagan. I don't know what they would have done to him." I said it like I was feeling upset again.

"All right." He stood up like we'd talked enough and he was ready to take action. "We need to go get some lunch. While we eat, you can tell me how you ended up in New York with the Sicari's serum in ya."

I knew I didn't want to do that, but it was bound to come up at some point. I would just make something up that would sound good, like I had so far. He would believe me, then we would move on. "Fine," I said as I got up and followed him. I was hungry as well and didn't want to skip another chance at food.

After talking over lunch, the planning began. We would leave for Nashville within the week, after we had gathered provisions for the trip. Once we got there, we would scout out the area and find an escort contact to lead us into the city. From there, we needed to find Miller. If he was in the city, we would wait for the right time to deploy, get him alone and interrogate him.

For me, it was a win-win. I knew the closer we got to Miller, the better my chances of killing him, especially if I had a fellow trained agent at my side. I also knew that's where Jake still had a house and maybe if I was able to find it I could also find a way to reach him, potentially by phone. The mission didn't sound easy, but from my memory none of them really were. I wasn't excited to be back in the field but I was excited to finally have a chance to avenge both Marcus and myself. I wouldn't have known it without having my memory back, but killing Miller and the other four men that raped me was my new mission. One that I had hoped I would accomplish by the time Jake was able to find me.

4

BEFORE ALL THE LIES

"Kaleah, this isn't you…"

I knew I was dreaming again. I knew Jake wasn't really here talking to me, but just seeing him, I didn't care. I didn't want to wake up. I missed him. I needed him. If the only way to see him was to dream, then I would sleep, even if I wasn't tired.

"You're not Eva," His eyes were so sweet, I couldn't remember a time they looked sweeter.

"What do you mean? I am Eva…"

"No, this isn't you… it doesn't have to be. You don't have to be hard, you don't have to kill anyone anymore." I could hear what he was saying but I couldn't understand the intent behind his words.

"But this is me, Jake. Eva is who I am. I can't be anyone else."

"Yes, you can. Remember at the cave, when you gave yourself the serum, you said you wanted to be Kaleah again, my Kaleah…"

"I can't be Kaleah," I couldn't stop myself from arguing with him even though I knew it wasn't real. "Kaleah is nothing but scared, and pathetic, and soft, and—"

"You're wrong!" He said, with passion in his face. He did love me. "*Eva* is scared. That's why she pretends. She pretends to be strong, she pretends that she doesn't need anyone else, but it's not true, she does…

You do! Kaleah, can't you see? Eva is afraid of you. She's afraid to let go and be you."

"Why?" How could he see it when I couldn't?

"Because Eva's afraid to love again, that's why…" He said it softly as he pushed my hair from my face like he always did.

I understood him. He didn't have to explain it anymore. I knew what he was saying. I knew he was right, too.

"What are you afraid of, baby?" His eyes looked so sincere as he asked, genuinely wanting to know.

I couldn't help but begin to cry as I thought about my answer. "I'm afraid I'll lose you like I lost Marcus." I leaned into him and let him wrap his arms around me. The tears didn't stop. They continued as I began to sob.

"I know, baby, I know…" He whispered softly as he held me.

The longer I sat there crying the more I thought about my plan and what I still needed to do in Nashville. He was telling me I didn't need to kill anymore, but that's exactly what I felt like I needed to do. "I'll be your Kaleah again. I just need to kill Miller first, that's all, baby. I have to kill Miller." I didn't know if he would understand but I wasn't sure if I could ever let that side of me go until Miller was dead. The things Miller did to me were what created the monster that was inside, the side of Eva that Jake didn't like. I didn't know how I could let go of her as long as Miller was still alive.

"Revenge won't complete you, baby." He said it so calmly. "Do you love me?"

"Yes, you know I do, Jake!"

"Then let your love complete you, not hate. Killing Miller will never be enough. It won't bring Marcus back and it won't make you forget the evil things that were done to you, either, Kaleah…" He pulled away to look me in the eye again. "You can't go back to Nashville."

"I have to, Jake… I'm sorry. I have to." I wanted to do as he said but I knew what I had to do.

"You can't, Eva… You promised your father you wouldn't."

I felt myself beginning to wake up as I thought about what he said.

I didn't... did I? No, I never promised. I couldn't remember. *What if I did?* If I did, and I went back anyway... then I would be breaking a promise. But I had to go back. I had to. My mind began to toil the more I allowed it to think. Then the more I thought, the more I woke, and the more I woke the quicker I lost sight of Jake. He wasn't in front of me now. I couldn't see him anymore, either. I opened my eyes and looked around; it was still dark. *Go back to sleep,* I thought. *You might see him again. Go back to sleep.*

"Y ou're grounded."

"No, I'm not." I knew the consequences of talking back to my father but even though I did care, for some reason I still couldn't stop myself.

"What did you just say to me?" He furrowed his brow and raised his finger to point at me. He was clearly angry. He hated when I talked back.

"All you ever do is treat me like a child. It wasn't even midnight when I got back last night!" I didn't intend to raise my voice, but I did.

"You *are* a child, Jayde. You're only fourteen! As long as you live in this house, you're going to abide by my rules, and *midnight* isn't when your curfew is. It's ten o'clock and you know it!" He didn't have any problem raising his voice back. "You want to tell me what you were doing out so late?"

"No!" I wasn't about to give him any information he could use against me later.

"Jayde, why do you have to be so stubborn?" Ellice must have been listening and thought she would interject.

"Ellie, baby, this is between Jayde and I, go back downstairs please." I could see the way he talked to her was different. He never yelled at her like he did me.

"Okay, daddy." She didn't argue. She just turned around and did exactly what he asked of her, like she always did. *She's his perfect little angel, something I'll never be.*

"Jayde," his voice wasn't as harsh anymore. He probably didn't want to continue to argue where Ellice could hear us. "Tell me where you were or I won't let you go out again. And don't even try to lie, you're not good at it."

He was wrong; I *was* good at it. I lied all the time, and he never caught me. "Fine, I was with Nora. I lost track of time and I came home as soon as I realized how late it was."

"Nora?" He didn't look like he believed me. This time I really was telling the truth, though. That's why I felt like I had to lie so much; he didn't want to believe me when I really was innocent. "Jayde, you were with Weston again, weren't you?"

It didn't matter what I said, I couldn't win. I never won. To him I was stubborn, and rebellious, and incapable of making him proud, despite what I actually did or tried to do. "No," I said quietly. I didn't want to keep arguing with him, either.

"That's another week then, Jayde. You're grounded for two weeks now since you think you can lie and get away with it." He sounded like he always did, like he was disappointed in me.

Something caught my attention behind him. I looked and saw Ellie peeking over the top stair. But as soon as she saw my eyes connect with hers she quickly ducked.

"Jayde, are you listening to me?" Dad reached out and grabbed my arm and jerked it, forcing me to look at him again.

"I understand," I said. I really didn't want to fight with him. "Can I go to my room now?" I didn't feel like I had any more energy to stand there. I was tired and just wanted to go back to sleep.

"No, it's Saturday. You know your mother has a trial on Monday that she's preparing for, and I have more campaigning to do. I need you to stay out here and watch your sister."

"She's eleven. She can't watch herself?" I was getting frustrated again.

"No." He'd already turned to walk back toward his office. "That's part of your punishment, Jayde. You do the crime, you do the time."

"She doesn't need me, though." I looked back toward the stairs as I said it to see if she was still there.

"You're right," he said now yelling through the doorway. "But you need her. Maybe she'll rub off on you… maybe she can teach you how to behave."

It hurt hearing him say that. He had no idea how hard I tried to make him happy with me.

"Come on, Jayde," she finally popped her head back up over the top stair again. "Let's go play together."

"I don't want to play, Ellie!" I didn't know if I wanted to disobey and go to my room to lie down or do what he asked and follow her back downstairs.

"You have to… Daddy said so." She grinned as she slipped her head back down slowly below the stair.

"No, I don't." I said, walking toward her. "Just go watch tv, and leave me alone." As I got to the stairs, I looked down at her. She was sitting all curled up on the fourth step down.

"Pleeeease play with me, Jayde. I'll let you decide what we do." She made it hard to refuse her.

"Ellie, I'm too old to play." I actually wanted to, but I didn't feel like I could be playful like that anymore.

"Jayde, what do you wanna be when you grow up?" I looked at her, confused, wondering where that came from.

"I am grown up," I said as I stepped over her to proceed down the stairs.

She grabbed a hold of my ankle before I got it past her. "Then what do you want to do now?" She knew I wasn't, but she didn't even try to argue with me. She just carried on with her questions.

"I wanna be a doctor," I said finally, giving in.

"Why?"

"So I can save people." It was true. But deep down, the real reason was hoping I could finally do something that would make my dad proud of me. That's what I really wanted, for him to look at me the way he did Ellie. I wanted him to love me like he did her.

"Good, then you can be the doctor and I'll be the nurse," she said as she let go of my ankle and perked up. "We can make Reggie the patient." She stood up and quickly walked past me down the steps like she was excited to get started.

"That would make me a vet. It's not the same." I said, following her.

"I know, but I won't tell him if you don't." She giggled. "Reggie! Come here, boy!"

"E va," my name was called out loudly as I saw a blinding light shooting through my eyelids.

"Reagan!" I yelled, recognizing his voice.

"Sorry, I tried waking you up nicer and you see how that went." He didn't really sound sorry at all. "Get up and get ready. We have a few more things to do before we leave."

"Like what?" I asked, still covering my eyes with my arm. I'd thought we were as prepared as we needed to be.

"Like you still need your physical. Parker said she won't let you go back out without it."

"My physical?" I tried to think about what it meant when he said it. It had been so long I couldn't remember what they did when we had physicals. "So I have to see a doctor?" I hoped that wasn't what it meant, but I knew better.

"Ah yeah, that's generally what a physical is… A doctor looks at you and says you're approved for duty. Oh, and I'm sure you'll get more shots… Who knows what diseases you picked up out in the wild over the last five years," he chuckled after he said it so I knew he was joking.

I uncovered my eyes to look at him finally. "You're not funny," I said in all seriousness. I realized he didn't know it but I had developed a pretty deep fear of doctors.

"What's wrong?" He must have sensed I was hesitant about the idea. I could see on his face he looked confused.

"I don't think I need one." I said, hoping I could get out of it. "I'm afraid of needles." That wasn't really my problem but after being erased so many times, I don't think it was actually that much of an exaggeration.

"Well, too bad Parker doesn't accept excuses as currency." He said with a smug grin. He must have been enjoying seeing me squirm now. *There's the asshole I remembered.* "So are you gonna get ready or do you want me to have the doctor come in here?" He was probably trying to hurry me along seeing I still hadn't gotten up.

"Shut up, Reagan," I said without thinking as I sat up on the edge of the cot.

"Eva..." His voice sounded tight.

I looked up at him, squinting my eyes; they were still having trouble adjusting to the light. "What?"

"You can't talk to me like that. I'm your superior now, remember? I know you've been used to being on your own and all but, you're going to have to remember how to be an agent again." The way he said it was kind and not controlling like I remember Marcus being.

"I'm sorry," I really was. He was right. I had forgotten how to control myself and I didn't want to let it keep happening. I was better than that.

"I understand. Just don't let it happen again and we'll be cool." He smiled, then shut the door behind him as he left.

So many things were going through my head. I had the dreams, then the mission, now the physical. I got up and began to get dressed again as I thought about it all. I missed Jake and really didn't want anything except to see him again. I didn't want to go on the mission if I thought it would make him upset with me, but I really didn't know. I tried to think about where he might be, and what he might be doing.

I hoped he would have stayed in New York and not tried to come to the Praetorium to find me. Surely he knew that was too dangerous, even if he did bring multiple men with him like he did when he rescued me from Luca. The longer I thought about it, the more frustrated I could feel myself get. We'd never discussed a scenario like this, if I was taken again, where we should rendezvous. *How did we not think to have that discussion?* I wondered. Even though I felt like him staying in New York was probably what he should do, I knew that wasn't Jake. If I wasn't there, he probably wasn't either.

Chicago, where the Praetorium was located, was the only city the Sicari ever held a stronghold in. It wasn't as large as New York but it was definitely more fortified and extremely dangerous for a Coldier. All I could think of was how awful it would be if he tried to come here. He couldn't come here. He couldn't be that dumb. *He's smarter than that.* I tried to convince myself that he knew better than to attempt it.

If that was true and he knew not to come here, but I knew he wouldn't stay in New York, then where would he go? The question was difficult for me. *Nashville?* Something in me wondered. What about Nashville? He had a home there, but he also knew Miller was there and from my recollection, I don't think they were happy with each other.

It didn't take long for me to decide what I needed to do. I would proceed with the plan that Reagan and I had. It only made sense. I would kill Miller first and get that out of the way then when I got a chance, I would try to find Jake's house and go from there.

"So… I hear it's been a while since you've had a physical?" I didn't recognize the man that was the doctor now.

"Yes… It has." I didn't know if he could tell I was nervous but I was. I felt sick to my stomach and hoped we could get it done and over with so Reagan and I could leave as planned.

He didn't say anything else as he walked around the table I was sitting on with a small tool in his hand. He used it to thump each of my knees, making my legs quickly spring out toward him. "Good," he said quietly to himself after each one. "So, do you have any injuries that I should know about?" He spoke louder finally talking to me again.

"Um…" I didn't respond right away. I wanted to think it over to make sure first. "No… well, I was poisoned a few months back."

"Ha, oh really?" He said, surprised and slightly intrigued. "Go on, tell me more."

"Oh, there's not much to tell, really. I felt like I was dying and I've died before so I know what the feeling is like. My heart was beginning to slow down; I know that. But then I drank a bunch of water with activated charcoal… I don't remember much after that. I just woke up later and wasn't dead so…" I shrugged.

"Okay, well… hmm," He stood up, stopping what he was doing

and looked down at the floor, probably thinking about what impact that could have. "If you feel fine now, I guess it isn't a problem," he said, smiling as he looked back up at me. "Any pregnancies?" He asked next.

I could feel my expression change as he asked it. I didn't know how to answer him.

"Don't worry, Eva," he said, looking down at my chart, probably checking to see if he was calling me by the right name. "Whatever you tell me is confidential." He smiled again after he said it.

I knew he meant the best but by the way he said it with his smile; I also knew he was lying. "I know," I said finally, seeing I couldn't trust him. "Nope, no pregnancies," I smiled back.

"Okay, great." He sounded like he believed me.

After a couple more minutes of him listening to my breathing, he moved over to the counter and started to put his tools away. For a second, I felt relieved when I thought that he was done. Then, before I had a chance to relax, he pulled out a few vials, each with their own syringe.

"Wait... what are those?" My nerves quickly ramped back up. My breathing began to pick up pace as well.

"Just your shots, no big deal." He really didn't act like they were a big deal, but they were to me.

"Well, what are they? I need to know what's going into my body." I meant it but mainly I wanted to hear him say he wasn't going to erase me again. I already knew I could read him if he tried to lie. So if I got any inclination he was up to something, I was prepared to choke him out like I had almost done to Reagan the morning after we arrived.

"Just normal shots..." He said as he proceeded to draw liquid from one of the vials into a syringe. "This one is your birth control. Then I have a few other vaccines you've missed over the last few years."

I could tell he wasn't lying so I would allow it but I wasn't sure how I felt about the birth control. I didn't know how long it would take for me to be back with Jake but once I was I didn't want anything to stop us from having kids again when we decided it was time. "Well, uh, how long will that last?" I asked, trying to sound like I was just curious.

"Six months," he said as he brought the syringe closer, ready to inject it into me.

"Wait…" I knew I shouldn't have said it but I couldn't help it.

He looked at me oddly. "Agents can't have children, Eva… Surely you remember that."

I nodded not knowing any way to argue against it. "All right, go ahead," I said finally, ready to receive it.

5

HONORABLE INTENTIONS

"Reagan?" I looked around frantically like I had lost my dearest friend. "Where's my gun? I packed it, but it's not here…" I couldn't find it even though I knew exactly where I'd put it.

He didn't say anything at first as he continued to drive. Then he reached up to scratch the back of his neck, probably trying to think of a good lie to tell me.

"You took it! You son of a—" I stopped. I knew I couldn't talk to him like that, even if he was a thief.

He quickly looked over at me with warning in his eyes, making sure I wasn't about to say it as well. "I'll give it back after we get there."

"What? Why did you even take it?" I suspected I knew the answer, but I wanted to ask him anyway just in case I was wrong.

"Because I don't really trust you yet, Eva. You said it yourself—you get what you earn."

"Ugh, whatever…" I said, complaining while trying not to argue. "Fine, as long as you know it's your fault if we get in a situation and I need it to back you up, but can't."

He didn't respond, no smile or anything. He just kept driving like I wasn't there.

"Well, aren't you a ton of fun... I can already tell this road trip's gonna be a blast." I said sarcastically. I expected that might get him to respond as well, but still nothing. I just stared at him, watching as he stayed completely focused on the road. He didn't look anything like Marcus but at the same time there were parts of his face that were familiar enough that I could faintly catch some resemblance.

"What's your last name... your real one?" I asked, hoping a change of subject would make him finally respond. I remember thinking I wanted to marry Marcus but what bothered me was I didn't remember how genuine that feeling was. I never asked him what his real last name was. How could I be in love with someone so much that I would want to marry them and not know what my new name would be?

He looked over at me finally after I asked the question. "Why do you want to know? Did Marcus never tell you?"

"No," I said softly as I looked away from him and out the window. "Honestly, I never asked, and I don't know why. It bothers me."

"Thompson," he gave it up without a fight or argument.

"That's it?" I don't know why I was surprised, but I was.

He laughed as he glanced at me, then back to the road. "Yeah, what were you expecting?"

"I don't know... something not so English sounding..." I was expecting something more Spanish from the color of their skin. They both had a darker yellow undertone that tanned easily. I didn't know what their ancestry was but Spanish was my best guess.

"You sound disappointed. Did Marcus make you believe he wasn't American?" He asked now sounding more lively. I could hear the similar Southern accent in his voice that I remember Marcus having.

"No," I slightly chuckled. "I knew what he was... or well..." I answered before thinking. "I don't actually know. Maybe I don't..." The more I thought about it, the more I wondered if I really knew Marcus as well as I thought I had or if he'd been lying to me the whole time, like I had him.

"Ok, well I don't guess it'd hurt to tell you about our family..." As soon as Reagan said it I could feel myself get a little excited, until he went on. "You should tell me about yours first though…" He said as he turned to smile.

Darn it, I thought. He really was smart. "Um…" I started while trying to think about what I felt comfortable telling him. I knew I had to lie, but I still wanted to be as honest as I could be as well. "Okay… well… I have one sister. She's younger than me. She'd be about, uh 22 this year, yeah… that sounds right."

"What's her name?" He sounded like he was being genuine with his question but I knew I couldn't be honest with him. He could use it against me.

"Lilly," I said quickly. I knew if I hesitated he would know I lied. That was actually my real middle name, the best I could come up with as fast as I did and remember in case he asked again later.

"That sounds like a sweet name, is she?" He asked.

"I haven't seen her in years. She was fifteen when I left…" It was hard to think about her. I didn't want to give it too much thought, or I knew I would start to miss her and I didn't want to cry. "Yes, she's the sweetest person I've ever known." I thought about Bethany as I said it, but I wasn't lying. Ellice was sweeter.

"Which side of the war did your family choose?" He continued with his questions. I knew he was just making small talk, but I was beginning to feel uncomfortable.

"They're Gypsyins… they didn't choose anything." I said it like I was slightly disgusted, though I knew it was a lie. *They're Coldiers, just like my Jake.*

"And your sister?"

"I don't know," I said. I suspected she chose to be a Coldier just like my parents but I really didn't know. "She knew I was leaving to join the Sicari. I think I broke her heart that day. She didn't understand. I begged her not to tell my parents though, and she promised she wouldn't." I made it up. In reality, I actually didn't remember when I left, or even how I left.

"What was your reason? What did you tell her?" I knew he was probably asking more because he was curious why I choose the side I did.

"I didn't give her a reason. I just said I had to do what I had to do, and hopefully she would understand later, when she was older." I made that part up too. I actually had very little recollection of the events leading up to me joining the Sicari, oddly enough. I had an idea in my head of what happened and how, but no actual visual memory. Those pieces of my puzzle were still vague at best.

What I do remember was after the war started, it was clear my father, Elijah Jordan Prescott, EJ for short, was quickly making rank. It was in the beginning when the sides were still being established, so they dished out tags to their loyal followers. I knew with his political and military background he was going to end up high. He never asked me to be anything. He didn't want me to be an agent for either side.

I thought I remembered wanting to join the Sicari but there was no memory corroborating that idea. I do remember wanting to make my father proud though, and I felt like the only way to do that was to show him what I was capable of. I could be on both sides. I could play the enemy. The thought of taking something away from the Sicari and bringing it to him, surprising him, that's what I lived for—until I fell in love with Marcus, anyway.

"That's the benefit of Marcus and I both going in together," he said. I guess he'd heard enough of my side and he was ready to share his.

"He never talked about his family to me." The thought saddened me. The more we went on, the more I realized Marcus hadn't told me much about his real life at all. "Was it just the two of you, or did you have other siblings?"

"We were the only boys, but we have four sisters."

"Wow, really?" I had no idea.

"Yeah, I'm the oldest, then Marcus. Our youngest sister would be about your age now."

I was surprised at how honest he was being. I didn't guess he felt like giving me the knowledge put any of them in danger though, so it probably didn't matter. "Are they all Sicari?"

"No," He said it solemnly like it was hard to admit it. "The war split our family in half. My father wanted one thing, my mother wanted something completely different. Marcus and I chose a side before they did. We assumed they would follow us, but I guess it wasn't that easy." I could tell he was intentionally being vague.

"Is that why you suspect he was a double?" I asked it gently, knowing it was a hard subject for him.

He didn't say anything, he just nodded.

"Did you lie when you said you'd decommission him if you found out that he was a double?" I knew it was another hard question, but I needed to know. His answer would tell me a lot.

"No," he quickly glanced at me as he said it, probably trying to see my reaction. "That's the benefit of having you with me though, Eva. When we find him… he doesn't have to tell me what he's been doing. I just want to make sure he's alive. Then you can go back to him… When I get back to the Praetorium, I'll just blame you. Like you said, you didn't make a promise to Parker like I did."

I understood what he was saying. Even though it sounded harsh, it was kind. "I like that plan. I know it'll be hard for you, but thank you." I wanted him to know I appreciated it, even though I knew it could never happen like that. "There's just one problem… Parker would never rest until she found me again. I can't remove the tracker from my head like you guys can your arm."

"That doesn't have to be a problem," he said, clearly knowing something I didn't.

"What do you mean?" I was eager to see if he had a solution.

"If you and Marcus still want to run away together, I know how to deactivate your tracker." He said calmly, apparently having already thought of the entire plan in his head.

"I do." I tried to hide my excitement, but it was difficult. "Reagan, I do!" I wanted him to know what that meant to me. "How? I didn't know it was possible?"

"I'll tell you after we find Marcus." He knew it meant something to me, enough he would use it as leverage, like any smart agent would.

"Deal!" I didn't care if he waited, just knowing it was possible was exciting. I didn't know if he'd intended for it but I also realized he was more valuable to me now. Whatever we came across in Nashville, I needed to keep him alive and by my side. At least until I came up with a plan to extract that information out of him, anyway.

"Eva, I know you and me haven't gotten along very well in the past, but I want to put that behind us. I think we can work really well together, if we both give it our best... We have to, for Marcus' sake."

Interesting... He's never been this nice. He has ulterior motives, surely. "Can I speak freely?" I wanted to make sure he wouldn't get upset if I called him names.

He nodded like he already knew what I was about to say.

"You were a jackass, Reagan. I couldn't stand you. I don't think I've ever met anyone more pompous and arrogant. Not only that, you were also a—"

"I was jealous, Eva." He cut me off.

"What?" I heard what he said, but I was confused by what he meant.

"You could have been mine... I'm not saying I feel for you like that now, I'm just saying... Marcus had something I didn't. Actually, with you, he had a lot of things I didn't. It was more than love. He had a partner—a Gypsyin partner. I wasn't the only one envious of him for that either, by the way." He paused but I could tell he wasn't done.

"He was happy. He seemed like it anyway, you know? Especially when he thought you were pregnant. You should have heard him when he told me. I could tell he was scrambling, like he wanted out of being an agent but he didn't know how... We were in this together, Eva. Like... it was me and him against the world, then came you. He wanted you, not me. I mean, I understand, that's natural. You're a smart, attractive woman, but... it was something I didn't have. I didn't have an Eva, and well... I regret it, because I could have." I'd never heard him express himself like that. Reagan was always the type to keep everything close and to himself, a lot like Jake was, really. But here he was, laying it all out, and I didn't know why.

"You're not telling me something..." The more he told me the more I realized even though it was probably true, he was using it as a cover for something else. There was a reason he was being so nice, and

I wanted to know it. He wasn't the type to show feelings like that, not without a reason.

"I'm telling you a lot. What do you mean? I'm actually telling you more than I should." His voice went back to his usual closed-off self.

"The reason you found me, was it really just to help you find him? What do you want with me?" I asked. I could tell he was taken aback by my response to his opening up.

He hesitated for a second to think. "Things don't make sense, Eva. Marcus knew the intel was dangerous, but he didn't warn you. He knew you were pregnant, but he asked for you to be reassigned... The last time I talked to him he told me he loved you, but..." he paused again like whatever he was about to say he had intended to keep a secret. "He made me promise if something happened to him and he didn't make it back that I would take care of you and his baby."

"Oh," I was trying to process what that meant.

"I promised him, Eva..." he sounded more upset than before. "I promised... but I couldn't find you. I've been looking for you both for 5 years every chance I got. If something did happen to him, not having you and the baby safe with me felt like I broke it..." He shook his head like he didn't want to think of it but he had to. I hoped you had just run away together but when your tracker came back online at the Coldier base, I knew that wasn't the case.

I appreciated where he was coming from but I couldn't let him feel responsible for me. Not with everything I knew I was, all the lies I'd told him; it didn't feel right. "You can't love me, and I won't love you. I'm sorry, Reagan, even if he is gone... we can't." I looked out the window so he couldn't see my face as I said it.

"You don't have to love me, Eva. I wouldn't ask that of you. But if something did happen to Marcus..." he paused to take in a deep breath. "If something did happen, then I need to take care of you. I promised."

"I can take care of myself, Reagan. Look, I have for the last five years." It was honorable what he was trying to do, but I didn't like it. I couldn't help but feel uncomfortable. The nicer he was the more guilty I felt for what I was, what I'd already done to Marcus and for all the lies I'd been telling.

"Well, too bad you don't have a choice." He said, making it clear that him fulfilling his promise meant more to him than my freedom and happiness.

I didn't know what else to say to him. I didn't want to argue or sound unappreciative even though I didn't like it. "I need a nap," I said, pulling the lever next to my seat and leaning it back all the way.

"Be my guest. We still have quite a while until we're there. Do you want me to wake you up to eat when I stop to put the gas in the tank?" I could tell he was ready to move on to a different subject just like I was.

"No," I said, balling my jacket into a makeshift travel pillow to lean my head against. "I'll wake myself up when I need something," I continued, then took the end of my jacket's sleeve that was next to my face and shoved it in my mouth and closed my eyes.

"What are you going to name it?" I couldn't go anywhere without constant questions about my stomach. You look too big, you look too little, how many are there in there, I bet I know who the dad is… It had to be obvious who the dad was. Jake never left my side.

I looked down before I answered the woman and rubbed the side of my bump in a circular motion. She was always on that side, kicking the other. "We don't have a name yet," I said as I looked over at Jake, rolling my eyes. "He can't decide," I went on, this time with a smile.

"Yeah, I can. I told you I like Henry." He grinned back.

"Ugh." I couldn't help but roll my eyes again. "It's not a boy, Jacob. And besides, you can't use your cousin's name. That's weird." I knew they were close, but I had to draw the line somewhere.

"What? He said he'd name his first boy after me, so…" He shrugged like that was normal behavior.

"That doesn't even make sense. Why don't you each just name your son after yourself? That's what they make the initials jr. for." I was perplexed that they thought that was a good idea.

"That's why men shouldn't name babies," the older woman decided to interject again.

I smiled at her, trying not to laugh. She had a great point.

"So, it's a girl then?" She asked, seeing I was now ignoring Jake and looking at her again.

"Oh ah, I believe so… But we won't know until I have her."

"Him!" Jake added with a big grin.

"Well, my dear, you seem like you'll make a great mother. I assume this is your first?" She smiled as she continued to finish the flower arrangement for me.

"Um…" I was about to answer when I stopped to think about the others I'd lost when I heard Jake.

"Yes," He spoke up, answering for me. "We had another, but we lost it. So this will be our first."

"Oh, that's a shame. Well, congratulations on this one. It's not all that common to see kids these days." She said like she was excited for us.

"Right…" I turned to look at Jake. It bothered me thinking about the other two that I could have had but didn't. Even though I lost them, it felt like they were both taken from me. It wasn't fair.

He looked at me and furrowed his brows a little like he could tell I was upset, but didn't understand what was the matter. "Jayde… Are you feeling okay?"

"No," I actually wasn't when I thought about the question. "Jake," I looked at him, feeling more upset. "They were taken, they were mine, and they were taken…"

"Oh, baby…. Shh, I know… It's okay…" He said like I had become frantic and he was helping me calm down.

"But it's not, Jake!"

"Jake?"

"Jacob?"

I felt myself suddenly wake up. *Oh shit.* I hoped I hadn't said anything out loud.

"Eva?" Reagan asked.

"What?" There was nothing in my mouth. My jacket must have slipped out.

"Are you okay?"

"Um… yeah, why?" I had no idea how much he'd heard.

"It sounded like you were crying."

"Oh…" If that was it, I felt relieved. "No, I'm fine, thanks."

Dammit! I didn't want to hesitate, but I didn't know how to answer him. "He's a Coldier that works for Miller." I said the first thing that came to mind.

"All right," Reagan said calmly as he nodded. "When we take care of Miller, we can take care of him too, then."

Shit! I didn't respond. *What have I done?*

6
STAKEOUT

MI L... L... E... R... Backspace, backspace, back...space... *I can't, dammit.* I knew what we were doing here. We were supposed to find Miller but I couldn't help but feel guilty. Neither Jake nor my dad wanted me to be back in Nashville. I didn't know if I would ever have this opportunity for vengeance again, though. I was torn. Their names were so similar, I couldn't help but wonder what would happen if I searched for Miles instead? I knew he had a house in Nashville, too. What if I could find him first? *He's not in Nashville, Eva, don't be ridiculous,* I thought, then felt torn again. *But what if he is?*

I didn't know how old the system was and if his name would even be in it but it was worth a shot. Reagan was waiting for me though, so I knew I needed to hurry. If either of us were caught at the library, it would be game over. I typed in the missing letters, E... S... then hit enter.

It was there; it worked. I was astonished. I quickly took the tiny pencil and jotted his address down on a small square of scratch paper that I found next to the computer. Those computers were normally only used for searching for books but thankfully I remembered from my training a back way into the city's directory.

I suspected it was the same way Reagan found me in New York. *Smart little shit,* I thought as I mentally congratulated him on such an outstanding achievement. It couldn't have been easy for him to out-smart Jake. The more I thought about it the more I wondered if finding Jake's house instead of Miller's was a good idea, or if it would end up being more dangerous for Jake.

I quickly folded the piece of paper and shoved it into my pocket, then sat there staring at the computer. I wondered if I should look up Miller's too, or if that would just complicate things. "Ugh," I tried not to express myself out loud but I could tell I was getting frustrated not knowing what I wanted to do on top of having to hurry to do it.

Backspace, backspace… L… E… R… Enter! "Error, no address found." I read it out loud under my breath. I couldn't believe it. *There's not one single person named Miller in this whole freakin' city?* That wasn't even realistic. That was a pretty common last name. How could it not exist anywhere in a city as big as Nashville? I sat there and stared at the screen. I couldn't help but feel dumbfounded as I thought about why that would be and what I should do about it.

"Ugh…" I cleared the screen as I got up, then turned to walk back out.

"May I help you?" a voice called out but I couldn't distinguish where it came from.

I slowed my pace to look around and see who was talking to me. *That's not the plan. You can't get caught,* I reminded myself. When I didn't see anyone, I picked up my pace again and walked as quickly as I could—without looking suspicious, like I had just stolen a book—back out to where Reagan was waiting for me.

"Hey, babe, you find the book you were looking for?" He asked with a bright cheery smile, one that looked completely absurd coming from his face. I knew we'd discussed the fictitious roles we would need to play while in the city, but hearing him call me 'babe' felt weird and awkward. He was nearly fifteen years my senior and already had salt and pepper hair. I doubted we actually looked like a real couple.

"Um, yep." I didn't know who was around so I had to play along. The more I thought about what I actually found though, the more I realized that I couldn't tell him the truth. I couldn't tell him we were going to Jake's house and not Miller's.

"Great, are you hungry?" He sounded too upbeat. I had half a mind to tell him he was a horrible actor, and it was going to give us away but I didn't. I didn't want to break his spirit. At least he was trying, even if he was awful.

"Rea… uh I mean, Ryan… you're a little too happy," I whispered. "Yep, I'm starving." I followed it with a normal voice. The walk back to the car was a lengthy one, so I hoped he'd listen and take my advice.

"That's not the name I picked," He whispered back. "It was Tony."

"Yeah well, you look more like a Ryan, so…" I shrugged as I continued to walk slightly in front of him.

"Ev… ugh… Kaleah," He reached up to grab my arm, probably so I would slow down. "Well, I don't really like yours either but you picked it so I'm going along with it."

"What do you want from me, Ryan? Do you think this is a good place to stop and have an argument?" I asked with my normal voice as I quit walking and turned toward him.

I could tell he was getting frustrated with me as his eyes widened. He quickly looked around, making sure no one heard me. "Ugh, *Kaleah,*" he whispered, seeing we were alone. "If you really were my wife, I swear…" He pushed me gently to start to walk again right next to him.

"What, Ryan? What would you do?" I grinned, knowing I was taunting him at this point and there was nothing he could do about it.

He tightened his grip on my arm but didn't say anything. He just kept walking next to me like we were a couple.

"Aww, I love you too, sweetie." I said, smiling really big then took the arm he was holding and wrapped it back around behind his waist.

He followed my lead and wrapped his arm around my shoulder and pulled me in tight to him, then whispered again. "If you're trying to earn my trust, you're doing a shitty job. I moved my gun. It's not on that side anymore. Now I think I'll keep yours for a few more days."

I didn't move my arm to his waist to look for his gun; I was just trying to keep up our act. I'm sure he thought he was clever though, keeping mine from me, but he wasn't. That was a dumb move. Whether he felt like he could trust me or not, I needed my gun if I was going to protect him and until I got my tracker deactivated, that was my plan: keep *Ryan* safe.

"I hope you don't wind up regretting that." I said softly.

"Are you threatening me?" I could feel his hand tighten at my shoulder. He obviously took what I said wrong.

"No, baby." I stopped and turned to look at him. "I need to keep you safe, I need you..." I smiled. "So if you make it hard for me to protect you, then I just hope neither of us regrets it later, that's all." I smiled again, then leaned in to give him a quick kiss on the cheek.

He relaxed his grip as we turned to walk again. He didn't say anything at first; I think he was still thinking about the kiss. Even though it was relatively benign, I wondered if it meant more to him since he'd probably not been kissed in years. "Is this how you acted with Marcus?" He asked me finally after walking silently for a couple of minutes.

"What do you mean?" I didn't understand his question.

"Did you really love him or were you pretending? Because you're really good at it, I can't tell the difference." I looked at him after he asked it. He was serious, not joking or anything.

"Get off me," I moved so his hand would fall off my shoulder, while I pulled mine back from his waist. "I can't believe you..." I didn't even want to answer him. I was upset that he'd even asked me that.

"Be mad all you want, but answer the question, *Kaleah*," he didn't sound phased by my response.

I knew we were almost to his Jeep, but I stopped and turned toward him again right there on the sidewalk. "I loved your brother more than anything. It wasn't an act. He was the best Sicari agent I've ever seen, a hell of a lot better than you'll ever be. Because of that, I was devoted to him..." I could tell I was beginning to feel emotional. "Too bad you'll never know how that feels, *Ryan*."

"Get to the Jeep now!" He was looking at something behind me when he said it. At that moment, I realized what I'd just told him, and what could happen if someone heard me.

I turned to walk again, but picked up my pace to get there quicker. He continued to walk next to me but I could tell he was keeping an eye on something across the street. I knew better than to turn and look at whatever it was myself. That could alert whoever was there that I knew too, and we were suspicious. "I'm sorry." I said quietly but where he could hear me.

I could see the Jeep finally, only a few yards ahead, right where we parked it. "Get in and lock the door." He said as he quickly went to his side.

"I'm sorry, Reagan." I said again as I shut the door behind me and locked it as he instructed.

He didn't respond; he turned the key, put it in gear and pulled away as fast as he was able to.

I didn't say anything else; I felt bad. I knew my mouth could have just gotten us caught.

"I believe you," he said finally as he slowed down to a normal speed when we got far enough from where we were parked to feel like we weren't being followed. "We were trained to hide our emotions… When you don't, I know you're being honest."

I nodded, but I didn't want to say anything else. I wanted him to know I appreciated that he saw the truth, but I couldn't tell him he was right. He needed to trust me, and if that was how he did then that was good for me to know.

W e found the address. I never told Reagan that it was actually Jake's house, not Miller's. I didn't see any benefit in telling him the truth. I explained to him, from what I remembered, Miller had many houses within his multiple-city jurisdiction, so he might not be at this one for a while. We agreed to sit and watch for any movement in or out until dark. If we saw nothing before dark, then we would reassess at that point if we would continue to scout longer or agree to move in and search the place.

It was bigger than I'd expected. However, the more I thought about how big both Jake's parents' house and Lane's house were, the more it made sense that that's what a high ranking T&C Agent would live in. It didn't look like it would be difficult to break into but I wasn't sure considering we could only see the front and not what kind of security measures he might have in the back.

We were sitting there for hours barely talking to each other since the sidewalk incident had made tensions high between us. I could tell I was getting bored and wanted to fall asleep, but assumed Reagan wouldn't approve. All I could think about was poor Lane. This was his job in the agency. How could he do this all the time? Maybe that was why he still had a decent outlook on life, because he probably didn't have to fight, kill people, or be manipulative like other agents had to… like *I* had to.

"Oh my gosh… I'm a spy!" I'd known it before that but it was like the sudden realization came out of nowhere and hit me. I remembered being at Jake's parents' house and telling him I thought it would be fun to be an agent, to be a spy… and here I was, a spy. I looked at Reagan, feeling excited. Just the thought that I had achieved something like that was monumental in my mind.

He furrowed his brows and tilted his head, looking at me puzzled. "What did you think you were?"

I couldn't help but chuckle at the thought. Then I got quiet again to think about the answer. "A nobody," I said softly, looking back at him. "I thought I was just a Gypsyin." I smiled, "but I'm not… I'm—"

"A Sicari!" He finished for me, with a smile.

"Um, yeah," I said, trying to still sound enthusiastic and proud. I realized I was more than that though, even more than he knew. I was a Sicari spy with a Gypsyin tag in a Coldier city, in front of my secret Coldier Agent lover's house… I was amazing, that's what I was…

"Since you won't give me a gun, if we come across someone when we go in, can I kick their ass?" I asked. I didn't expect anyone to be in there but if Miller had confiscated Jake's house and there *was* someone in there that worked for him, I was in the mood to fight.

As I asked, Reagan was in the middle of taking a gulp of water and spit about half of it out all over the steering wheel. He quickly brought his hand to his mouth, swallowed then used it to wipe up his mess as he answered. "By all means, yes, I wouldn't dare stop you…" He used his sleeve to finish the task then brought it up to wipe his mouth again. "Honestly, if nothing has changed, you're better at fighting than you ever were with your gun, anyway."

"Really?" I said like I didn't know any better. Though, the more I thought about it, the more I knew he was right as I thought of memories that went along with his hypothesis.

"You still remember how to fight, right?" He asked, now uncertain if he should still keep my gun from me.

"If I say no will you give me my gun back?" I smiled, hoping that was the case.

"No… now answer my question." He was direct, as usual.

"I think so." All I could remember though, was my pathetic attempt at taking Lane down and him winning.

"We'll just see when we get in there then," he said nonchalantly.

"I'll be honest with you, Ryan," I said with a smirk, "I haven't gotten to really fight with anyone in years, I don't know if I'm still good at it or not but my spirit is still there. So how about we make a deal… Whoever we come up against, will you give me a chance to take them down first before you shoot them? I need to practice, and I doubt you want to spar with me…" I smiled again so that he knew I was actually serious. I had more motive than just practice, though.

"Why not?" he said nonchalantly, looking back out his window. "But if you're not as good as you used to be and they use you as a human shield, where would you like me to shoot—his head or his leg?"

I knew the dilemma he would be in if that happened, although protocol was to shoot anyway. He was probably a good enough shot that he wouldn't hit me but that wasn't my issue. If it was Jake that was holding me, I didn't want him to shoot either of us. "Neither, you could miss and hit me!" I answered finally like I had forgotten protocol and expected something different.

"Eva… that's not how it works… but don't worry, I'm a good shot. If I go for the leg, I'm sure I'll miss you, the head… ah well—"

I interrupted him before he could go on. "Not the head. You can't kill him, remember? Whoever it is, they might know where Marcus is. If it's Miller—"

"You're right, that would be a problem then." He interrupted me back, "If we need him to talk, he can't be dead. But he can't have you either. I won't let that happen. So what do you propose, then?"

I was surprised he was asking me when we both knew he was just as strategically intelligent. I wondered if it was a trap again to see if he could trust me. "Okay… well, we can't make strict plans. It'll just handicap us." I knew from working with Marcus anytime we ever made plans that were too detailed it was harder to go with the flow, which was necessary in a combat scenario. "How about you let me fight and promise not to shoot unless I give you the signal?"

He leaned his head back against his headrest while he listened to me, but continued to watch the house out his window. "What's the signal?"

"I yell, 'Reagan… shoot!'"

He looked over at me with a befuddled look. "You're serious?" He asked, dryly.

"Dead serious," I said, smiling really big.

"Marcus, never let you make plans did he?"

"Nope," I said, trying not to smile too big. Marcus really didn't, but I was happy to see Reagan was hopefully willing to.

"I can see why," he said, turning his head toward the window again. "What if he's bigger than you?"

"Uh…" I thought about both Miller and Jake as he asked. Jake was bigger than me for sure but Miller wasn't all that much. "I can take a bigger guy… they're slow, you know? Those are the one's I'm good at fighting. I'm faster than them. It's the smaller ones I would be concerned with if I were you. Be prepared to shoot the smaller ones." I hoped I was able to cover my bases by saying it like that. I would have loved to tell him, more or less, don't shoot the man I love, shoot the asshole that deserves to die, but I couldn't.

"Well, that's different. You never had the big guys before, at the academy." He remembered.

"Oh, you know I haven't seen Johns in years… How is he?" I asked as I leaned my seat back like I was going to take a nap. I wasn't, but I wanted to distract Reagan from his last question while at the same time changing the subject.

"Sit your ass back up, Eva…" It worked. He didn't sound happy with my perceived lethargy. "You should have no reason to be tired. I need you to help me watch."

"Oh, sorry," I said, raising my seat back, "I'm just bored. This scouting shit isn't for me."

He relaxed against his seat again and returned his face to the window. "If I see someone walk in, I need you to tell me if it's Miller or not."

"Right… gotcha…" I said, putting my attention back on the house. *Man, wouldn't it really suck if I got the address wrong?* That thought was funny, but I knew better than to laugh. "I bet I know why they don't assign females to be scouting agents," I said as I thought of something else that was funny.

"Why?" He asked with a sigh, like he didn't really care.

"'Cause I have to pee… and I doubt you have a bottle big enough for me to go in, too."

"Eva…" He snapped his head around to look at me, "You better not pee in my Jeep."

I laughed at his response. "Yeah, that would suck wouldn't it? You'd have to go back to your horse."

"You're not funny and I'm serious." He said, looking down to make sure that I hadn't already had an accident. "Hold it!"

"I'll try…" I said, trying not to laugh again. "But I'm not making any promises." I grinned. "Sorry!"

7

THE HUNTER IS HUNTED

We had barely gotten inside before I felt my adrenaline surge to an ungodly level. If we did find someone, I knew it could be anyone. It could be Jake, it could be Miller, it could be Jake's dog... *Did he have a dog?* The whole situation was unsettling yet exhilarating at the exact same time. This had to be why I wanted to be a spy; the rush was unreal. My thoughts were bouncing around from one thing to another, but I stopped them just long enough to give myself a pep talk. *If you find Miller, kill him. If you find Jake... don't kill him... Don't even hurt him. Whatever you do, don't hurt Jake... Wait, what if he hurts me?*

I was quickly distracted by Reagan turning around, making a hand signal. We were there, inside, armed—him, not me, because he's a dick—and ready. We walked into a small hall off the back entry we came in through. We were at a split; he motioned for me to go right and he would go left. Somewhere inside, I felt like splitting up was a bad idea but I really didn't expect anyone to be there so I ignored my intuition. We hadn't seen any activity anywhere around the house so I was pretty sure it was vacant.

Go right... Ok, I'm going right then. I walked the way he suggested. I didn't have a gun, so I kept my arms to my sides, tiptoeing around things, trying to be as stealthy and silent as humanly possible. I walked until I came to another split. One door went back outside and the other doorway led upstairs. The house was dark enough as it was but I could tell it would get much darker if I went up the stairs. I stood there and looked up toward the top to see if there was a door or if it was an opening that I would encounter. It was too dark to tell which. I would essentially be walking into a black hole. I had no idea what was there. *Ugh, the dark is my freakin' kryptonite.*

Even though it looked scary, I didn't hesitate for more than a moment. I didn't want the adrenaline spike to wane; I needed that spike to fight at my best. I started to ascend them as quietly as possible, putting my feet on the sides of each step as close to the walls as I could, hoping there they would be the least likely to creak under my weight. As I made it to the top, I reached out in front of me for a door but there wasn't one.

I stood there for a moment hoping my eyes would adjust to the lack of light and maybe give me some idea of where I should go next, but nothing. I couldn't see anything other than a small glowing sliver of light over against what I assumed was a wall. It looked like maybe a small bit of moon seeping in under the blinds, nothing more.

I didn't understand why it would be that dark upstairs; it didn't make sense. It was almost like it was on purpose. I took a step to my left then hesitated as I looked back to the right. What if there was something to the right? *Holy shit.* Immediately I realized what the feeling was that kept tugging at the back of my mind. Something wasn't right. It felt like a trap. I was in a trap…

I took a step backward; I didn't want to go any further. I needed to turn around and either go back down the steps or find a light switch. As soon as I decided which of those I was about to do, it was too late. I didn't even get a chance to spin on my heel when I felt someone grab a hold of me. I opened my mouth to scream, but I never got the chance. A man's large hand quickly covered my mouth, pulling my head to his chest. At the same time, an equally beefy arm wrapped around me, pinning my arms to my sides and drawing my back to press tight to his torso.

Shit, what have I done? I got myself captured... I couldn't help but think if this was Miller; I was screwed. *Fight, Eva!* I couldn't give up. I had to fight, that's what I felt like I was made for—fighting. As soon as the thought hit me, my instincts kicked into gear and I began. I knew I needed to get loose from him before I could do anything else. I pushed with my feet off the floor like I was trying to jump with both of my legs. Then, as quickly as I could afterward, I brought my feet up, using my body weight as momentum to let gravity take me back down.

It worked a little. I could feel his grip around my torso slip slightly but I wasn't heavy enough to slip away from him completely. He quickly readjusted, tightening his arm more than it had been to start with. My next attempt was to bite his hand, but I didn't get a chance before I heard him do more than just grunt at me. "Eva?" the man whispered. It was Jake's voice. It had to be his voice. It was lower and more horse than I remember but it had to be his voice.

I stopped trying to fight. I didn't wiggle, squirm, nothing. I just stood there waiting to hear him again, hoping he understood the relaxation in my body was my answer to his question.

"Eva... it can't be you... that wouldn't make sense..." he whispered again. Why was he being so quiet? I wondered. Who was he up here trying to trap?

I nodded my head, then tried to open my mouth wide enough to lick his hand. I figured that would show him it was me. Only Eva would lick someone's hand.

As soon as my tongue hit his fingers, I felt him release me. I turned around, still not seeing him well but I could feel him, and smell him now. It *was* Jake. I buried my head in his chest. He smelled exactly the way I remember him smelling, like a man, musky and woodsy with a hint of citrus from his deodorant.

"Jake..." I said finally, so he knew it really was me.

"Oh my gosh, Eva, baby... How are you here? I can't believe it... Are you serious?" He whispered again. I could tell by his response he really hadn't expected to see me again, not so soon or like this, anyway.

"Jake, I..."

"Shh, baby, don't answer, just let me hold you," He whispered as he tightened his arms around my back. I didn't know what he was doing there or why I needed to be quiet but I listened. Then, before letting it continue for too long, I realized I couldn't. He was in danger. Reagan was downstairs with a gun, ready to shoot anyone who wasn't a female named Kaleah.

"Reagan," I whispered, "he's down there with a gun, he thinks you're Miller… You can't kill him though, Jake, he knows how to deactivate my tracker."

He brought his hand up to pull my head in tighter to his chest. "Okay, baby…" he said softly, still whispering. "Andry's down there. Hopefully Reagan is still alive. Has he hurt you?"

"No…" I couldn't think of anything he'd done that he needed punished for.

"Good… He thinks I'm Miller?" I could tell he was thinking about what that meant. After a moment, he finally responded again. "Do you wanna play prisoner, then?" He asked, then leaned down to give me a quick kiss on top of the head.

"Sure," I didn't know exactly where he was going with it but I trusted him.

"Okay, turn around and I'll cuff you…"

I did what he asked; I turned to where my back was at his front. He reached down and took a hold of both my hands, pulling them behind my back. Then, without hearing the rattling of the chain I felt the cold metal of cuffs being put on my wrists.

"I'm going to cover your mouth again. It'll be more believable. Anything else I need to know first, though?" He whispered.

"He knows what Miller's done to me, he's Marcus' brother… He brought me here to look for him, he doesn't know he's… uh…"

"Got it…" He said, knowing where I was going with it. Then he put his hand over my mouth again, but gently this time. From there, I expected him to move, but he didn't. He was hesitating for some reason. He let his hand fall from my mouth and turned me back around. "I love you, baby," he whispered as he leaned down and kissed me. "I love you so much… You have no idea how much I've missed you…" I could hear his voice starting to break. "I can't believe you're here... in front of me again..."

I couldn't see him but I'd hoped this wasn't a trick. It couldn't have been. I'd know my man from anywhere, even in the dark. It was him. I knew it. I couldn't believe he was really in front of me again, either. It felt all too real in that moment. "I love you too, Jake..." I said, then leaned in for another kiss. "It better be you, Jacob Miles!"

"It's me... I think we need to get your eyes checked though, baby..." Apparently he didn't have as much trouble seeing my outline as I did his. "Now, you ready to be a shitty prisoner again?"

"Yes," I said smiling. Even though I knew he couldn't see it, I hoped he heard it.

"Good!" He kissed me again, then spun me back around and returned his hand to my mouth. He pushed me toward the top of the stairs like I expected this time but then he let go of me again. I was about to ask him what he was doing when I heard him draw his pistol, release the magazine, and cycle the action as quietly as he could, probably to remove a chambered round.

When we got to the bottom of the stairs, I nodded in the direction I had last seen Reagan and we started moving that way. I didn't hear anything, so I was concerned about what might have happened to him. I hoped Andry hadn't killed him already. Then the closer we got to what looked like the living room I heard him finally. He was groaning and sounded hurt.

"Hey, Boss, caught one." Andry said, watching Jake lead me around the corner into the room.

"I did too," Jake said, pushing me. Andry's face initially looked confused, then he corrected it quickly. I suspected Jake probably winked at him or something.

I looked down and saw Reagan laying on the floor cuffed as well. He wasn't dead, but he looked like Andry probably socked him pretty good. He must have caught him early on, right when we got there. Reagan was a good agent. I figured the only reason we both got caught was because they were lying in wait, but for whom I didn't yet know.

"Sit up, you little shit!" Jake pointed the gun at Reagan as he motioned for Andry to help Reagan sit.

Andry took one large step over toward him then nudged him with his boot. Reagan looked up finally and saw me then sat up. "Kaleah… I'm sorry, honey." In that moment, I realized I forgot to tell Jake that Reagan and I were also role playing.

"What are you doing in my house?" Jake asked, speaking to Reagan again.

"I'm not telling you shit! You caught us both already. What good would it do to talk now?" Reagan sounded upset. Since I knew he'd never been erased before it was easy to assume he'd never been caught before either. If this was his first time, I could see why he'd be frustrated.

"I need to know there's not more of you," Jake said as he held his gun up to point it at my temple, while still covering my mouth with his hand.

I began to squirm and whine like I believed there were bullets in it, and I was concerned. Reagan's face quickly went from being frustrated to terrified. "Dude, stop! There's no one else, okay? Put the gun down, please!" I could tell he felt panicked, unsure what to do, or say. "She isn't a threat… We're just Gypsyins looking for food. We thought the house was vacant. I swear man, please… check her arm, you'll see."

I felt the release of pressure from the gun barrel at my temple. Jake didn't move his hand from my mouth yet but I felt him tugging my sleeve up, checking for my tag. He slipped his hand in up my shirt around my waist as well, surprising me and making me jump with a squeaking sound. "So, she is a Gypsyin… a nice looking one at that." If he was pretending to be either Miller or the standard Coldier agent, he was doing an amazing job. He went right where I'd have expected him to, acting like the first thing he'd like to do was take me for himself.

"You son of a bitch, that's my wife… don't you touch her!" Reagan was upset again, and for good reason. If he still thought Jake was actually Miller, he knew what sort of things had been done before and what he could do to me again.

"Your wife, you say…" Jake was having fun taunting Reagan. "I don't see a ring on her finger… she looks like fair game to me." He was probably enjoying tormenting him, just like I'm sure the way he felt after Reagan took me from him in New York on top of shooting Lane.

"Please, man… just let us go. We don't have anything you need. We're just Gypsyins."

"You might be… but this one seems awful familiar…" Jake continued as he let his hand run up my front until he stopped right above my navel. "Andry, watch him. If he moves, knock him out, I don't care. I'm gonna take her to go have a closer look." I tried to shake my head like I didn't want that to happen as I continued to make noises under his hand. "You better not fight me, woman… you'll make it worse for yourself."

I didn't listen to him. I wanted to make it believable for Reagan so I was going to play the 'shitty prisoner role' as best as I could. I continued to wiggle and squirm like I was trying to get away from him.

"Kaleah, sweetie…" Reagan sounded concerned; my acting must have been working. "You're going to be okay. We'll get out of this, all right?" He said, looking at me then took his focus back to Jake, "If you hurt her, I swear I will find a way to kill you." I could tell he meant it. He must have never been in a situation like this before, since it didn't seem like he was holding anything back. I wasn't sure that was the smartest approach. If Jake really had been Miller, Reagan's poor strategic word play wasn't all that encouraging.

Jake didn't hesitate any longer. He pulled me, making me walk backward until we were in a separate room, one that was just off of the back entry where we came in. "Eva, oh my gosh, baby!" He said softly still whispering as he shut the door and turned me toward him. "I didn't know if I would ever find you again. How did you get here?… Why are you here?" He sounded relieved as he wrapped his arms around me again while I rested my face against his chest.

"Jake… I have so much I have to tell you." I said, thinking about all that had happened and where I was now. I didn't know where to start. There were so many things I needed him to know. At the same time, we needed to continue what we were doing until I figured out how to convince Reagan to tell me how I could deactivate my tracker.

"I know, baby… I know…" He said as he pulled away to look at me. I couldn't help but tear up when I saw his face in front of mine. I missed him so much and seeing him here right in front of me again felt unbelievable. "Oh, baby… don't cry… shhh, you're okay now, I've got you." He said, pulling me back in. "I've got you, baby… you're safe now…" He whispered, as he began to stroke my hair. I'm sure he was as relieved to see me as I was him. "Here, turn around now. Let me get the cuffs off of you."

"Jake, I have my memory back now… I'm Eva again." I said, facing away from him, waiting to feel the metal fall off my wrists.

He didn't say anything for a moment and I wasn't feeling the cuffs fall off, either.

"Jake?" I said, waiting for a response.

"*Eva…*" He said it softly, thinking out loud. "Kaleah? Can I trust her?"

I thought it was odd what he was asking me but then I remembered the cabin and suddenly knew why he asked. "Yes, Jake… You can trust me, baby!" I said, hoping he believed me, since it was true.

He didn't remove the cuffs, he just spun me back around. "I'm sorry. I really am, but I can't yet." He said, looking at me, his face looked sincere.

"Jake… I don't understand." I really didn't. I'm sure he could see the confusion all over my face.

"I love you, baby, but I don't know if I can trust Eva again yet… Talk to me, tell me how you found me." He took a couple of steps back toward a bed behind him then sat down, "Come here, talk to me."

"I didn't find you," I said as I walked over and sat down next to him. "I mean, I hoped you were here, but I didn't know that you would be. I didn't know where you were. If you stayed in New York with Lane or… Oh my gosh, how is Lane? Is he okay? Did you get to him? He's okay, right?" I quickly became distracted from the subject we were on as soon as I thought about Lane.

Jake smiled and brought his hand up to push the hair from my face.

"Lane's fine, baby. It'll take him a while to recover but he should be fine. He told me everything that happened." Jake's face suddenly got serious after he said it like he was thinking about something else. "Wait, why are you in Nashville?"

"Marcus is Reagan's brother… Reagan thinks he's still alive. He thinks he rescued me when he took me from Lane in New York. I agreed to help him find Marcus, but only because I didn't see another way out. That was the only way I could get away from the Praetorium and back to you. I told them I didn't have the intel. Marcus was the only one who had the intel. Oh, I have something else to tell you, too. I'm not who you thought I was, I—"

"You don't have the intel?" He asked before I was able to finish.

"What?" I was about to tell him about my father, my past, my real name, everything, but then stopped. *Why did he care about the intel?*

"You said only Marcus had the intel. So you never had it?" I couldn't read him. I didn't know why he was asking, if he was genuinely curious or if he had ulterior motives.

"Why are *you* in Nashville, Miles?" I wondered the same thing. What was *he* doing here?

He furrowed his brow, confused by my question now.

"You weren't trying to look for me were you?" I asked. I could tell my mind wanted to split, as it had the first time Eva returned and tried to take Kaleah's place. A part of me wanted to trust him, but another part of me was just as suspicious of a Coldier agent as I was a Sicari. Agents are agents. They all lie at one point or another. *Even I do.* We all have ulterior motives. I wouldn't suspect Miles would be any different.

"What? Of course, I was trying to look for you." He sounded defensive like I'd thrown him off.

"Well, if you knew I wasn't in Nashville, what are you doing here?" *Reporting to Miller?*

"I was here to recruit men to go with me to Chicago to get you back."

"Then why are you interested in the intel?" I didn't want to catch him in a lie but it would be dumb for me to play naïve and not even try to ask him the hard questions. *If he's a back stabbing traitor, it'd be better to catch him now before he really got a chance to screw me over.*

"Look, baby, this isn't how I wanted this to go. I'm sorry if you're upset 'cause I didn't remove your cuffs, but you can trust me."

"But you can't trust me?" I didn't care about the cuffs, I wanted to see where his head was at.

He didn't say anything, he just looked away from me, thinking about what I said. "Fine, you're right." He said, finally looking back at me. "Turn around, I'll remove them."

I turned away from him like he said, but continued to talk. "I have just as much suspicion of you as you have of me. Who were you waiting for upstairs?"

"Miller... he was supposed to be home this afternoon. I was going to detain him and use his men. I was forming an army to take to go find you."

I turned back toward him after I felt him remove the cuffs. "What do you mean he was supposed to be home? This isn't *your* house?"

"No," He furrowed his brows again with the response. "Why... Eva, how did you find it?"

"The library," I said suddenly thinking about what I saw. "I looked up Miles in the back end directory. This address came up. When I looked up Miller's, nothing came up."

"Holy shit," the look on his face drastically changed suddenly. "It's not safe here for you. We gotta move." He said quickly as he stood up.

"Okay," I said, realizing he was right, and we were all in danger. I stood up next to him, then turned back around and put my hands behind me for him to re-cuff them.

"No, baby, we don't have time now. I gotta get you out of here. You won't be able to fight if I put them back on and if Miller or his men are around, you need to fight."

"Jake, I know but you have to... Reagan needs to believe that you're Miller. He won't deactivate my tracker if he finds out who you really are. He can't find out that I'm in love with you and not his brother!"

"Ugh…" I could tell he was torn. "Fine, I'm gonna make them loose though, so if you need to get out of them you can, okay?"

"Okay," I said, expecting him to hurry.

"Eva… I love you, baby, remember that okay?"

I turned back toward him when I felt he was done. "Jacob…" I said, looking directly into his eyes. "I love you too! You can trust me. I'm still your Kaleah… Eva's on your side, okay? I'm on your side, baby." *I always have been.*

He looked confused, but he nodded like he understood. "Okay… I believe you. Let's go now. I need to get you out of here."

8

FORGOTTEN LIES

It was so obvious; I was kicking myself for missing it. Miller must have doctored the data in the library's central archive, erasing all signs of himself while putting Jake's name on Miller's own house. He knew Jake and I had been traveling together and must have assumed that if we were ever separated, I would look for his house in hopes of reconnecting. Jake obviously didn't know Miller had done this, so he was lying in wait for Miller while Miller had already set this trap for me. The plan made so much sense. Miller was smart, but I wasn't sure how smart.

"Jake… How would Miller even know I'm here? Can he see my tracker? I didn't know the Coldiers had that technology…" He was clearly in a hurry but I was still tying to make sense of it all.

"No, baby, just knowing he set a trap for us is why I wanna get you the hell out of here. He shouldn't have any way of knowing either of us are here. He probably set it up after I saw him in Nashville when I came to get your antibiotics. Good thing I turned my tracker back off in New York." He was talking quickly without paying much attention to my face. I don't think he even realized what he'd just told me.

"What?" I would have taken my hand to stop him so he'd look at me but I couldn't move either of them. "Jacob... stop! What did you just say?"

He was in the middle of putting his boots back on. He must have removed them to be more stealthy. He looked up at me quickly, then back to his boots. "I said we gotta get out of here... but don't worry, Miller can't track us."

"That's not what you said..." I never knew he saw Miller at Nashville when he came to get my medicine. He told me he hadn't seen him. *Holy shit, I caught him in a lie.* He lied... He promised me he would never lie to me... *What did this mean?* My mind was reeling at the thought. He promised!

"Baby, we gotta go. We can talk about this later, all right?" He asked, clearly clueless that I just experienced an epiphany of that magnitude.

"Sure," I said quietly under my breath, but I felt frozen. I didn't want to move. I didn't want to run, to fight. I didn't want to do anything but sit in silence and ponder what it meant. Had he been deceiving me this whole time? *Was* he actually working for Miller? Why would he lie? Not only that, why would he turn his tracker back on when he got here? It made no sense. The more I thought about it though, the more memories began to make sense. That was probably why there was a Coldier agent that Luca found dead in the grotto lands. That's how he found us. He was tracking Jake... The more I thought about it all, the worse I felt. I felt sick and chilled like I was about to pass out.

"Eva?" Jake asked. "Are you all right?"

I turned my face to look up at him but my eyes barely connected with his when I saw a gray fuzzy tunnel closing in on my vision.

"Eva!"

"**K**aleah... wake up... Kaleah... Oh my gosh, you son of a bitch! What the hell did you do to her? I swear when I get free I'm gonna kill you. I swear it!"

"You won't be getting free…"

"Kaleah… come on, yeah there you go… wake up." I could hear Reagan's voice next to me. By the movement, it felt like we were in a vehicle.

"Owe!" My forehead hurt. I tried to reach up to feel it but I couldn't, then I remembered I was still cuffed. I sat up and looked around. I was in the back seat with Reagan, but both of us had our seat belts on so I knew I couldn't move over closer to him.

"You're bleeding… She's bleeding, you bastard." Reagan shouted again.

Jake was driving, and Andry was in the passenger seat. I could see Jake look at me through the rear-view mirror but he didn't say anything. Andry turned to look at me as well. "She is bleeding, Boss. You wanna do anything about it?" He said, looking back over at Jake.

Jake didn't reply for a moment, probably thinking about how to handle it. "She's fine." He said, suddenly cold and calloused, just like Miller would. I couldn't help but wonder how much of it was an act and if any of it could have been real.

"You *are* a son of a bitch, a *lying* son of a bitch!" I said it where I knew Jake could hear me. I meant it, every word. I hated his mother, so it didn't bother me to call her names. At the same time, I knew that Reagan would be suspicious if I didn't fight back with my mouth. After all, that's what he knew me to be good at, running my mouth.

Jake didn't respond. He just glanced at me again through the rear-view mirror, then back to the road.

We drove for what felt like a couple of hours without anyone else talking. I think everyone knew better than to say anything, especially me. I had no idea where Jake was taking us but I hoped it wasn't back to New York. If Reagan was going to deactivate my tracker, I doubted he'd have what he needed to do it in New York. I suspected he would need to take me back to the Praetorium to do it, but I really had no idea. I don't think Jake did either.

"Where are you taking us?" I broke the silence finally speaking to Jake. Reagan was leaning against his door and looked like he was asleep but I knew better than to believe it. You can't trust a spy, especially not when they're asleep. We were trained to listen while we slept, always be listening. Always be on alert for any edge, any angle, any intel that might be of use later. You never know what advantage it could give you, especially in a situation like the one we were both in currently.

"Why would I tell you that?" Jake said, still sounding impudent.

"I don't know… maybe because I asked, dip-shit!" I wasn't all that happy with him but I didn't care if he suspected it or thought I was still acting.

"Do you think calling me names will make me want to answer you?" This time, he sounded more like Jake talking to Kaleah.

Too bad I still felt like speaking to him the way a scorned Eva would. I especially liked that I could get away with it since I was expected to be acting. "Do you think lying about your real intentions with me will make me love you? The chances are about as high I think!"

I couldn't see much of his face but I could tell that one puzzled him. His brow furrowed at the same time he squinted, the classic expression when confused. "Maybe it's best that you don't know where we're going then… That way when I release you later, you can't make plans for where to escape to." It sounded like he didn't know what to say but was still playing the role we devised unaware I wasn't completely acting anymore.

"Release me and see what I do to you." I said, looking out the window even though I couldn't see anything since it was still dark.

"I don't know what you think you're gonna do, but I sure have plans for you… If you've got a problem with that, you can show me in the morning." The way he said it made me think he had caught on to my secondary message.

"So, I guess that means we won't be there tonight then…" I tried to lean as far as my seat belt would allow to look at what time the clock on the console read—twelve, twenty-three, just past midnight.

"We'll get there when we get there. Why don't you just go to sleep like your *husband*…"

I didn't say anything else. I just sat there and thought about what I wanted to do. I *was* tired actually and the thought of resting sounded nice. I would have done it sooner if I'd have been able to get comfortable but I couldn't with the seat belt on.

"Hmm," I looked down at where the belt was buckled into the seat. It didn't look like it would be hard for me to undo if I got my hands around to it. Being small had its advantages. I wiggled and turned where my fingers could reach the red push button on top of the buckle. If I wanted, I knew I could pull my wrists loose from the cuffs to do it but I didn't want to take the chance that Reagan might see me, so I didn't.

It worked. As soon as I pushed the button, the seat belt began to retract, slowly sliding past me back into its spot behind the doorjamb. I looked over at Reagan; he didn't look comfortable either but I knew I shouldn't unbuckle him. I edged over closer to him, then turned to where I was facing the seat so I could curl up with my back to the front of the car. Once I got comfortable enough, I lay my head in his lap. It looked like the most comfortable thing around so I figured it'd due.

The thought of it bothering Jake was also a bonus. Until I figured out why he would lie to me, I didn't care how chummy it looked like I was getting with Reagan. As far as I knew, Reagan hadn't tried to deceive me yet, so he wasn't as high on my shit-list as Jake currently was.

It must have woken Reagan up when he felt the pressure of my head laying on him. He opened his eyes and looked down at me. It looked like he wanted to smile, but didn't. He was probably still torn up with the idea that we'd been caught and he didn't know what was about to happen to us, namely me, since 'Miller' didn't seem very nice.

"Are you okay?" He whispered but I couldn't tell if it was loud enough for Jake to hear him or not since I had one ear muffled by his thigh.

I nodded, "Are you?" I mouthed back.

He nodded, then looked up toward Jake. "Did he hurt you?" He spoke softly again, looking back down at me.

I wasn't sure how I wanted to respond. Technically he did, emotionally anyway when I found out that he'd lied. And technically, I had a nice bloody spot on my head, probably from hitting something when I passed out. So telling Reagan 'no' might have made him suspicious since all the evidence showed otherwise.

"Yeah," I whispered back, "but I'll be fine." I forced a smile. It wasn't genuine, and I figured he'd be able to see that.

He half-smiled back, trying to encourage my optimism. "Did he tell you where—" He started to whisper again, but then stopped and shook his head. "Never mind," he mouthed. I wondered if he was trying to see if I had learned anything about Marcus, but I wasn't sure since he didn't finish.

I nodded. When I felt him relax back against the door now done talking, I shut my eyes.

"Reagan! Man, it feels like it's been a whole month since I've seen ya." Marcus sounded excited, which wasn't all that common for him. He quickly walked over and gave Reagan a big hug like he had missed him.

"Hey, man…" Reagan sounded like his usual self, dull and boring. "Was it a good one?" He asked still looking at Marcus. I assumed he was talking about the mission we'd just been on.

"Yeah, we got a lot done. It went well." Marcus said now pulling back from their hug.

Reagan looked at me, then back at him. There was something about the look that was unusual, but I wasn't sure what it was. I didn't say anything. I just sat there waiting for them to finish, like I usually did, hoping they'd hurry so we could get back to our room.

"That's good to hear." Reagan sounded upbeat, but I didn't believe it. "Parker has me assigned to a Gypsyin now too, so we'll see how that goes. We're leaving for our first mission tomorrow morning."

"Really? Okay cool." I could see something about Marcus' face change when he heard it.

It didn't take long for their conversation to be over and Marcus to decide it was finally time to go. He was quiet the entire way back to our room. When we got inside, I asked him what was wrong. I could tell he had something on his mind.

"Nothing, baby. I'm fine." I knew by the way he said it he was deflecting, hoping I would leave him alone.

"Marcus…" I said so he would look up at me, and he did. "Do you not think I know by now when there's something off?"

He rolled his eyes, knowing I was right and I wouldn't leave him alone until I got it out of him. "Reagan lied, all right?" He said, finally giving in and telling me.

"Really? About what?" I hadn't been listening to most of their conversation so I wasn't sure what he was referring to.

"About having his own Gypsyin…" He said it as he began to remove his clothes, getting himself ready for bed.

"Why would he lie about that, and how do you even know he did?" I asked.

"I don't know why. That's what bothers me. Parker told me the unit was closed… They were having issues with the current Gypsyins going missing so they've suspended the program until they figure out what to do about it."

"What? Why didn't you tell me?" I couldn't understand why he would hold that kind of information from me, and for how long, I wasn't sure either.

"Because, when I asked her what they planned on doing with the current ones in the field, I knew you wouldn't like the solution they came up with. So I didn't see any reason to tell you until you needed to know."

"What?!" I couldn't express my shock enough. "What is the solution and when the hell did you think it would be a good time to tell me?"

"Eva, don't talk to me like that!" He said coarsely now standing in front of me without his shirt on. "I couldn't tell you while we were in the field, you would have run… I couldn't allow it."

"What the hell, Marcus?" I couldn't control my mouth, not when I was as upset as I was. "I would have run? What the hell are they going to do to me?"

"Eva, I told you not to speak to me like that. I won't warn you again!" He sat down on the bed and started to remove his socks. "You don't have a tracker like we do. They're going to put a tracker in you, that's all." He said it like it wasn't a big deal but I knew he wasn't telling me everything.

"If it's not a big deal, then why did you say I would have run?" I was still upset, but I tried not to cuss at him anymore. "I don't understand. If they put a tracker on me, won't that negate the whole Gypsyin part? Then you'd see I have a tag!"

"No, because they're going to put it in your head." He said it calmly like he was expecting me to get further upset and he didn't want to fuel it more than his answer was already likely to.

"What? They're gonna put it in what? And you're okay with this?" I couldn't believe him. He was too calm. How was he not as upset about it as I was?

"This is why I didn't tell you, Eva, because I knew you would freak out." He looked back up at me finally.

"Where at in my head?" Maybe it was too late to run but if I knew where it was, that didn't mean I couldn't try to remove it later.

"I'm not telling you. It'll be good for you to have a tracker. You need one. It'll keep you safe." I could tell he believed everything he was saying.

"No, it won't," I tried not to yell, but it was difficult. "It won't keep me any safer than I am right now… That's not why they're doing it, they're doing it so they can keep tabs on me, so they won't lose another agent. Do you think they give a shit about my safety, Marcus?"

"You're an agent!" He stood up and started yelling back at me. "You signed up for it. You knew what you were getting into, and you knew there's no way out. You're going to get your tracker and you're not going to fight them, do you hear me? That's an order!" He had gotten up in my face but was still yelling like he was farther away than he was.

I didn't think about it before I did it but I reached up and slapped him. I could tell instantly by the look in his eyes that that wasn't a good idea, and I immediately regretted it. "I'm sorry, Marcus." I said quickly, so he knew I hadn't thought before I did it.

"Turn around now." He ordered. I wasn't sure what he was going to do, but I was scared it would be something I didn't like.

"I'm sorry!" I said again, trying to plead with him.

"Now, Eva!" He didn't relent. He continued with his order.

"No, I said I was sorry!" I didn't know what else to do, but I didn't want to turn around.

He grabbed me by the arms and forced me. I didn't want to fight him but I didn't want to listen either. Once he had me spun around, he held my arms behind my back, up tight against him as he moved me backward.

"Why are you doing this? I said I was sorry." I didn't know what he was going to do with me but I stopped any attempt at fighting. I knew it would just make it worse for me.

"I'm restraining you." As soon as he said it, I felt him putting the zip ties from my bag onto my wrists. "Then I'm going to get dressed again and take you to Parker. Your surgery wasn't until tomorrow but I'm sure she can make other arrangements if I bring you in early."

"What? Marcus, please, you don't need to do this. I'm sorry, baby. I'm sorry I hit you." I didn't intend to cry but I could tell I was beginning to the more I begged him to reconsider.

"I wish I didn't have to treat you like this, Eva, but you fight me when you shouldn't. You need the tracker, whether you think so or not." He didn't sound remorseful at all.

"So that's it? You're just gonna turn me over to her?" I couldn't believe how easy it seemed for him to be okay with it. "I hate you, Marcus," I didn't mean it but I was mad and I knew he couldn't do anything worse than he was doing to me already, so I didn't care. "I hate you… I freakin' hate you…"

"Eva, stop it! You know you don't mean that." He sounded more calm, probably because he knew he had me restrained and I couldn't fight him anymore.

"No… I do mean it," I continued to cry. "I hate you. I wish I had never been assigned to you. I wish Reagan took me. He wouldn't have treated me like this."

He was quiet for a second as he pulled me over to sit on the bed, probably so he could get himself dressed again. "If you believe that, then you're delusional. The one thing Reagan doesn't have is a soft side, especially for mouthy women."

9

LAST SECRET

"Grab him, I got her." Jake spoke up immediately after the car stopped. I didn't get a chance to fully turn over and open my eyes before I heard the doors of the vehicle open, then shut, then open again. I glanced down at my feet; Jake was standing there, staring at me. He didn't say anything, but he didn't look thrilled with how I was laying or how close I was to Reagan, either.

After a moment, Reagan's door opened, startling him to finally wake up as well. He looked down at me, then over at Jake. I turned from looking at him over to Andry. He didn't smile or say anything either, he just grabbed a hold of Reagan's arm and pulled him from the seat at the same time I felt Jake grab my ankle.

"No, wait…" I yelled. I wasn't sure why that was what I yelled but I figured it fit into character well enough it would do. "Stop! Wait…"

Jake didn't respond. He just kept dragging me further along the seat, closer to him, until he could reach my waist. I tried to kick him but I did it playfully so it wouldn't actually hurt. He smiled like he felt ornery, then tugged me harder. "Let's go, Gypsyin!" He said finally in his raspy lowered voice.

He had me; he pulled me from the car and stood me on my feet. Even though he was playing rough the way his hands held me still felt loving. I wanted to stand there and let them continue to touch me, then before I got too carried away, I remembered I was mad at him. *He lied,* I reminded myself. *Don't give in to anything until you find out why he lied.* That was a grand idea, but I knew it probably didn't matter.

I looked around as he moved me and shut the door. It was light outside now but I couldn't tell where we were. "Where have you taken us?" I asked but not very loud just in case he wanted to whisper back an actual answer.

He brought his face down next to mine, close enough I could feel his beard tickle my cheek. "My parents had a vacation cabin. Hopefully, it's still the way they left it before the war." He whispered.

"Okay," I said softly again. Then he quickly kissed my ear before he pulled his face away again to walk with me over to the entrance and inside.

"Set him down on the floor, Andry." Jake said as he pushed me over to Reagan. "Sit!" He said now talking to me. "Andry, stand here and watch them. I'm going to take a look around and make sure we're alone." He pulled his gun from his holster, then walked off.

"Andry… that's not a common name, is it?" Reagan must have felt like talking, I didn't know where he was going with it but I was intrigued and interesting in seeing how he was going to attempt an escape solely with his mouth.

"It was my father's," Andry said, I think trying to make a joke but he didn't smile or anything after he said it so I didn't know what he was doing. I didn't really know him well enough to know what to expect from him. Although, from my memory of how he had reacted with me and Luca, I got the idea he was great with guarding prisoners.

"How tall are you? You have to be well over six feet?" Reagan continued to be cordial.

"Six-eight, actually," Andry answered, being polite back.

"Wow, man, that's tall." Reagan went on like they were old friends. "Is the rest of your family tall like that?"

Andry smiled, but not like he was enjoying the conversation, more like he knew what Reagan was trying to do. "Want some advice?" He asked as he looked at Reagan, before quickly glancing at me then back.

"Sure." Reagan sounded like he really thought Andry was being sincere.

"If you want to make it out of here alive, just give my boss whatever he wants and he won't kill you." Andry actually did sound sincere when he said it, to my surprise.

"Okay, what is that?" Reagan asked as he leaned forward a little, ready to listen.

"Her…" Andry said as he let his eyes drift over to me.

Reagan turned his head to follow Andry's eyes. Then he sat there and looked at me, trying to think about how to respond. "I can't do that, Andry," he said calmly, still being cordial. "She means too much to me to just walk away."

"Shame… I thought you'd say that." Andry said, done with the conversation. I had no idea what Jake had told him but I hoped he wouldn't say anything else that would make Reagan suspicious.

We sat there and waited for Jake to return for another couple of minutes until finally I saw him as he walked back through the front door again. This time, he was carrying two of his black duffle bags with him and another smaller gunny sack. As he walked over toward us, he threw the gunny sack down at my feet, then took the two duffles down the hall into a different room.

After a minute, he started talking as he walked back down the hall toward us. "Andry, un-cuff her, but keep a close watch. She's a tricky one." He said, looking from Andry to me, then he continued to talk to both me and Reagan. "There's some food in that," he pointed at the gunny sack. "You might ration it if you don't want to starve. I don't know how much more I'll have for you. Kaleah, I'll let you decide how much you want to take for yourself and how much you want to feed your *husband*… Oh, and just so you both know, this isn't an area I'd try to escape from if I were you. I doubt the bears up here have had fresh meat in a while; they're probably ravenous." Thankfully, his threat sounded realistic. So I didn't figure it would be hard to keep Reagan's mind off of the idea of escaping since I didn't actually want to.

I didn't give Andry a chance to un-cuff me before I decided to act up. "I'm not hungry," I said as I kicked the gunny sack away from my feet.

Jake smiled like he didn't mind because he had other plans for me, anyway. "Well, isn't that perfect? You're not hungry and I'm tired… Let's go." He said quickly, walking over to me and reaching down for my arm to pull me to my feet.

"No, wait… I'll eat. I'm not tired. I didn't mean it… I'm hungry now."

"Too late," he said as he looked back at Andry. "Watch him, same orders as last night, clear?"

"Sure, Boss," Andry nodded as he looked down at Reagan. He didn't look tired at all. Maybe he was able to sleep in the car like we did.

"Wait, no…" It didn't take Reagan long to begin to plead with him when he saw Jake was about to take me away again. "Let her go, please!"

"Don't worry," Jake said as he spun me around, ready to walk out. "She says she's hungry… I'll bring her back to you nice and full."

Reagan and I both continued to argue with him as he proceeded to walk me back to the room where I assumed he had taken his bags. Once we got inside, though, I stopped and didn't say any more. I just sat down on the bed and waited for him to remove the cuffs. I knew better than to say anything to him this time that might make him leave them on like he did the night before.

He shut the door, then walked over to me. "Eva, baby, what's wrong?" He said softly as he started to remove them.

"How do you know there's something wrong?" I was surprised he could tell. I thought he was denser than that.

"You made it pretty clear by the things you were saying in the car. I doubt you'd have said that stuff to me if I was actually Miller."

I turned to face him when I felt the cuffs fall off. I didn't know if I should be completely upfront with him or try to get it out of him another way. If I just came out and told him he lied, he could come up with another lie to cover for himself, then that wouldn't do me any good. But we were also supposed to be trusting each other, so I was at a standstill mentally on how to proceed. "No, you're right, I wouldn't say *anything* to you if you were Miller. I'd just lay here and beg to die as you tortured me. But you showed me you're not the man I thought you were, either."

"What?" He looked confused. Then I saw his eyes go up to my forehead then back down to my eyes. "Oh, baby, is it 'cause I didn't stop and do something when Reagan said you were bleeding?" He raised his hand to my forehead, ready to inspect it now.

"No," I batted it away. "It's because you're a liar…"

"What?… What have I lied to you about?" He asked, genuinely unsure.

"I don't know… Why don't you tell me? The last thing I remember was you making a promise to me when we were at the cabin that you'd never lie to me again… about *anything*!" I hoped he could tell that I was upset, and it was a serious subject. I didn't like being lied to, not when it was from the man that was supposed to love me and want to marry me. I especially didn't like that he broke his promise, either. That was foul in my book, very foul.

"I don't understand, I haven't li—" He stopped mid-sentence like he realized what he was saying wasn't accurate. "The girl…" He said suddenly, but that didn't mean anything to me. "You don't remember do you? You were drunk…"

"No," I said as I furrowed my brow. I couldn't even really remember the few times I'd had alcohol, never mind how many times I'd been drunk. I had no idea what he was talking about.

"Ugh… Okay…" He sighed like it was going to be a long story and he had other plans that would now be delayed.

"What does this have to do with you lying to me?"

"I didn't lie… uh, well… I did, but I was sorry. I didn't feel like I had a choice, and I told you the truth as soon as I felt like I could."

"While I was drunk?" I said flatly, so he got the idea it didn't count.

"Uh well, maybe…" I could tell he felt apologetic, but that still didn't cover for his horrible decision making.

"Jacob!" I hoped if he felt a little scolded, he would stop dancing around it and just tell me already.

"Oh my gosh, Eva, fine…" It sounded like my tactic worked. He went on with more of the actual story. "I knew I did something that would make you really angry but I didn't feel like I could tell you right away. And I wouldn't have done it but I had no choice. Then after you got poisoned, I felt awful and knew I had to tell you but I still didn't want to see you upset with me so I might have thought you being a little tipsy was a good time to tell you… I guess once it was out I figured I was in the clear and—"

"You weren't," I interrupted him.

"Well, I see that now…" He sighed.

"I can't believe you, Jake." Nothing he was saying was making me feel any better. Now I was just more confused than before. "Who's the girl? *Were* you cheating on me?"

"What? No, Eva, I promised you I'd never do that."

"You promised me you'd never lie to me again too, Jacob, and look what happened. I don't know if I can believe anything you tell me now. That's the cost of lying!"

"Well, you're not so innocent yourself then, either. Are you, *Eva*?" His tone changed from being defensive to stern.

I was about to tell him I never lied to him but then I realized I couldn't actually say that either. "Fine, I never told you everything, but I also never promised you that I would. Who's the girl, Jacob?"

"Who are *you*, Eva? You tell me who you really are first and I'll tell you everything about her."

Miller already knew who I was, so I didn't guess if Jake was really working with him and trying to deceive me that it would matter for him to know now, too. "My name isn't Eva." I said, then swallowed when I realized I was about to finally let him in on everything, my last long kept secret. "It's Jayde Lilly Prescott. I'm Elijah Jordan Prescott's daughter. I have a sister too. She's younger than me. Her name is Ellice Prescott. My father never knew, but I signed up under the Sicari, intending to be a double agent. I wanted to do something that would make him proud of me. That's the only thing I lied to you about, Jake. I promise."

I could see from his face after I said it—that wasn't what he'd expected whatsoever. His mouth wasn't open, but it looked close to it and his eyes weren't their usual almond slivers, either. They were widened like he was surprised or shocked, maybe both.

"Are you serious?" He said softly, still unable to believe it.

I nodded.

"Oh my gosh, Eva… Do you even realize what that means?" He asked it as he slowly looked away, like *he* didn't even realize what it meant, but was doing his best to think about it.

"I probably don't." I said, being honest. "Oh… Reagan told me I'm also the last living Gypsyin from my Sicari unit. So, yeah… unless I can get deactivated somehow, it doesn't matter who my dad is, the Sicari will never stop trying to find me."

"Okay…" he said softly, probably now thinking about the implications of that and what it meant as well.

"Who's the girl?" I didn't want to wait, I wanted to know.

He nodded, knowing it was his turn then he proceeded, "She's nobody… I mean I didn't know that at first. When I went to Nashville to get your medicine, I went to see Miller too… I know I told you I wouldn't but I… Honestly, I intended to kill him. When I thought about all the things he'd done to you, and I was so close to him, I wanted to kill him more than I wanted to keep my word to you that I would stay away." He looked up at me, seeing if I believed him.

"Okay, go on…" I said.

"Well, when I got there, not only did he act like he knew things about you that I didn't know but he also had a picture of this little girl. He said she was your daughter, and honestly, she looked just like you, like… *just* like you, you know? He said that he erased you and sent you away after you had her. He told me you weren't who I thought you were, and that you were lying to me just to keep the intel safe."

"What? My daughter?" I looked away from him as I thought really hard about that period in time.

"He said he'd kill her if I didn't cooperate with him. He made me turn my tracker back on and he said I needed to get the intel from you if I wanted him to let her go. But don't worry baby, she doesn't exist. She wasn't ever real! Okay?"

I felt more confused the longer he went on. "What? How do you know that?"

"I don't trust Miller. He's a liar, among other things. I knew he wanted the intel, but if he'd kill you for it, he'd do other things too. At first, I really didn't know what to think. If she was real, I didn't want you to lose another baby, you know, since… yeah. Well, so after I got you back from Luca, I sent Andry to spy on Miller and get the truth."

"Oh…" Things were beginning to click now. "That's the girl you were talking about when Andry was at your mom's house."

"Yes!" He sounded excited that I was beginning to understand. "Andry told me he couldn't find anything that made him think she was real, so we both just assumed it must be a picture of you as a child. The only thing that kept bothering me was I didn't know how he would get your picture, and what he meant when he said you weren't who I thought you were. Do you think he knew that you're E.J.'s daughter?"

"I know he knew," I said as I thought back and sifted through different memories. "I think that's why Marcus is dead. The bridge that day was an ambush… I sent a letter to my father telling him I was coming, and I had intel, but not to hurt Marcus, to just have agents ready to capture us. When they shot him, I assumed my father never got the letter, because he wouldn't have ordered that." *He wouldn't have betrayed me when I finally was about to come home to him.*

"But Miller would…" Jake added.

"Yeah…" I said softly, "Miller would… When he caught me, I'd decided I wasn't going to share the intel with him. I wasn't going to give it to anyone but my father. My dad was a good man. He'd know what to do with it. Before Miller interrogated me, I told him I was EJ's daughter. I figured that would make him stop, but he didn't. I think it made him want to punish me more. After he initially erased me, I have a few memories of where I can see him talking to me again, but that's all. He erased me so many times, everything around that period is fuzzy. I just can't remember it."

Jake leaned in to hug me as soon as I was done telling him. "I'm sorry you had to go through all that, baby." He said as he stroked my hair.

"So the girl's not real, though, right? You're sure I don't have a daughter?"

"I can't be sure of anything, Eva, but I don't believe so."

"Why did you not tell me all of this when I was sober?" I was suspicious Jake had more of a reason than just not wanting me to yell at him.

He was quiet for a moment still holding me, then let out a big sigh before he answered. "Because, baby, I knew if you thought you had a daughter in Nashville, you'd go there to try to save her. And I don't want you anywhere near that place, not as long as Miller is still alive."

"But what if she's real?"

"One step at a time, baby… Let's see if we can get you deactivated first. Then I'll take you back to New York. You can see your family… We'll decide what to do then, together… agree?"

That sounded like a good plan but I wasn't sure if I could agree so easily. I really didn't like the thought of having one of my babies anywhere near that monster.

"Eva…" Jake pulled back to look at me. "I'm almost certain she's not real. Miller will do anything for the intel. This is just another one of his tricks. We'll decide together, after you're safe, I promise."

Together… "All right," I said. "If you promise…"

IO

DOUBLE SIDED WHISPERS

He smiled as he continued to look into my eyes. "I still can't believe you're actually here with me. I didn't know how far we'd get, but I was preparing to gather a small army to come and take you back."

I reached up to stroke his hair. I loved that he was willing but more than that I was happy that he never got a chance to. I knew they wouldn't have made it far. The Praetorium was more fortified than anywhere else in the country as far as I knew. "So, you did miss me?" I grinned.

"You have no idea," he said it softy as he let his eyes drift down to my lips.

I didn't say anything else. I just sat there waiting for him to make his move. I knew he wanted to.

"Are you tired, baby?" He looked back up into my eyes as he asked.

"No, I am hungry, though."

"You are? I was just saying that about the food in the sack to sound mean. I have more for you if you really want it."

"No, baby, I'm just... Don't worry about it, I can eat later. But you're tired, aren't you?" I started to wonder if that's why he asked if I was. His eyes looked like they were heavy. Surely, he had to be since he was up driving all night without a break.

"Yeah," he said as he reached up to touch my cheek, "this has been a difficult conversation. It's kinda worn me out."

"I understand. I should go back out there then." I thought it might be weird if I stayed in the room with Jake too long, but I didn't know exactly how Miller would treat his prisoners, either. Maybe that actually would be normal behavior for him.

"No... Don't go..." He said softly, then without warning, finally leaned in to kiss me.

I knew he was tired but apparently that didn't affect the intensity of what he was feeling. The kiss was strong and passionate, exactly how I would have expected it to be now that we were finally getting a chance to reconnect.

"Eva... you have no idea how much I missed you, baby." He whispered as he took his hand from my hair to my waist, pulling me in closer to him.

"I think I do." I said, searching his eyes. "I missed you just as much, I'm sure."

"Ugh... I doubt that." He teased, then slowly rested his forehead on my shoulder. "I don't want to just kiss you. I want to really reconnect."

"You're really tired though, aren't you?" I could tell there was something wrong. That must have been it. "If so, it's okay, I understand."

"No, baby... well, I am, but right now that's not as much my issue." He lifted his head to look back down at me. "I have to control myself... I can't get you pregnant again, not yet."

"That's it?" I reached up to rub his cheek. "Oh, baby... that's not a problem."

"Eva, I'm serious." He stopped me before I had a chance to tell him why. "I made a promise to my dad, and until we're married... you know... Plus, it's still not safe for you yet, not while you're still a Gypsyin."

"We can still wait, that's fine, but..." I paused. "I can't get pregnant now."

"What?" His eyes softened with concern.

"Before I left the Praetorium, they gave me a physical and a bunch of shots. One of them was birth control. I intended to tell you because it's supposed to last six months, and I didn't know if you'd be upset or—"

Before I got a chance to finish, he leaned in to kiss me again. "Oh, baby, you had me so worried. I had no idea what the Sicari might have done to you while they had you." He blew out a silent breath as he relaxed again.

I smiled up at him. "I love you."

"I love you too, baby." He leaned down to kiss me again, this time slow and gentle. "I'm not too tired to wait, unless you want to?"

"No, I'm good." I said, running my hands through his hair.

"Good." He said as he turned to sit on the bed, pulling me toward him. "'Cause I miss my girl."

***

"You don't act nearly as tired as you did," I said, resting my head against his shoulder while snuggling up next to him.

"Well, I feel it." I believed him when he said it. I lifted up to look and his eyes looked like they weren't even their usual almond shape. Now they were mere slits, I'm sure making it hard for him to see anything.

"Do you feel better now, more relaxed?" I leaned on my elbows to stare down at him.

"So much better," he said, smiling, "but that's how it is every time I'm in you, so..." he shrugged.

"Are you going to take me back out there now?" I assumed it would be the best place for me since I could help Andry watch Reagan. That way, Jake could sleep more comfortably, knowing he was safer.

"I don't know… I don't really like you being around him." He said, rolling over to sit up, then stand by the edge of the bed.

"Why? He hasn't hurt me. He believes I'm a hundred percent on his side, too. I think he's safe… for me, anyway." I said as I crawled over to the edge where I wrapped my arms around his thighs and looked up at him.

"You just looked a little too comfortable earlier, that's all." He said as he began to stroke my hair down and away from my forehead as he looked down at me.

"What do you mean?" I couldn't think of a point when I had really been comfortable at all.

"When you had your head in his lap…" He widened his eyes after he said it probably to help emphasize what he was talking about.

"Oh… that bothered you?" I had considered it might, but didn't really know that it would. "I just needed a pillow," I said, then leaned my head into him as I pulled him closer to me.

"Well, you might have been innocent thinking it's just a soft place for your head but all a man sees is how close you are to his crotch…" He wasn't holding anything back, making it clear why it bothered him.

"Ohhh," I said as I pulled back to look up at him again. I really hadn't thought about it that hard. I guess I didn't really know how men thought at all, but it made sense. "I'm sorry, baby."

"Come here." He brought his hands under my arms to help me stand. "I'm not going to lose you again," he said as he wrapped his arms around me. "If he tries to take you again, I don't care what he knows about your tracker. I'll kill him. And I'll kill any Sicari after him that tries to come for you again, too."

"I know… you're a lean, mean, tired killing machine." I said with a small laugh as I pulled away to look at him. "Why don't you take me back out there so you can come back here and lie down to rest? You can't go forever with no sleep. You're not that good."

He smiled, then leaned down to kiss me again. "Okay…"

"Good," I said then looked back over toward the bed where he'd left the cuffs. "I guess we'll need those."

"Right," he leaned on the bed, then reached to grab them.

I looked down at myself. I needed to put my pants back on. I didn't know if I looked like Jake'd had his way with me enough though, so I reached up and pulled on the top of my shirt, trying to break a couple of the buttons holding it together.

"What are you doing?" He asked as he stood back up off of the bed. I accidentally broke more buttons that I intended and apparently he noticed.

"Whoops, I guess I'm stronger than I thought." I said, trying to smile like it wasn't intentional and it wouldn't be a big deal.

"Eva, dammit… Now if you move the wrong way he can see your entire chest." Jake said, eyeing the damage.

I didn't know what else to say even though he was exaggerating, so I shrugged with an apologetic look on my face.

"I don't have another shirt for you." He turned to look inside his bags for something to cover me, anyway.

"It's okay, *Miller.* I gotta look like you did it… Remember, you don't care if I'm covered, you're an asshole." I said as I put my pants back on, then picked up the cuffs and tried to put them on myself as well.

"Nice try, Eva…" he mumbled, rummaging through his bags. He didn't sound thrilled.

"I can't go back out there in one of your shirts… it'll make him suspicious." I really did feel bad for my mishap but I didn't think trying to salvage it was a good idea either.

"Ugh…" Jake was clearly frustrated with me, but probably knew I was right. He zipped his bag back up and turned to walk back over to me. "Fine…" He sighed, returning his eyes to mine. I turned around without him asking so he could help me with the cuffs and so he wouldn't see just how open my shirt actually was now, either. "I know we need him so I won't kill him but if I catch him looking at you, I won't hesitate to make him a eunuch. He doesn't need his that part of his body to deactivate you."

I laughed, not being able to stop myself from picturing it in my mind. "Aww poor man, that wouldn't be nice."

"Well, you want me to pretend to be Miller? That doesn't sound so far off, I don't guess." He said as he finished the cuffs and spun me back around.

"You're so sexy." I didn't even realize I'd said it. I just couldn't get over the sight of him in front of me again. I missed him so much and didn't want to leave his side.

"Okay? That was random." He said, confused.

"I just missed you so much. And well…" I stepped back and let my eyes slowly glide down his body. "I'm not sure I can get enough of you."

"Well, good. I think I might just have you come back to my room again tonight." He took a step to close the gap between us, then leaned down and kissed me again. "Now, let's go, Gypsyin!" He said loudly as he took a hold of my arm firmly and opened the door. Before we exited the room, though, he reached down and adjusted my shirt so nothing would be showing.

I didn't say anything else. I just followed his lead until we got back to the living room where we'd left Reagan and Andry. I saw them both as soon as we walked in. They were sitting exactly how we left them. Andry didn't appear to be in the best mood and Reagan looked frustrated as well. I suspected Reagan had probably tried to talk to Andry again and didn't get very far.

As we got to Reagan, Jake pushed me a little, suggesting I sit. I tried my best to have a face that looked like I was scared but it wasn't easy since I actually enjoyed our time together.

"Watch her now too, Andry. I've had my fun. I'm done with her… *for now*." Jake said where we could hear him, then he leaned in to whisper something to him that he didn't want us to hear.

"Are you okay?" Reagan whispered to me when he saw Jake taking Andry's attention.

I nodded. I didn't want to say much though since if what he thought just happened to me really had happened I knew I wouldn't feel like talking. When the real Miller raped me the first time, I felt silenced for days, if not more, until he erased me. The moment he used me felt like he took more than my body for his pleasure. He took a piece of my spirit. He took my power and replaced it with a sense of vulnerability and shame. Even though I was innocent, he made me feel guilty and dirty… filthy… unwanted, unlovable…

"Are you sure?" Reagan continued to prod, breaking me from a trance I'd fallen into.

"I don't want to talk about it," I whisper-hissed back.

"Kaleah… I'm sorry…" He said sweetly, something I didn't remember being an aspect of his personality until that point. Maybe he did care about me and he wasn't just using me to find his brother.

"Are you hungry?" I asked, looking at the gunny sack, trying to change the subject, but when I looked back at him, I saw him looking down at my shirt. At that point, I wasn't sure he even heard the question. "Ryan!" I tried to still whisper but say it loud enough to get his attention.

"What?" He quickly brought his eyes back up to mine.

"You can't look at me like that," I said as I quickly looked back at Jake and Andry, making sure neither of them noticed. "Miller seems like he's pretty possessive of me now. He said he'd kill you if you got too close to me again." I said softly under my breath as I looked down, trying to make it look like we weren't talking.

"But I'm your *husband*," he winked.

"He doesn't care…" I said, widening my eyes to insist he cut it out. "Are you hungry?"

"No…" He turned away and leaned back, also trying to act like we weren't talking. "I can't eat when I'm stressed." He whispered. That was good for me to know. I honestly hoped he didn't want to eat. If he didn't eat, I knew he wouldn't have as much energy. Maybe that way he wouldn't be as likely to escape and try to fight with Jake. "Are you?" He asked now trying to pull the gunny sack toward us with his feet.

I shook my head. "I'm just tired."

"Okay, you can lean on me again if you want."

I looked down at his lap, then looked back up to see if Jake had left yet. I knew what he'd said but I couldn't help but think about how comfortable it would be compared to laying straight on the floor.

"It's okay…" Reagan said, seeing I felt torn.

I nodded, then wiggled over toward him and leaned my head on his shoulder. "Elbow me if I start to talk in my sleep, okay?" I whispered.

"Okay," He whispered back.

II

TWISTED PLANS

I was awakened by a sharp elbow in the side. "Owe," I opened by eyes to look over at Reagan. *Holy shit, what did I say?* "Ryan?"

"Shhh, Kaleah," he looked at me, then back to Andry who was sitting on the couch across from us now asleep as well.

"Oh my gosh," I whispered when I saw him. I didn't know what that meant other than Reagan probably saw it as an invitation to try to escape. *Shit... Really, Andry?*

"You started to talk in your sleep, too. I was afraid it'd wake him up," Reagan whispered, as he leaned over closer to me.

"What was I saying?" I hoped it wasn't something that would blow my cover.

"I don't know. Something about a man named Miles. I didn't let it go on long because you were getting loud."

"Oh, okay," I nodded. That was close. I was glad it wasn't anything worse. "How are we gonna escape?" I figured that was probably the first thing on his mind and he'd want to start discussing it now that Andry wasn't listening. I intended to do my best to interject ideas that weren't realistic.

"I was thinking about that... I'm not sure you're going to like it but, we can't... well, we shouldn't."

"What?" I acted like that was the worse idea in the world but deep down I was ecstatic that it was his idea, not mine. "Why?"

"If Miller knows what happened to Marcus, we're not going to get that from him if we escape. That's if it goes well and we get away. If it doesn't go well, one of us could get hurt or killed, not to mention he was right. It's not safe to travel down a mountain."

"Why not?" I figured I knew, but I wanted him to tell me. That way, it would solidify in his mind that he had come up with it and it was his idea. If he had any pride in him, hopefully, then he would be less likely to change his mind later and go back on his own plan.

"Miller's smart… if we're on a mountain then he knows if we try to escape, the only safe way down is on the road. He'd find us again."

"Ugh." I rolled my eyes like I knew he was right. "Ok, what should we do then?"

"He wants to see you again later, right?"

I furrowed my brows. *What the hell, dude?* I glared at him for a second before subduing my anger with where I knew he was taking this and reminding myself to play along. "I… well…" I looked down and away like I was thinking about it, "yeah, he's twisted. Of course he isn't done with me."

"Okay good… You're probably not going to like this but I have a plan then."

Probably? "No, I'm not going to like it… I'm not a whore, *Ryan!*" I acted like I already knew what he was alluding to and it wasn't something I would be willing to do.

"Kaleah… please," He widened his eyes, telling me to calm down. "You're a spy… it doesn't make you a whore… it's part of the job."

"What the hell, Reagan…" I whispered through gritted teeth. "What do you think you want me to do?"

"For one… I don't care if we are both currently captives. I'm still your superior and you're not going to talk to me like that. Clear?" He said sternly under his breath.

Reagan-the-asshole is back. He's suggesting I willingly go be tortured, and he's upset that I'm cussing at him?? I can't believe this guy! Thank God it was actually Jake that captured us and not the real

Miller. I'd never let that bastard touch me again just for the sake of intel. Even though I was upset at Reagan's lack of compassion, I knew I had to keep playing along. I nodded, trying not to roll my eyes. He sounded just like Marcus did every time I cussed at him. Poor men don't know how to handle a feisty woman. Seemed pretty pathetic in my book.

"Good, now listen... When Miller comes back out here, you're going to let him take you again." He stopped, knowing I'd try to argue, so I did right on cue so he wouldn't be suspicious.

"Are you serious?" I made a face like I thought he was insane.

"Kaleah... please listen... You can do it, remember your training... You need to do what he wants until you can get close enough to ask about Marcus."

"But won't he be suspicious... If I'm supposed to be your wife, he'll know I'm playing him if I just give him what he wants?" I was trying to cover my bases with enough questions that Reagan didn't suspect anything.

"I don't know how to help you there... I just gotta trust you know how to manipulate him. You did a good job acting with me when we left the library. Enough that I still didn't trust you with your gun."

"Okay..." I said like I was finally giving in. "I'll do it."

"I'm sorry about that, by the way." He looked like he meant it. "We might not have been in this situation if I had let you have your gun back before we went into the house. I just..." He looked away from me like he genuinely felt bad. "I didn't know if I could trust you yet. And in all honesty, I didn't think anyone was inside."

"I know..." I said, softly. "I forgive you."

He smiled, appreciating my response.

"Are you hungry yet?" I asked, since I definitely was now.

"Yeah, I could eat." He said, then leaned up and grabbed a hold of the gunny sack and set it between us.

"Ryan! Where are your cuffs?" I instantly realized he wasn't still restrained as he should have been. Then I looked back over at Andry to make sure he was just asleep and not dead.

"Shhh," He quickly hushed me as he put his hands behind his back again. "Espionage training day two, how to escape restraints… Don't you remember?" He whispered it lower than his normal whisper.

"No… well—" I stopped to think. I knew I could do spy things—things that didn't make sense before when I was erased—but I never remembered the day I was trained how to. "I guess." I said finally. "Have you been free this whole time? You could have stopped Miller when he—" I stopped again to think about the implications.

"Yes, shhh, I'm sorry…" He hushed me again. "I'm sorry he's done more things to you… but I couldn't stop him. We have to find Marcus. It's a necessary evil…"

Necessary evil? I stared at him blankly, trying to keep my temper in check. I didn't know what to think when he said it. Obviously, I was glad that he didn't hurt Jake when he apparently had the chance to. But the other part of me that was used to being defended by my partner was a now in shock that he would just sit there and let what he thought Miller was doing to me, happen again, all for the sake of intel. "Okay…" I said. I knew it wouldn't do any good to argue with him, not when he was exactly where I wanted him to be—believing I was completely on his side and willing to whore myself for the cause.

"Here… let me help you out of your cuffs so then you can eat." He brought his left hand over to my back.

"No, I'm good." I said, slipping my hands out from behind my back as well.

"Wow, so you do remember." He looked surprised.

"I just needed reminded," I smiled as I took a hold of the gunny sack and opened it. "Miller apparently was okay with me not having them on since he told Andry at first to release me to feed you. But I don't think he'd be as nice if you left yours off." I said, suggesting he put his back on.

"You're right. I don't think he sees you as a threat since you're a woman."

"Here, let me help you. Turn around." I said as I reached down for his to reposition them on his wrists, tighter than I suspected they had been before.

"That's good… Kaleah, that's good," he whispered louder.

"Oh, sorry… It's okay, you can just get out of them again, right?" I was curious how he had done it since I couldn't remember the technique exactly. I'd only been able to slip from mine since Jake hadn't tightened them down as well.

He turned back to me. "Ugh, I'm not sure now… You made them really tight." He sounded frustrated.

"Shit… I'm sorry." I said, but I wasn't. "Here, let me feed you," I hoped feeding him would help him forget he was now upset with me. I reached down into the gunny sack and pulled out a little brick of cheese. "You're not lactose intolerant, right?"

"Shhh," he hushed me again, but I didn't think I was being loud that time. Then, when I looked back up to see why, I caught a movement from Andry out of the corner of my eye.

"Oops," I mouthed to Reagan when I saw Andry wasn't still napping.

Reagan leaned over toward me like he was going to rest his head on my shoulder now. Then he started to whisper again, "Tell him you have to pee. He'll get Miller to take you so he can keep watch of me. That'll be your way in… You can do it, Eva, I know you can. You'll be all right, you're tough." His encouragement was impressive yet irritating at the same time.

"All right," I whispered back. "Andry…" I said louder so he could hear me. "It's Andry, right? I have to pee!"

Andry didn't look enthused. "I don't guess that Boss would be happy if you pissed yourself," he said like he got the idea and needed to do something about it. "Boss!" He yelled over his shoulder, "Cupcake thinks she's gotta take a piss."

It was the most I had really heard Andry say the whole time I'd known him. I did everything I could to not laugh when he said it.

It didn't take long before I heard the door open and I saw Jake walking toward us from down the hall. "Oh, I guess she's ready for round two." He said with a deepened voice like he'd just woken up.

"No!" I said emphatically. "I just have to pee!"

Jake smiled like he felt frisky, but that quickly changed when he looked down at my hands and saw I didn't have my cuffs on. "Where're your cuffs?" His face changed to his stern one.

"Aww shit," I said like I hadn't intended for him to see even though it didn't really bother me that he had.

"Get up now…" He ordered me. "Andry, check him, make sure his are still on and tight. If she got loose, I don't know what she did for him." He pointed to Reagan.

"Sure, Boss." I could see on Andry's face that he felt bad. He knew he fell asleep and probably figured that I knew he fell asleep, too. Whether that was intentional, accidental or whatever, I doubted he wanted Jake to know about it.

"Get your ass in there and go pee!" Jake didn't sound happy with me but I knew he was acting, and doing a great job of it. He pointed to the hall where I had seen earlier that there was a bathroom across from the room we'd been in.

I walked down the hall toward it only looking behind me to see where he was. He hadn't followed me yet; he was still in the living room, probably making sure Reagan really was still cuffed nice and tight. I walked into the bathroom and shut the door. Then, while in there, I assumed it probably wouldn't hurt to actually use it, so I did.

Before long I heard banging on the door, "Let's go, cupcake…" It was Jake's voice.

I wasn't in a hurry myself, so I took my time to fix my hair while I had a mirror. Before I got a chance to finish, though, I heard a loud noise that made me pause. It was distinctive… *Holy shit,* I thought, *I know that sound.* It was a gunshot. If Jake was at the door though, and Reagan didn't have a gun or the will to escape, who the hell would be shooting a gun?

I reached down for the knob, ready to walk out and see what happened when Jake suddenly opened the door and stuck his head in. "Hide! I'll be back for you!" He said quickly as he locked the knob from the inside and shut the door behind him.

"Hide?" Where the hell did he think I was going to hide? The room was tiny and not well lit. All I could really see was what contrasted well with the white tub and toilet. The light from the small window above the tub wasn't really giving me much to work with.

I looked down at the vanity to gauge how big it was and if I could fit inside of it. Then I looked over at the tub. "Ugh…" I was frustrated. Neither of them looked like good hiding spots. I knew I couldn't fit inside the vanity and without a shower curtain I might as well hide sitting on the toilet than pretend like the tub was going to do anything.

Before I had a chance to think about it too long, I heard men talking. I walked over and put my ear to the door. At that point, I figured standing behind the door was probably the best hiding spot in there, anyway.

"I could ask you the same thing, Miles… What are *you* doing here?" It was a man's voice, one that I recognized from somewhere. I waited to hear more before I tried to make a judgment on whose voice it could be.

"I was trying to interrogate *him!* How did you find us?" Jake growled.

"Oh, that's nice… I haven't heard from you since you went rogue, and now you think you can just come and go through Nashville without stopping to say hi?"

Holy shit! I instantly realized whose voice it was—Miller's! *Holy shit, holy shit, holy shit…*

"How did you find me, Miller? I'm not working under you now. I'm working under Voss, that's why I'm here. So unless—"

"Voss? Bullshit… You still work for me, Miles. Remember our deal? You bring me the intel, I give you the girl… So where is she? Where is your little Gypsyin? You've had long enough to get the intel from her!"

"What do you think I'm here working on, Miller? You just shot my only lead! He was the only man that knew… I needed him, dammit!"

"What? Him? Who is he?" Miller sounded like I remembered, loud and raspy. He was probably still ugly, too.

"He stole her from me in New York! He's another Sicari! The brother to the man you shot in Nashville when you first found her."

"What the hell were you doing with her in New York?"

"She erased herself! I couldn't get any intel out of her if she didn't remember it," Jake snapped back. I was starting to feel concerned about how their conversation was going. Jake sounded a lot like he was on Miller's side, but at the same time I knew now that he was a decent actor too so it was all confusing. I couldn't tell whose side he was actually on. He started to remind me of myself. It felt like the more I played the double, the more it was hard to distinguish which side *I* was even on.

"You idiot, she lied to you! If she didn't remember the intel after she'd been erased, then why would she send that letter to her father? You know, the letter I gave you when I sent you to find her? It said she had intel and needed picked up. You should have remembered that! You read it like fifteen times!"

"Her father? Who's her father?" Jake asked like he didn't know. "And how did you get the letter if it was sent to him?"

"It doesn't matter, just follow orders and do what I say… Find her or the girl is as good as dead."

"I'm not an idiot. I know the girl's not real, Miller. You can stop lying to me now. I'm on your side, all right?"

Miller didn't respond right away. I assumed he was thinking about if he believed Jake or not. "If that's true, then why were you at my house?" Miller said finally, sounding unsure if he wanted to trust Jake.

He didn't deny it… Miller didn't deny it! Is that proof that she's a lie? I could only hope.

"Andry's tracker… That's how you found us…" Jake said suddenly, having figured it out. "We were there because I saw you changed our names in the city records… I needed to find her and I hoped she'd come back to look for me at *my address*. I set a trap, but this Sicari was the only thing I found. I brought him here to interrogate him. I didn't figure you'd want the blood on your carpet."

"And? What did you get out of him?" Miller asked. He sounded like he was falling for everything Jake was giving him.

"Not enough! I know he's the one that took her and who his brother was but that's it. I was about to work on him here again soon until you all decided to barge in."

I caught the word all. *Shit,* I thought, there must have been a bunch of them. That made more sense why Jake was going down the path that he did. I couldn't help but wonder about Reagan now too after hearing them. The way they kept referring to him was like he was dead. I didn't know if I should have felt relieved or upset. On one hand, I didn't have to worry about him catching me being a double and taking me back to the Praetorium. On the other hand, I still hadn't had a chance to learn how to get myself deactivated. I also felt concerned now that I didn't have a fellow Sicari on my side, so if Jake was lying to me, I would be all alone.

"So, you don't know where she is?"

"No!" Jake sounded irritated. "As far as I know, she could be sittin' pretty at the Praetorium. And if she does remember the intel, she might have already given it to them. You just shot my only lead!"

"Dammit, Miles… you better not be lying to me!" Miller barked back, ready to move on. "If I find out you're lying, I'll find her myself. Then you wanna know what I'll do with her…" He paused as if he really expected Jake to respond, but then continued when he didn't. "I'll erase her again. Then I'll tell her she was mine this whole time. You can watch me do whatever I want with her before I send you away to never see her again."

"Look, you know I don't give a shit about the intel, man. I'll give it to you as soon as I find her again. But threatening me isn't going to help your situation. You know she's mine, and she's staying mine."

"That's exactly what I wanted to hear." Miller sounded heinous when he said it. "I knew you were the right man for the job when I first sent you to find her. You fell in love just as I hoped… She was such a pretty girl. I guess you better find her before I do, Miles…"

"You're never gonna touch her again." Jake didn't sound happy whatsoever with the exchange.

"Look you li'l shit… She was *mine* first! You're just lucky I'm being lenient with you. Now do your job and you can have her, but backstab me, and I'll make her watch as I slowly torture you! Love has a way of making people talk… get me?"

Shit. That *was* his plan. *That's been his plan all along.* I suddenly felt like it was hard to breathe.

12
WHO TO TRUST

"**A**ndry, get your shit together. You're going back with us. Baker, you stay here with Miles. Make sure he does what he's supposed to, ya hear?" Miller gave the men orders but something he said stood out. *Baker…*

Baker… I repeated the name to myself, trying to think about why it meant something to me when I realized he was one of the five. He was one of the bastards that watched as Miller did what he did, then joined in when Miller allowed it. Initially, I didn't know how to feel about him being left there to join Jake but it didn't take me long to decide what that meant for me.

I listened longer, waiting to hear the voices leave. I was curious to hear what Jake was going to say to Baker. I wasn't sure how he was going to deal with him, especially knowing I was still in the bathroom waiting.

Before long, I heard the front door slam and several voices fade like Miller and his men had left the cabin. Then I heard Jake again in the living room. "I guess if you're here to take Andry's place, you can start with cleaning up this mess."

"I wasn't left to help," I heard another man's voice. It had to be Baker.

"I don't care why he left you, you're gonna do what I tell you." Jake didn't hesitate to show his rank.

I didn't care what they were arguing about; I saw their discord as an opportunity to proceed with a plan I'd just made up five-seconds before that. I quietly unlocked the door and turned the knob, then slowly opened it enough to create a crack to peek through. I couldn't see anything in the living room from my vantage point down the hall, which was perfect. That meant I knew they couldn't see me.

As they continued to bicker with each other, I took the opportunity to use their voices as cover to quietly tiptoe down the hall until I got to where I could see their reflections in the glass from the dining room sliding door. Just as I had hoped, it was only Jake and another man, *Baker*. I couldn't see Reagan and I couldn't hear him either so I really wasn't sure what condition he was in. I knew it would be hard for Jake to do anything to a fellow agent even if he was one of Miller's loyal men, so I decided I would handle it for him.

I didn't have a gun, but I knew exactly where Jake carried his and just the right amount of pressure it took to pull it from his holster, since I had done it multiple times before while helping him undress. I knew I had to be quick if I was going to have the element of surprise, which I needed for both Jake and Baker. I stood there and watched them in the reflection for a minute, waiting for Baker to turn and Jake to hold still.

"Well, now without a lead, I'm going back to New York. You can follow me if you want but it won't do you any good." Jake said as he took a half-step back toward the hall. He wasn't blocking his holster, so I knew what I intended to do would work perfectly.

"You're not leaving his jurisdiction again, not with me, you're not!" Baker had his arms crossed like he didn't feel threatened by Jake and was trying to look like he had superiority.

I watched and waited until finally he turned just as I needed him to. Then, without missing a beat, I sprung into action. In two quick steps, I was behind Jake, with my hand on his gun. As soon as I had it in my hand, I leaned around him and fired. Before either man even knew what was happening, just as I had trained to, I sent two bullets to Baker's chest and one into his forehead. He didn't have a chance to see me so he didn't know it was coming. He fell to the floor before Jake even had a chance to turn around.

"Eva!" I think I shocked him. I wasn't sure if he was happy, upset, surprised or just what. I stepped around him to look at my handiwork, but I didn't get to say anything before I saw another man walk in the door.

I hadn't expected him. I held the gun back up and was ready to shoot again when I heard Jake yell at me to stop. The man didn't reach for his gun. He just looked at both of us and held his hands up.

"Why can't I shoot him too?" I asked Jake while I kept an eye on the man. I could still feel the buzz from killing Baker and I wasn't sure I was ready to stop, especially not if it was another one of Miller's men.

"Eva, that's Turner," Jake didn't hesitate. He walked over to me and slowly took the gun from my hands. "He's on our side." He turned toward the man to address him. "Did he leave you too?" He asked as he held the gun, waiting for an answer before he re-holstered it.

"Yeah, man... Holy shit, what just happened in here?" Turner said, as he turned to look at Baker.

"What were you doing outside?" Jake asked, finally putting his gun back.

"Before they drove off, Miller told me to stay back and watch you two. He thinks I'm loyal like Baker was. I was waiting to see what he was going to pull before I decided to show myself. When I heard the gunshot, I figured you'd had enough of him... but..."

"Yeah, I know..." Jake interjected, looking down at Baker. He didn't actually sound pleased with my achievement, though.

"How does she know how to shoot that well?" Turner asked, looking back up at me then over to Jake.

Jake didn't say anything at first so I was about to respond for him when he finally spoke. "It's complicated."

Turner looked confused.

"I'm an Agent," I added.

"Eva?" Jake said it with a sort of frustrated disbelief at my bluntness. He didn't sound happy that I'd decided to just come out with it. "Turner, don't worry about it. I can explain it all to you later. Right now we need to address this," he pointed at both the men now laying on the floor.

It was the first chance I'd had now that everything had cooled down to get a good look at Reagan. I didn't hesitate; I walked over and knelt down next to him. From what I could tell, he was only shot once, although it was in the chest. "Reagan!" I said, trying to see if he could still respond. "Reagan…" I shook his shoulder.

"Eva, baby… I'm sorry, he's gone." Jake said calmly from behind me.

"You don't know that… he could be pretending." I tried to shake him again. "Reagan!" I shouted, as I pulled his shirt up to look at where exactly he was shot and how bad it looked.

"Eva, get up, baby." Jake said softly. "You're just gonna upset yourself seeing the blood. He's gone."

I didn't want to listen, but I had a feeling he was right when I pulled my hand back and saw it now had blood on it. "Why the hell was he even shot?" I asked, turning to look up at Jake. I knew he wasn't in the room when it had happened but I thought maybe he'd know why Miller had done it.

"Eva… stand up, please…"

"Tell me now!" I didn't know why but I could feel myself getting disproportionately upset. I wondered if I was more attached to Reagan than I realized. Even if he was an ass at times, I couldn't help but tread through the different memories I had of him, Marcus and I all together. In a strange way, it felt like losing a brother.

"When Miller was here, how much did you hear?" Jake asked, staying calm, unlike myself.

"All of it!" That wasn't true, but I felt like I'd heard enough. Maybe that's why I was upset. I still wasn't sure where Jake and I actually stood.

"It's 'cause Miller's an asshole, Eva!" Turner spoke up, maybe hoping to relieve the tension he saw building between me and Jake.

"He's right…" Jake sighed. "Miller's an idiot. He's impulsive. He saw I had a hostage, and that's as far as his thinking went. If I didn't have what he wanted, which was you, then he was going to punish me by taking what I did have. It doesn't make sense, but for him, it doesn't have to."

"I needed him!" I said, as I turned back around to look at Reagan again. The coloring in his face was already starting to disappear as the bloodstain on his shirt got larger. I reached down and held his hand for a moment as I let myself digest my feelings. After Marcus died, Reagan was the only other Sicari that I ever considered anything like a friend. I blinked hard to try to hold back any tears. I didn't want to cry right now, not in front of Jake, not over a Sicari. I leaned forward and pushed his sleeve up, revealing his tag. Now that his life source had been drained from him, the three red dots had more contrast against his pale, colorless skin. So much contrast that the red of the dots was now a deep, rich, almost vibrant color. They looked like three red rubies.

"Jake, you know Baker being shot is a problem, right?" Turner asked, more concerned about their dead agent than mine.

"Yeah," Jake said with a sigh.

"Oh, I'm sorry." I said sarcastically, as I gently wiped my hand off on Reagan's pants and stood back up to look at Jake. "I didn't realize that bastard was so valuable to you."

I didn't wait for him to respond. I walked back toward the room when he reached out his arm to stop me. "Eva, wait…"

I didn't wait; I kept walking, pushing his arm out of the way as I went.

"It's all right, Miles. I'll take care of the body and remove his tag. We can take it with us. You go talk to her, I got it."

"Okay, yeah, good thinking about the tag. You know Miller is gonna track it with yours so it'll have to go too. Let me take care of her and we can talk about where we're gonna go next. Thanks, man." Jake said. "Eva, I'm coming… please don't lock the door."

I had just walked into the room when I heard him. I had thought about locking it since I wasn't thrilled with him but I didn't. I figured we needed to talk again and resolve whatever he thought I heard him tell Miller.

"You're mad at me aren't you?" I asked as soon as I saw him enter the room.

He didn't shut the door behind him, he just moved over close to me and motioned to the bed. "Why don't you sit down?"

"Fine," I said, taking a seat. Then he sat down next to me.

"I'm not mad, just frustrated. I had it under control... I had a plan and it wasn't for you to shoot him."

"Well, sorry I didn't ask for your permission but he needed shot. I wasn't going to let you bring him along with us like you did Seth."

I could tell that didn't make him feel much better. He reached up to rub his forehead, like he really was frustrated with me.

"He was one of the men that raped me, Jake. I wasn't going to let him live." I said it softly.

He stopped what he was doing and let his shoulders relax as he looked back over at me. "I didn't know that."

"Well, it doesn't matter, he's dead now... hopefully." I wondered after I said it if he actually was. I wasn't sure since I didn't technically check him myself.

"He's dead, all right." Jake responded as if hearing my thoughts. "Turner's right, you're a good shot. You're quick too. I didn't even know what had happened until I saw you beside me, pointing my gun at Turner."

"Can you trust him?" I wasn't sure I could trust anyone that was with Miller even if they acted like they weren't.

"Yeah, he's a good guy. I wouldn't worry about him." Jake reached down and took a hold of my hand.

"Can I trust you?" I asked, pulling my hand back.

"Is it what I said to Miller? Is that your problem?"

"Depends... Do you want the intel?" I wasn't in the mood to dicker around. I figured we should get right to the point.

He sighed as he looked away and stood up to shut the door. "Do you have it?" He asked now softly almost as a whisper.

"Why does that matter?" I whispered back.

He looked down at me, thinking, "Eva... if you have it then that means you're in more danger than if you don't."

"How do you know? You don't even know what the intel is?" I said, thinking back to what Parker had said and how she had told Marcus about how dangerous it was to carry it.

"You're right, I don't know what it is but I know Miller will kill us for it…" He paused, hesitating to go on. "I know I said I'd never ask but—"

"You want it, don't you?" I interrupted him.

"Eva… It's only to keep you safe."

"I can't believe you…" I really didn't know if I could trust him, not if he was now asking me for what he had said he'd never ask me for. "How the hell will me telling you what it is, keep me safe? Unless you think you're going to give it to Miller, is that what your plan is?"

"Stop, please." He whispered. I wasn't as quiet as he was being. I assumed that's what he was referring to. "I don't intend to give Miller anything. But you have to understand where I'm coming from. I love you and I don't know if you should be risking your life over trying to keep a secret."

"You're right. It's because you don't understand. It's not just a secret. It's intel… It's knowledge that can change the war… Who's on top, who's on bottom, who's dead, who's alive, who's in control… everything! That's why Miller wants it, for the control."

"Shhh… if that's the case you shouldn't be so loud." He said softly as he stepped over to the bed and sat back down.

"I thought you trusted Turner?" I was confused why he wanted me to be quiet.

"I do, but that doesn't mean he needs to know more than he already does." He said as he rubbed his knees. "So, you remember it then?"

"Yeah," I said softly, with a small nod.

"Did you remember it in New York?" He asked as he looked back up at me.

"Are you asking because Miller said I did and that I was lying to you?"

He nodded.

"No," I answered. "He was wrong. I didn't remember it in New York. The serum really does erase it."

"Then how did you write that letter?" He asked, sounding just as leery of trusting me as I was him.

"The one he said I sent my father?"

He nodded.

"I had a location code memorized. I must have done a good job memorizing it too because the serum didn't take it like it did a lot of my other memories. Since those codes aren't like postal addresses, I didn't know exactly where it went to, the Sicari or the Coldiers. I just knew if it was important enough for me to have it in my head, then it went somewhere. I hated the Coldiers, so I'd assumed it went to the Sicari's central station. That's why I wrote in there that I was a Coldier Agent. I intended for the Sicari to get it. I thought they would be happy that I was turning myself in, and come get me even though I thought I was lying." I paused to think back about it. "I really didn't know what I was doing. I was just lonely and wanted someone to come get me. If no-one showed up, I decided I was going to take my life within the week. I didn't really want to do that though, so…"

"You never told me that." Jake said softly.

"Yeah, I really was ready to die when you showed up. That's why I let you take me, I thought if I let you guys kill me it'd be a lot easier than doing the job myself… I'm a big chicken when it comes time to actually do it, though, you know… that's why I didn't jump in New York either."

"Miles…" I heard a knock at the door. Jake stood up to answer it.

"Yeah, man, are you done already? Or… what do you need?" Jake asked after he opened it to see Turner standing there now with blood splattered across his clothes.

"Ugh, yeah, I got his tag out but I'm not sure what you'd like done with his body now?"

"How well did you know him?" Jake asked. I wasn't sure why but I was interested in seeing what Turner said.

"Decently well, I guess." Turner looked from Jake to me as he answered then back to Jake. "He was a patriot before the war. He was hardcore loyal to Miller, I know that. If Miller said jump, that dude'd leap! Honestly, that's probably why he picked him to leave here with you." Turner looked over at me again after he finished.

"Okay…" Jake said, looking down, thinking about what to do. "Well, he was one of the men that raped Eva, so… I'm not sure I want to do anything with him now. I think he'd do best to lay there and rot. What do you say?"

Turner was quiet. He didn't respond right away. He looked like he was thinking about what Jake was saying when finally he just nodded to agree and that was it.

"Okay good, don't mess with him anymore then. I'll get his gun and check what else he has on him before we go. We're going to need the tag off the Sicari too, if you don't mind. He's being tracked as well and I don't want his lack of movement to look suspicious."

"All right…" Turner nodded, looked at me again then turned to walk back down the hall.

"Why do you want Reagan's tag?" I asked as Jake shut the door and turned back around to walk over and sit on the bed again. I suspected a reason, but I wanted to hear it from him.

"Well, if you and him are supposed to be a team and your trackers get split up and his stops moving… I don't want them to think you killed him, you know? You don't need them after you for something like that on top of the intel."

I knew he was right, and I was happy to hear he'd thought it through so thoroughly. "Well, now that he's dead I guess I won't be able to get my tracker turned off." I said like the thought was upsetting.

"That's not true, baby." Jake reached over to hold my hand again. "I know we can't find out from him anymore, but just knowing it's possible is a good thing. We can be hopeful now, at least. We'll find a way… I promise."

"Jake, don't make promises you're not sure you can keep."

"Those really mean something to you, don't they?" He asked.

I nodded. "They're supposed to, that's why they're promises."

"Okay…" He said like he was thinking about something. "Is there something that means more to you than a promise?"

"Yes, a vow… That's like the holy mother of promises. You break that and you're cursed."

He smiled, "Okay, well, I want to settle something between us once and for all, then."

"All right?" I said, not sure where he was going with it.

"Eva, Kaleah, Jayde… whoever you want to be… I vow to you that I do love you, and you can trust me. I'm not working for Miller, and if I do ask for the intel, it's not so I can turn around and backstab you, it's only so I can help you carry the burden."

I still wasn't sure if I wanted to tell anyone, even him, what the intel was but it was nice to hear him say all of that. "Okay… I'll try to trust you again, then." I smiled.

"Good," he smiled back. "'Cause I mean it, baby… You're my world. All I want is to make sure you're safe. All right?"

"All right…" I said, leaning into him.

13

DEADLY SUSPICION

"We don't have enough gas to go straight to New York. I used too much going south. Driving up into the mountains takes a lot. The closest city where we can get more is Charlotte." I overheard Jake discussing with Turner the best way to proceed. Turner seemed like a nice guy and it was easy to see Jake trusted him but I wasn't so sure of him yet.

"You don't wanna go back up to Nashville to refuel? It's closer." Turner sounded sincere, however stupid-ass ideas like that were what made me second guess who he was actually loyal to.

Jake's face said about as much when he heard the question as well. "Hell no! I'm not taking her back anywhere near that place."

Turner just shrugged like it was an innocent suggestion and he would say no more.

"How much gas do we have, exactly?" I thought if Jake would allow me to chime in on the discussion, maybe I could help with a better idea than what Turner had come up with.

Jake looked at me, blinked a couple of times to think, then finally answered. "Probably only enough to get halfway to Charlotte."

"Okay?" I looked at him, then at Turner who shrugged again then back to Jake. "How far could we get to Nashville?" I asked. I didn't like the idea any more than Jake did but I wasn't sure making it only halfway to Charlotte then going the rest of the way on foot was any better.

"Eva, it doesn't matter, I've already—"

"All the way." Turner interrupted him then quickly looked away like he realized that might not have been the best idea.

"Dammit, Turner!" Jake said, giving him an unsettling side eye.

"Well, I don't think it'd do you any good to try to lie to her. I mean, she should have some say here, too. It's her life you're—"

"Trying everything in my power to protect!" Jake interrupted him back, now looking more irritated than he had. "I wasn't going to lie to her... I was just going to say, I've already decided."

The way Turner talked to Jake didn't sound like the way I remember Jake's other men talking to him, but I thought surely he wasn't as high of a rank as Jake, either. Maybe Turner just wasn't as respectful of Jake's rank as Andry was.

"Okay, well what have you decided then, is it Nashville or only halfway to Charlotte?" Turner continued to pressure Jake for an answer, which I thought was quite bold.

"Are there no other cities where we can get gas before Charlotte? I mean, don't Coldiers control all the cities?" I knew my Coldier knowledge probably wasn't nearly as extensive as theirs but I was confused why those two cities were the only options.

"Yeah, ugh... never mind, maybe she shouldn't have any say." Turner looked at Jake puzzled by my question, then back at me. "I thought you said you were an agent?"

"She was confused... like I said, it's complicated. You have no idea how many times she's been erased." Jake quickly interjected, to dismiss Turner's question. "Eva, baby..." Jake turned to look at me, "We only control the major cities and no, between here and New York there are only two, which are Charlotte and D.C."

"All right..." I shrugged like I was willing to pull myself from the conversation. Obviously, I was erased too many times to help make a decision on how to proceed and I should step back and let the 'men' handle it. It was hard for me not to roll my eyes but I didn't.

"You realize the other problem with going to Charlotte is the mountain pass might not even be passable, right? I'd hate to use the only gas we have left and get stuck. That honestly could be more dangerous for her than Nashville." Turner actually brought forth a more realistic reason to go back to Nashville than *'just because.'* "If you get stuck on a normal road, you can just find another way around. There aren't other ways around on a mountain. There could be a rock slide or anything… You don't want to get stuck up there."

"Dammit…" Jake mumbled as he looked down, thinking about it. I could tell everything in him wanted to do the opposite, and he was willing to take the chance of going by foot. Now he knew the chance wasn't as good of one if we got stuck at the top of a mountain, though. "Fine." He said like Turner was actually able to change his mind.

"All right then… What else do we need to do before we can get going?" Turner asked, ready to take action.

"Wait…" Jake said, holding his stance firm, clearly not ready. "I get it… that's the best way, but if we're doing this… she's not stepping one foot back in that city!" Jake said it, looking at Turner then he turned to address me. "Eva, I'm not gonna take the chance. While we're on the way, I'll think of what we can do to make it safer for you. Sound good?"

"Okay," I said, agreeing to his conditions. I had no problem with them. I was just curious to see if Turner did.

"Sure, that sounds great. Now, what else do we need before we can get on the road?" Turner sounded like he was in a hurry but I wasn't sure why. "Do you want me to do some of the driving while you guys nap, or do you wanna stop somewhere for the night to camp? I'm good with either." He looked at me while he asked it, allowing me back into the decision-making process again.

"I don't want either of us driving at night if we don't have to." Jake said, leaning against the car. I could tell he still felt tense about the idea of where we were going. He'd crossed his arms now, looking at the ground to think. I wasn't all that thrilled myself but I knew the number of miles we were going to travel wasn't the problem. It was the time it took to get there. Having to go so slowly to navigate all the abandoned vehicles is what felt daunting to me.

"Okay, well..." Turner looked up at the sky, apparently able to tell by the sun about what time it was. "I'm thinking it's probably not even noon yet. If we get a move on it, we could make a good bit of headway by the time it's dark. We can stop and make camp wherever you think is best, then."

"That's fine." Jake dropped his arms and pushed off from the vehicle to stand up straight. "Eva, baby, are you done with everything inside? If so, do you wanna just wait out here in the car for us?" I figured he was asking because he didn't expect that I would want to return to see any more of the two dead bloodied bodies in the living room.

"Well... I would like to check and see what Reagan might have been carrying on him." The thought of seeing what secrets Reagan could have been hiding was alluring to me.

"I'll check him, baby, I don't want you to have to see that..." Jake responded how I expected him to. Even though I really thought I would have been fine to see it, I knew he wouldn't want me to.

"Jake... I've killed people before. I'll be fine. I can check him myself." I insisted.

He nodded as he reached out to put his arm around me and bring me in closer to him. "Turner," he said, looking away from me for a moment. "Go on in and get my bags for me if you don't mind. I think that's all there is that we need to get. I'll be in there in a second, all right?"

"Sure, man!" Turner didn't hesitate. He spun around and walked back into the house.

"Jake, I really think—"

He stopped me before I could go on, "Eva... baby..." He said as he gently put his hand up to my mouth like he knew I was going to try to argue with him. "I know you think you'll be fine, and you probably would be, all right... I just... I don't think you should get used to seeing that, it hardens a person and I don't want you..." he paused to select his words carefully. "I don't want you any more hardened than you have to be… all right?"

I took a deep breath in. "Fine… I'll sit out here and wait on you, then."

"That's my girl," he smiled as he looked me in the eye then leaned down to kiss me. "I'll let you know what I find as soon as I come back out."

"All right." I said as I turned to open the back door of the car and get in.

"I love you, baby." Jake said as he leaned down and peered in at me.

"I love you too," I replied. He gave me a smile and shut the door, then walked back toward the house.

I wasn't sitting there long before Turner opened the door to set Jake's bags in beside me. "You gonna be good with these up here, or would you like for me to see if I can get them to fit in the trunk? With all the gas cans though, it might make them smell…" He bent down to look at me as he said it. I think it was the first time I'd had a chance to talk to him without Jake there.

I didn't say anything for a second. I just looked at him. I was hoping I could get a better idea of how well I could trust him by looking into his eyes.

"You all right?" He asked like either I took too long to respond or he was used to working in a faster gear than most people.

"Yeah… sorry, um… I can handle them back here. That's fine." I figured I could lean on them if I wanted a nap. There was also something comforting about the idea of having something of Jake's so close to me.

"Or if you'd like, I could ride back here and let you sit in the front with Miles." He said as he lowered himself to squat next to the car like he intended to speak with me for a moment.

"No, I'm good back here."

He nodded, then leaned forward to stand back up before I stopped him. "Wait, I wanna ask you something."

"Sure, what'cha got on your mind?" He seemed pleasant enough, but I hadn't gotten a sense of his sincerity yet.

"What do you know about me?" I asked, as I kept my eyes locked on his.

He furrowed his brow, unsure why I asked him that, but then shrugged it off like he was willing to answer, nonetheless. "Um… Well, the first time I saw you was when we went to get you from the doctor guy… Uh…" He looked away to think of what to say. "You're Miles' girlfriend. You said you're an agent but then you don't act like an agent and you don't have a tag, but you apparently shoot like one. So yeah, that's a little confusing to me." He stopped, then looked back at me again. "You wanna explain that?"

"I think you know more than you're letting on." I said it before thinking, since it was the first thought that came into my head.

He squinted his eyes again as he readjusted himself using the car door. "Um… Well… Sure, I'll be honest with ya. I have some suspicions. I'm not sure you've told Miles everything about yourself and that makes me a li'l nervous. You know, 'cause he's a good friend of mine and I don't wanna see him hurt."

"Oh, yeah?" I was now intrigued. "What do you think he doesn't know about me that you do?"

"I'm not saying I do know anything. I'm saying I have suspicions. It's different."

"What are you afraid I am?" I pushed him to continue.

"A Sicari," he didn't hesitate, he just came out and said it.

"That would be bad, wouldn't it?" I didn't deny it. I wanted to see how he would respond.

"Yep," he said still staring at me, trying to gauge my responses as well.

"Well, why would you think that?" I asked like I was confused by his suspicions.

He shrugged. "Just a few things that I've gathered, that's all. I haven't been with Miller's unit long but I've heard stories. Just that you have some mythical intel that he's obsessed about getting is one thing. Why would he think you have intel if you're just any li'l ol'

Gypsyin? Not to mention, you don't shoot like a Gypsyin... And I doubt Miles gave you his gun to shoot Baker with. He looked just as surprised that you had it as I was when I walked in."

From everything Turner was saying, he had a right to be suspicious. He'd be an idiot if he believed me, if I tried to deny it, anyway. "Well, where do we go from here, then?" I asked.

He furrowed his brow at me again like he finally knew he was right and he was thinking about how to proceed when I heard Jake speaking as he walked up to the car. "Okay, if you're good to go, I am!"

Turner looked back at him as he stood up and shut the door. "Sure, man!"

I couldn't help but wonder how awkward the rest of the trip was going to be after that little conversation now that I knew what he thought he knew, and he likely now knew he was right. I watched as they both got into the car and shut their doors. Turner looked a little uneasy now with his new knowledge and probably wasn't sure he liked that I was riding in the seat behind him. Jake looked just as oblivious to everything as he should've been.

"What'd you find on Reagan, Jake?" I figured I should ask while it was fresh in his mind so he didn't forget.

He didn't say anything at first as he started the car and began to drive, then after a moment, he responded. "Well, I didn't find anything at first, other than an odd tattoo on his arm that I couldn't read. Then, when I looked in his jacket pocket, I found a note. Here..." He said as he leaned to the side, reached down to pull it from his pocket and handed it to me over his shoulder. "I'm not sure it'll mean anything to you 'cause it's in another language but I think I saw your name in there somewhere so maybe I'm wrong. Look and see what you think."

"Okay..." I was intrigued. I took it from him and opened it to see what he was talking about. As soon as I got the paper unfolded, I recognized the writing. It was Marcus' writing. It was in Latin, so I understood why Jake couldn't read it.

"Can you read it, baby?" Jake asked, probably eager to see what it said as well.

"Um..." I wasn't sure if I wanted to tell him until I actually read it and knew what it said myself. "Let me try… I'm not sure." I said as I looked at it.

Frater, cras proximam missionem relinquemus. De hoc uno malo affectum habeo. Cur non certus sum, sed aliquid de eo ius non sentit. Si hoc non reddo, tantum memento te amo et pollicitus es ut custodiant Eva et infantem. Dic Eva doleo et omnia quae feci et facere pergo ex amore familiae meae. Memento operis tui, frater, perfice te. – M

I translated it in my head as I read it.

Brother, tomorrow we leave for our next mission. I have a bad feeling about this one. I'm not sure why, but something about it doesn't feel right. If I don't make it back, just remember I love you and please keep your promise to take care of Eva and the baby. Tell Eva I am sorry and everything I have done and continue to do is out of love for my family. Remember your work, brother, it will carry you through! — M

I understood it but I didn't all at the same time. I knew what it said, but I was confused by what it meant.

I sat there trying to think about it when Jake spoke up again. "What's it say, baby? Can you read it?"

"I don't think you really want me to do that."

I couldn't see his face but by his eyes, Jake looked puzzled after I said it. "What… why?"

"Turner thinks I'm a Sicari and said he'd have a problem with me if I was. So I'm not sure Turner would be any less suspicious of me if I was able to read out loud an encrypted note a Sicari had in his pocket." Both men suddenly reacted oddly. Turner about jumped out of his skin while Jake instantly froze.

"Eva, what are you doing?" Jake asked in his stern voice, probably trying to see where I was coming from.

"Well, you said you trust Turner, but I don't, since he works with Miller. And he doesn't trust me but he trusts you, so… I don't know, maybe if we got everything out in the open we could all either trust each other or umm… not." I didn't actually know what I was doing either but I figured it'd be best to get it all out there while we were still far from Nashville, just in case Turner wasn't what we thought he was.

"She is a Sicari isn't she, Miles?" Turner asked. Finally he realized Jake probably knew more than he had given him credit for.

"No…" Jake said as he looked over at Turner then back to me in the rear-view mirror. "I told you it's complicated."

"Why are you lying to me, man?" Turner didn't believe him, which I wasn't shocked by.

"What do you know about E.J. Prescott?" Jake asked, apparently going somewhere with it even though it didn't appear to have anything to do with the current topic.

"What? What does that—"

"Answer the question first, then I'll explain." Jake cut him off.

Turner turned to look out the window as he threw his arms up in frustration. After a loud sigh, he finally answered. "Um… I don't know… he's a first rank. I've never met the guy, so I don't know much, really." He said as he turned back to look at Jake. "The only other thing I can think of is a few years ago he opened up a special unit just to have men go search for his missing daughter."

"Right…" Jake responded like he knew what he was talking about even though it was the first that I had heard of such a thing. "Was Miller part of that special unit?"

"Miles, what does this have to do with Eva?"

"Turner, please… just… work with me, all right? I promise it'll all make sense when I'm done, okay?"

Turner nodded, then continued to answer Jake's question. "Um, that would have been before I was put under Miller, but from what I recall just by hearing him talk… yeah, I think he was. But seriously, he hates the guy, so that was probably a pretty big mistake on Mr. Prescott's part."

"What do you know about the girl… his daughter?" Jake continued with more questions.

"Uh… Not a lot. I think her name started with a J or maybe it was an L, I can't remember. When Mr. Prescott opened the unit, he said that she'd been abducted by the Sicari to use her as a hostage for negotiations between them and the Coldiers. I think there was a reward for a while to anyone who brought her in… Um and then, yeah… after a few years, I think everyone just thought she was probably dead and they closed the unit down… That's all, man. Now you wanna tell me what any of this has to do with your girlfriend being the enemy, and you being okay with it?"

Jake looked at me in the mirror, probably to see how I was taking the new information that I'd just heard. Then he looked back to the road. I wanted to blurt out 'what the hell,' and ask Jake why he hadn't told me any of that yet, but I was still in shock by it all and what it actually meant.

"Her name isn't Eva, Turner… It's Jayde Prescott… This is E.J. Prescott's daughter. She's not a Sicari! She might not have a Coldier's tag but she's just as much a Coldier as either of us!" As soon as the words came out of Jake's mouth I could see the realization of what he was saying hit Turners face as he turned to look at me.

"Are you serious?" Turner asked, speaking to Jake with wide eyes now locked on me.

"Yes! This woman has gone through more shit in the last seven years than any other agent I know has their entire life. Now that you know who she really is, you can show her some respect!" Jake said as if commanding it.

Turner nodded silently, having been put in his place then reached his hand out for me to shake it like he was meeting me for the first time. "My apologies… Ms. Prescott."

14

SAVIOR OR CAPTOR

"When were you going to tell me about my dad's special unit?" I asked Jake after we stopped for him to take a break from driving while Turner went to the bathroom.

He leaned his head back on the tree he was sitting against. "The next time we were alone. I'm sorry that you found out the way you did, though. I didn't know what else to tell him. Besides, it's the truth and I couldn't let him go on thinking that you were the enemy."

"Okay… I understand." I said, hoping he would see I wasn't mad at him.

"Now that you know… what do you think about the part about you being abducted for them to use against your dad? Like… I mean… how much do you remember about when you first were at the Praetorium?"

"I don't know… I thought I remembered enough to think it was my idea. But I'm not naïve. I mean… I realize I could've been brainwashed." I shrugged as I thought more about it. "It's possible that my dad could have just made the abduction story up, but at the same time, I can't actually remember leaving his house and traveling to the Praetorium either."

"I don't guess it matters how you got there as long as you aren't there anymore, right?" I think Jake was trying to make me feel better, but it wasn't actually that simple in my mind.

"Yeah, I guess." I didn't really want to talk about it anymore. I just wanted to sit and think about it to myself. I figured I would have plenty of opportunity to do that when we got back on the road.

"Now that Turner isn't around, do you wanna tell me what was in the note?" Jake asked as he leaned forward and took a hold of my hand. Maybe he could see I wasn't in the best mood, I wasn't sure, but the note was another puzzle that I hadn't figured out yet, so bringing it up wasn't helping my mood any either.

"Well, um… It's a lot… I mean, it's complicated. There's still a lot I haven't told you about some things I found out about Marcus after Reagan got me back to the Praetorium. The note was the last thing he wrote to Reagan before we went on our last mission."

"Okay?" He said slowly, listening.

"Jake, am I your family?" Something Marcus said in the note bothered me and I couldn't get past it. I thought maybe Jake could help me clarify before I told him any more.

He looked a bit confused by the question. "Um… Well…" I could see he was hesitant and didn't know where I was going with the question and probably didn't want to hurt my feelings with how he responded.

"It's okay, you can be honest. That's what I need. Do you consider me family?" I asked again.

His face got solemn like he knew his answer might sound harsh. "I love you, baby, and you're gonna be my wife, but um… no. I mean not yet I don't guess. When we're married, then yeah… Why do you need to know that?"

"Before we left on our last mission, Marcus asked for me to be reassigned." I felt like I was about to cry as I brought it up but I pushed through it, hoping I could get it all out before that happened. "I didn't know what the intel was about yet and how dangerous it was to carry it, but Marcus knew and didn't tell me." I could tell that bothered Jake by the way he furrowed his brow in disapproval.

"You just learned all of this when you were at the Praetorium?"

Jake asked as he looked past me probably to make sure Turner was still far enough to not hear us.

I nodded. "Reagan and Parker, my CO, were both asking me a bunch of questions about Marcus but I didn't understand why. They thought he was a double... or I was a double. I guess they were suspicious of one of us being one. I knew I was, so I kept deflecting the questions. Because I mean... if they found out I was, that'd be it for me, they'd decommission me for sure, but..." I paused, it was hard to consolidate my thoughts into what I was trying to really say.

"What'd the letter say, baby?" Jake apparently could tell where I was going with it and that it was bothering me.

I felt myself beginning to tear up as I swallowed, then took a deep breath to continue. "He was basically telling Reagan that he had a bad feeling about our last mission and he didn't think he was going to make it through it. He told him he loved him and asked him to keep his promise that if he lost him that Reagan would take care of me and the baby."

"The baby?" Jake's brow furrowed.

I blinked a few times to think about what I'd missed and realized I never had told him. "Uh..." I sucked in a deep breath, then went on. "Yeah, the last month I was with Marcus before we got captured I missed my period. I thought I was pregnant."

His face froze as if putting two and two together.

"It's not the girl." I said, stopping him if his thoughts were going down that path. "After Miller and the men all did what they did, I remember bleeding..." I stopped and closed my eyes tight to try to keep my tears at bay.

"It's okay, baby, you don't have to—"

"No, I'm fine." I said, trying to go on. "I honestly don't know if I ever was since I was on birth control. Or maybe I was and everything Miller did to me made me lose it. I don't know... I just know I bleed enough that... if I was pregnant, I wasn't anymore."

Jake's eyes were coursing with compassion or maybe it was pity but he didn't say anything, he just nodded like he wanted me to know he was still listening.

"Anyway, back to the letter... After Marcus asked Reagan to remember his promise he asked Reagan to tell me he was sorry and that everything he's done and continues to do is for the love of his family."

Jake tilted his head, thinking it was odd as well. "His family?"

"Yeah..." I took another deep breath. "On our way to Nashville, Reagan told me about their family. I loved Marcus, but it was then that I realized I didn't really know anything about him. We'd been together for three years and I didn't even know his real last name."

I started to cry as I said it. Jake took my hand and pulled me in closer to him then put his arm around me. "It's okay, baby..." He said like I didn't have to go on if it was too hard, but I wanted to.

"It was Thompson... Besides Reagan, the rest of their family were Coldiers..." I turned to look straight at Jake again. "They were Coldiers, Jake."

He nodded like he understood but I could see in his eyes it was hard for him to watch me cry. "Do you think he was planning to defect, or... do you think he was a double too?" He asked softly.

"I don't know... That's what bothers me... How could I have known him for so long and... I thought we loved each other, you know? Three years and I didn't really know him at all, and he obviously didn't know me... He was gonna leave me, he even knew I thought I was pregnant and he still was gonna leave me." I felt myself getting worked up the more I went on.

"Shh, baby... just relax, it's all right..." Jake said as he reached up and pulled the hair from my face then wiped my eyes with his thumbs.

"But... you don't get it... I've not even known you for more than a year yet and—" I couldn't finish before he stopped me.

"Eva... stop..." He said as he gripped my head firmly between his palms. "I'm not Marcus... Do you hear me?" He said as he looked at each of my eyes to make sure I was listening. "I'm nothing like him... I'd never leave you, okay? I love you, I loved our baby, I'll love any future babies we have too and that's all that matters... All right?"

I nodded as I tried to stop crying even though I wasn't doing a very good job.

"If it was ever in question, I'd pick you over my family… When I asked you to marry me, that's what I signed up for. You're gonna be my wife, baby. I'm committed to you… Now and after the wedding too… until death do us part."

Even though it was hard, I smiled when I heard him say it. "That's all I wanted, to know that I really did have someone that I could count on, someone who was my person, who wouldn't leave me, even if things got hard."

"Believe me, baby, you couldn't get rid of me even if you tried… Remember? Because you tried already?" He smiled really big, "And I wouldn't let you go, would I?"

I shook my head no, then brought my sleeve up to finish wiping my eyes.

"Come here," he said as he gripped my shoulders and pulled me to rest against him.

"I'm just scared, Jake." I said as I rested my head against his chest.

"I know, baby, I know…" He gently rubbed his hands up and down my back. "You're allowed to be scared…"

Neither of us said anything else for a few minutes. I just rested against him, enjoying his embrace for the moment. It turned out to be a short moment, as Turner came strolling back from watering the bushes and broke the silence. "You guys about ready to go? If you're tired, man, I can drive. It's no big deal."

"Nah, I got it, but thanks," Jake said as he gently moved me away from him so he could see my face. He continued to speak to Turner, but I felt the warmth of his gaze as he spoke. "You're right. It's been long enough we should get going again. I wanna try to make it as far as we can before dark."

I could tell the longer we were on the road the more bored I became. Jake and Turner didn't speak much and when they did, the conversations weren't the same as the ones when we were with Lane. Even though Turner seemed nice enough, he didn't have quite the same flare as Lane did to pull out the playful side of Jake, or me, for that matter. The radio didn't have music on it anymore like it used to when I was a child, either.

I enjoyed watching out the window but even that got old after a while. Maybe if we could travel at a faster speed, it could be fun to watch everything wiz by, but going a whopping 30-40 miles per hour didn't have quite the same excitement as I thought a quicker speed would have. After a while of window watching and rummaging through Jake's bags for something to do with no luck, I decided to just give in and take a nap. Since Turner knew the truth about me now, I wasn't as uptight about the potential of him hearing me say something in my sleep anymore.

I pulled the largest bag over closer to me and leaned against it, then closed my eyes and thought about the future.

"What's your name?" I was beyond confused about where I was or where he was taking me, but since I didn't know anything else, I hoped maybe the man in black would finally tell me.

"I'm not supposed to be talking to you. You shouldn't even be awake yet." He didn't say it mean, but I got the idea he still wasn't ready to tell me anything about myself or why I had no memory up until I woke up with him carrying me.

"Okay, I don't know what would hurt with you telling me your name, though... Or my name, will you tell me my name?"

"I already told you, I don't know your name. That's for you to decide later once I'm gone."

"Gone? What do you mean?" The idea of being alone made me frantic. "You can't leave me... Not without... ugh, you can't. You just can't! I don't know who I am, who you are, why I'm here, where here even is... please!"

"Calm down, Gypsyin! Look, I'm not here to give you answers, okay? I'm just here to make sure you don't die, not for the first few days, anyway." Him telling me to calm down didn't make me actually want to calm down. Nothing he was saying made any sense and didn't make me feel any better. I didn't say anything else. I was scared, and he'd made it clear that, not only did he not care, he didn't intend to tell me anything, no matter how much I asked.

"Walk this way," he said as he pointed toward the top of the hill. "We're going to stop on the other side. That's where I think it'd be a good place for you to make your home."

"My home?" I asked as I continued to walk.

"Yeah, don't worry, it might be a little rough for a few weeks but you'll learn quick. I'm gonna show you how to fish so you won't starve. It'll be like you're camping."

"Then you're gonna leave me?"

"You'll be fine. Keep walking."

"Do you hate me?" That was all I could think about. I didn't know him but he must have known me from before and hated me. He must have done something so I wouldn't remember him. That way, he didn't feel as bad when he abandoned me.

"No…" He squinted, not understanding why I would ask him that, then sighed loudly. "My name's Corbin. I guess it wouldn't hurt for you to know what to call me."

I glanced over at him after he said it. His face looked different like he wasn't as upset with me as he had been the whole time we'd been walking. I was surprised he finally answered one of my questions. I wasn't sure if I wanted to ask more or if it would make him mad again.

"Okay," I said, trying to sound appreciative that he would finally tell me. "Will you show me how to make a fire too, so I can cook the fish?"

He smiled for the first time since I woke up. Even though it was a small one, I took that as a positive sign. "Yes, I'm gonna show you how to make a fire. I'll show you how to build a shelter, too."

"Okay… thanks, Corbin." I didn't want to say much more since he seemed irritated and I didn't want to push him.

He nodded as he continued up the hill beside me. "I know you don't remember anything but I want you to know whatever this looks like to you and however scary it is… it's a better place than where you came from."

"Okay..." I said as I nodded back. I figured I'd take what I could get.

"The man that had you before this probably doesn't even know you're gone yet but he wasn't nice to you... I know you might not understand but I can't tell you much. I've done something that could get me in a lot of trouble."

"I won't tell anybody." I said, hoping he felt comfortable enough to tell me more.

"You're better off on your own out here than you were with him."

"Why can't you stay?"

He looked at me as if wanting to answer me, but then looked away like he was fighting it.

"Never mind... I'm sorry." I knew I was asking too much and was afraid it was making him shut down again.

"I'm sorry... I really just can't tell you much."

"Okay... but you'll teach me how to fish?"

His eyes looked like they were holding so much back. He nodded again. "Something else... don't go back into the city, all right?"

"Okay... which city?" I asked like it mattered before I realized I didn't even know where the cities were or what they were called.

"Any city... cities are bad places for you. To be honest, people in general are bad, all right? You need to just stay away from people. That's the only way you'll stay safe."

"Okay..." I sighed. "Will I get my memory back?"

He didn't respond right away, which in and of itself gave me an idea of what the answer probably was. "No," he said finally. "You might have dreams and maybe some things that were the most traumatic might still be in your memory but most things... no... I'm sorry."

"Okay..."

"We're almost there, keep going. There's a cave down here that'll give us shelter tonight."

"Corbin?"

"What?"

"Thank you."

"For what?" He looked confused again.

"For saving me."

"Don't do that..." He didn't seem happy with me again. "I haven't saved you. Far from it..."

"But you said you took me away from the mean man?"

"Saving you would have been taking you from him before he... never mind." He stopped, apparently realizing he was about to tell me more than he wanted to again.

"Was I a bad person?"

He stopped walking and looked at me then shook his head as he slowly let his eyes travel back to the ground and started walking again. "You didn't deserve anything that's been done to you."

"Kaleahhh... Evvaa... Babyyy... Wake uuup..." I opened my eyes to Jake sweetly stroking my face as he stood above me with the car door open looking down as if he'd been watching me sleep.

"We stopped for the night. You wanna get out and help us make camp? I figured you could get the fire started while we picked up some wood to keep it stoked over night."

I blinked a few times to help myself decipher my dream from what Jake was trying to tell me so I knew I was awake again. "Jake?" I said.

"Yeah, babe, you need help out of the car?"

"Did you ever know an agent named Corbin?" I didn't think and asked with my eyes still half closed so I didn't see the way he looked at me when he responded.

"Where did you get that name?"

When I finally opened my eyes again enough to see his face, all I could tell was he looked curious. "It doesn't matter, just tell me..." I wanted to know the answer before I told him where, just in case it changed how he wanted to respond.

"That used to be Miller's right-hand man. I never knew the guy though... He died before I was put under Miller."

"Oh… hmm… okay?" I thought that was interesting. "What else do you know about him?"

"Well, the other agents called him Robins, not many knew his first name, so it's odd that you'd know it. I'm not sure what he did but from the stories I've heard, Miller accused him of treason. He didn't make it to trial though. Before he could, some of the other men found him dead in his house."

The moment he said the name Robins, chills went down my spine and I realized who the man was and what other things he'd done besides save me from Miller. His too was one of the five names that was engraved in my memory. One of the five men that at one time I swore I would find to avenge myself, before Jake came along anyway.

"Eva… you all right?" Apparently, I was lost in thought and forgot to respond. "How do you know that name, baby?"

"It doesn't matter… I just dreamed it, that's all." I said as I sat up finally and got out of the car.

"That's not a common name. I've actually never known anyone else with it. You sure it was just a dream and not a memory again?" I could tell he wanted me to tell him more than I was letting on.

"I'm not sure of anything anymore, baby…"

15

COERCED AGREEMENTS

The sound of the fire crackling was soothing. I enjoyed watching it as well. In reality, I think it was having Jake next to me that actually made me comfortable, though. Just knowing he was with me and everything would be all right now that I was away from the Sicari and back in his arms was all I needed to feel secure again.

"Where'd Turner go?" I asked as I let my gaze break free from the fire for a moment.

"He knew I wanted some alone time with you so he agreed to go make his own fire and sleep by himself next to it tonight." Jake said softly as he rested against a tree, looking down at me with my head in his lap.

"Oh, well, that's nice of him." I said as I rolled to my back so I could look up at him.

"Yeah, he's a good guy. That's why I trust him. He's been a good friend to me." Jake smiled.

"How long have you known him?" I asked, hoping to get enough info that I could be convinced of his goodness for myself.

"I met him when I first came to Nashville to work under Miller… a little over a year and a half ago now."

"Is he the same rank as you? 'Cause he treats you like he is."

Jake half-smiled as he looked up and away for a moment, "Oh, he's just... you know... not all the men that are under me are the same. Some are more military minded, like Andry, so they treat me more like a CO and some are more like Turner... He treats me like a friend would, but I'm okay with that... when we aren't on duty, anyway... But no, he doesn't rank as high as me, baby... Most agents don't."

"Oh, ok, I guess that makes sense." I said as I thought about how I treated my previous superiors and realized I was just as guilty of doing what I was accusing Turner of. "Have you decided what you wanna do with me before we get to Nashville?"

Jake looked at me as I asked, then nodded as he recalled his decision. "Yeah... if you're okay with it, I think it would be best to leave you alone a little ways outside the city while we go in to refuel, then we can come back and get you. You have your memory back now and you know how to fight again, so you should be able to protect yourself... I'll leave you with a gun too so nothing bad should happen to you."

"Okay," I said as I thought about it.

"I don't want to send Turner into the city alone. It might take him too long. I also don't want to leave him alone with you while I go refuel because he still has a tracker on him... I don't want Miller to have any way of finding you, so the farther away from that tracker you can be when we're in the city, the better."

"Yeah, that sounds good." I said, as I looked up at Jake. There was something about the way he was looking at me though that I thought was off. "What's wrong, baby?"

He smiled, about to deny anything was the matter then began to stroke my hair away from my forehead as he looked up again. "Ugh... you know... I just..." He paused briefly, unsure he wanted to tell me. "Ugh, baby. It's just hard. I hate that we have to go back there. I don't want anything to happen to you again. It's stressful, that's all." He said as he looked back down at me. "I mean, I just got you back." He smiled again but I could tell there was a pain behind it. His eyes looked like they were beginning to get glossy as well.

"I know, baby…" I said as I reached up to rub his short beard. "Like you said though, I can fight now. I'm not just a scared little Kaleah anymore. So you aren't alone. I got your back like you've got mine. We'll be okay."

He forced a smile, then nodded.

"Plus, I don't know if it helps, but I got the idea from Turner earlier that most of Miller's men think the intel he's after doesn't even exist. So… I mean, if his men don't even take him seriously, that's gotta help."

"Turner said that?"

"Umm-hmm," I nodded.

"That's odd," Jake squinted a little, unsure of something.

"What?"

"That's the first I've heard of that. When I talked to Andry yesterday, he said that Miller and the men all were pretty well in one accord that getting the intel was top priority."

"Oh… Well…" I shrugged, "I don't know then, that's what Turner told me."

"Okay…" He said, letting his face get more serious as he thought about it. "You don't have to tell me what the intel is, but do you mind at least telling me what it's about?"

"Okay," I trusted him with my life so I realized I should be able to trust him with the intel too. "It's an eleven digit numeric code to the Armory vault at Fort Knox. There are enough weapons in there that if either side got them, they could end the standoff. They could win the war and fully take over… once and for all…"

The expression on Jake's face when I was done was exactly what I expected. He raised his brows, looking rather shocked. "That's what you've been carrying this whole time?"

I nodded.

"And you still know the eleven digit code, even after you were erased so many times?" He asked, sounding skeptical.

"Yeah… I memorized it… I don't know, I guess it's just one of those things. I knew how important it was when I got it so I locked it away in a place in my mind that was like a vault of its own."

His face was still full of shock like he didn't know how to proceed.

"What did you think the intel was?" I asked.

"I don't know… I guess I didn't have any idea. I had a hard time thinking whatever it was could still be relevant so many years later, but… that would be."

"Yeah," I kind of half nodded as I agreed.

"I can't believe you'd been carrying that all alone, baby…" He said as he looked down at me, knowing it was heavy.

"I wish I'd just forget it some days… but then others… I don't know… I'm the only one that's still alive that knows it. And I know how powerful it is, and what it could do. Before I trusted you, when I still wasn't sure about the Coldiers, when I still thought I hated you all… that's when I wanted to take it to the Sicari instead of my dad. I hated what Miller had done to me. I hated the Coldiers, even though I knew Dad was one. I just wanted to tell someone, so the war would end. But now… I don't trust any side with the intel, not really. I don't want the Coldiers to have it either. The Sicari aren't bad people, they don't deserve to die anymore than the Gypsyins or anybody else."

Jake didn't say anything. He just kept nodding with the same look of understanding, willing to listen.

"I don't know if Miller knows what the intel is about… I might have already told him before I was initially erased. I'm not sure. I know I never told anyone the code, though."

"Why would you have told him what it was about?" Jake asked, curious.

"When Miller first got me, I was so upset. They'd just shot Marcus, and he made me stab him so they couldn't use him against me. I think I was still confused too because I knew I sent the letter to my dad, but I didn't know why my dad would have had an ambush ready for us. Initially, Miller didn't act like… well the way I know him now. I think he knew who I was, so he acted like he was working for my dad, you know… It was so long ago and I was so upset… so many things happened that it's hard to remember. I can't think of any other reason why Miller would still be so dead set on getting the intel after so many years later, though. Not unless he knew what you know now."

"You're probably right." Jake said as he took in a deep breath like he didn't like it, but knew it was realistic. "That means he'll never stop looking for you." Jake's face looked distressed as he said it, then he looked away from me probably thinking about what all that meant. "And the only way he'll be able to keep finding you is because you're with me."

"Jake…" I didn't know where he was going with that, but I didn't want him to continue.

"You won't be safe with me, not until he's dead, Eva…" He went exactly where I was afraid he would.

"But you promised me… You said you were committed, you can't leave me!" I sat up to look at him so he would know I wasn't happy with his new conclusion.

"That's not what I am saying, baby. I don't want to leave you, don't think that. I'm just saying until Miller is dead, you're not safe around me. I need to hide you away somewhere, where he can't find you. Then I can go in and take care of him. That's the only way to make sure you're safe. We can get married after that."

"No!" This wasn't what we had planned, and I wasn't happy that Miller was messing it up, just like he had done the rest of my life thus far. "I'm not gonna go hide again, that's what we tried to do in the grotto lands, then in New York… I can't keep hiding from him. I won't!"

"Eva…" Jake huffed, probably wanting me to calm down, but I wasn't going to. He needed to know.

"No, Jake!"

"Please, just stop and hear me out… I can take you to your father in New York. You can stay with him until I get back. I'll get men, take care of Miller, then it can all be over with, once and for all."

"My father doesn't want me, Jake!" I said as I stood up. I didn't want to keep arguing. I didn't want to hear his plans any longer, not unless they were plans where we could be together. I didn't want to be away from him again.

"What? I'm sure that's not true… Please calm down. Just sit back down, please…"

"I need to think… just leave me alone for a minute." I said, as I turned to walk off.

"Eva! Where are you going?" He didn't sound happy.

"I just need to think… I'll be back."

"Stop, it's dark. You can't even see that well in the dark."

I turned back to look at him. "I just need to think… I won't go far. I'll be back."

"Fine!" He said, not wanting to fight with me, "But don't go far. Yell for me if you need me."

I didn't respond; I just walked toward where it looked like there was another large tree that I could sit down against to think to myself.

I wasn't sitting there long when I heard Jake. "Eva, baby, where are you?" It sounded like he'd followed me.

"Over here…" I didn't say it super loud, but apparently loud enough that he didn't have any trouble finding me.

He walked up and looked down at me. "The last time you walked off on your own didn't work out very well." He said, then turned to sit down in front of me. "I know you're upset, but that wasn't my intention, baby."

"I know you didn't do anything intentionally, but… I just don't like it when you make plans for our future and say it's for my own good, without taking into consideration what I want."

"Okay…" He said, thinking about what I said. "I'm sorry. I'll try not to do that anymore. Does that make you feel better?"

"A little."

"Just a little? Not all the way?" He said with a smile.

"No… I'm still a little mad." I said, trying to sound serious.

"Aww, baby, what are you still mad about? Let me fix it." He scooted himself closer to me.

"I miss Lane," I said, holding back a grin.

"Lane?" Jake huffed, jokingly. "What can Lane give you that I can't?"

"Lane can cook…" I couldn't hold back my grin any longer.

Jake chuckled, "Okay, okay… you're probably right…" He said as he leaned in to kiss me. "Still… I can do a lot of things that Lane can't." He said softly as he got closer to my ear.

"Are they as good as his pizza?" I asked as I leaned in closer to him.

"Better…" He whispered, then brought his hand up to sweep the hair off my neck.

"I don't know, Jake… His pizza is pretty amazing." I said, trying not to giggle.

"Lay down and relax. Take off your boots and give me your foot. Let me show you what's amazing." He whispered again.

I didn't say anything else. I did what he said and turned to lie against the ground.

"Comfortable enough?" He asked, as he turned and leaned to his side against the tree.

"Yeah," I said softly, bringing my right foot up so he could rub it.

"Close your eyes and relax… You're under a lot of stress, let me try to help."

"All right," I said, then did as he asked. Before long, I felt the muscles in my lower back relax along with my legs, as if all the tension was slowly releasing. It felt like it'd been forever since I was able to just relax and enjoy him taking care of me.

He didn't say anything else he just kept working his thumbs into my heel then slowly worked toward my ankle before he started on my calf.

"Jake…"

"Just relax, baby, you're fine."

"I don't know if I can stay awake, that feels too good."

"Then don't…" He said softly, sweetly.

"Okay," I whispered back, letting my thoughts and mind relax along with my body.

The longer it went on the more I wished it could last forever. It felt so amazing.

Then suddenly I heard something that didn't sound right. I opened my eyes to see Turner standing behind Jake only a couple of yards away, holding his gun. Jake must have heard him too, but by the time he pulled his hands away from me to reach for his gun, it was too late.

"I'm sorry to do this, I really am…" Turner said as Jake turned, putting himself between the barrel and me.

"What are you doing, man?" Jake asked calmly.

"I didn't want to, Miles… I swear I didn't… Take your gun and slowly toss it to me. Don't try anything, please… I don't want to but I'll shoot you if I have to."

"Turner?"

"Now Miles! Please…"

Jake did what he asked and slowly pulled his gun from his holster and tossed it to land at Turner's feet. "There, I'm not armed now. Will you put your gun down and talk to me… You haven't done anything yet, it's okay. We can talk." I could tell Jake was trying to deescalate the situation by staying calm, however I didn't feel so calm myself. Everything in me that was concerned about Turner and who he was really loyal to was now screaming at me—*I freaking told you so!*

"I have… Miller is coming. He's going to take you both in with him." Turner actually did sound apologetic as he said it, but I think we all knew that really didn't matter now.

"Eva, sit up!" Jake said as he brought his hand around his back to tap my leg. I bet he was thinking it might be best if I tried to get away, but I wasn't sure yet. "Why would you do that, Turner?"

"If she tries to run, I'm gonna shoot her, Miles. So don't tell her to do that… I don't want to shoot her."

"I won't, okay… Eva, don't run!" Jake said. "Now tell me why you're doing this, Turner. I thought we were friends?"

"We are, man… I swear I wouldn't have done this if I didn't have to. Miller has my son… He knew you trusted me so he took my son, man… I'm sorry… I really am sorry…"

"It's okay, calm down… He's not here yet… We still have time. I understand, Turner, I'm not mad at you, all right? We can work this out. Just put the gun down." Jake was trying the same method he used when Luca had a gun pointed at us. It worked that time so hopefully it could work again this time as well.

"I can't do that, Miles… You both need to be here when Miller and the men get here or he won't give Dillan back to me and his mom. Miller said I had to follow his exact orders or I wouldn't get my boy back and I believe him."

"How do you even know he's coming?" Jake asked.

"He told me when he left me at the house that if I saw you had the girl with you that I was to kill Baker and leave his tracker there."

"I don't understand…" Jake acted confused but I think he was just trying to get Turner to keep talking so he had time to think of a way out.

"Miller said he'd had enough of Baker and he'd been having issues with him following orders. He knew if I killed him it'd make me look more trust-worthy to you, too. I just didn't have to since she beat me to it. I did as you asked and took his tracker out, but when we left, I didn't actually bring it with us. I left it there with his body. Miller said if I did that then he would use my tracker to find us and come get you both as soon as night fell. I just needed to keep you here."

I think at that moment Jake had to see what I saw. There wasn't any way out, not without one of us potentially getting hurt. I knew what Turner said he'd do if I tried to run but I considered doing it, anyway. The idea of getting shot wasn't nearly as scary as seeing that bastard's face again. I hadn't had a chance to decide what I wanted to do yet, when I heard noise off in the distance; it sounded like Miller and his men were already here.

16
RELUCTANT RELIEF

"Good man, Turner! You followed my orders exactly. I was a little concerned there for a minute but you did well." The sound of Miller's voice brought back so many memories. I was having a hard time stopping myself from vomiting.

Turner didn't look as relieved as I'm sure he thought he would feel once his orders were complete. "You'll let my boy go now, right?" I could hear the trepidation in his voice.

"You help me and the men get these two back to my office without any mishaps and sure, I'll tell you where he's at, so you can go get him."

I wanted to scream out that Miller was probably lying, but I didn't want slapped across the face again. I looked over at Jake who was now bound and gagged sitting across from me still under gunpoint; he looked like he regretted being as verbal initially as he had been as well. I assumed the only reason Miller hadn't had me gagged along with Jake was because he was hoping I would decide I'd had enough and just give up the intel to make it all stop. I considered it, but I still needed more time. I didn't want either myself or Jake to get hurt but I knew how dangerous the intel would be in Miller's hands and I had a responsibility to protect more than just Jake and I.

"Wrap it up, boys," Miller said loudly, commanding his men. "Put Princess in my car," he said as he looked at them all still surrounding us, holding their guns out. Then he looked down at Jake. "This traitor will ride in the other one. Turner will drive. Simmons, Benton, you ride with them."

Jake didn't make any more noise or gestures. I think he knew it was a long game at this point and if we were going to find any way out of this, it'd be in time. I didn't know how many of the men that were surrounding us had previously worked with Jake but I hoped, like Andry, some of them had and might potentially be more loyal to Jake than Miller. Miller might have considered that though when he picked the men to bring because I didn't see Andry there, or anyone that looked familiar, for that matter.

Suddenly, one of the men grabbed me from behind to hoist me to my feet. I wanted to verbally assault every single one of them but I could tell by the way Jake looked at me the first time I was slapped for it; he didn't think I should do it again.

Just as Miller instructed, Jake and I were walked over and each placed in separate vehicles. For a moment I was concerned how they might treat Jake, then I realized I was probably the one in more danger of being mistreated, considering I would be the one in Miller's vehicle.

They put me in the front seat to sit next to Miller while he drove. Initially, I was upset to think I would have to sit so close to him, but then I decided to be thankful when I considered the situation could have been much worse. He could have had me sit next to him in the back seat. At least this way, his hands were occupied during the trip.

He tried talking to me initially, but I never responded. I didn't know what to say without making matters worse for myself. I also didn't want to give him anything to use against Jake, either. I tried the best I could to look out the window the entire time, then pretended to fall asleep with my head leaning against the door.

"Wake up, Princess... You're back home now, it's missed you." Miller shouted as we slowly pulled in to what I recognized to be the building his office was in. As I opened my eyes and looked around, so many memories flooded in of the time he'd kept me here after they killed Marcus. I felt my heart beginning to race at the thought of what this place represented to me and what had happened here.

"You'll have to kill me before I tell you anything." I said lightly under my breath, then realized that was probably antagonizing and it wouldn't do me any good so I shouldn't say any more.

Miller laughed, apparently having heard me. "I'm not worried about you talking, doll face… The intel is only part of the pleasure that having you again brings to me. Knowing that I have what your father doesn't—what he's spent the last seven years trying to get again— that's almost just as enjoyable to me." He said as he opened his door to step out. No sooner had he begun to order the other men in the car around than I saw the car Jake was in pulling up next to us. Even though he was tied up as well, just knowing he was close was comforting to me. I knew this whole time he was probably plotting and planning, hopefully trying to find a way out for both of us.

"Take them both to the loft," Miller instructed just before my door opened and a large man the size of Jake stepped forward to pull me from the car.

I looked around as I stood up slowly; I didn't see Miller anymore. I didn't know where he went, but knowing he wasn't around for a moment let me breathe a sigh of relief. "You don't have to do this," I said as the man began to push me toward the building. "Do you know who I am? My father has a reward out for me… He's a first rank. Let me and Miles go and I'll take you to him… You can have the rew—" a swift smack to the back of my head stopped me from continuing. The man didn't say anything, he just continued to push.

"Please…" I continued, despite his strike. I knew this would probably be the only chance I got to beg someone except Miller for my freedom, so I was going to take it, despite how much pain it caused me. "You can't let him have me. He'll torture me… please… you have no idea what he'll—" I couldn't finish before the man stopped and turned me around.

"Shut your mouth, or I will shut it for you, Gypsyin." He said calmly, with a fierce sternness to his face as he stood there and stared at me. Then he turned me back around and proceeding to push me again. I couldn't help but think of Jake when I saw it. It reminded me so much of him when he first captured me. He had no idea who he had a hold of; he was just blindly following orders.

"Shut it for me then…" The words slipped out of my mouth before I had time to think, and realize that was a completely idiotic response.

No sooner had I said it than the man turned me around again and raised his hand, about to slap me hard across the face. I winced while waiting for the strike when suddenly I heard him. "Nah, I'll punish you later…" He said with a smirk as he forcefully spun me again to continue up the steps.

It wasn't long before we made it up to the third floor where I remembered Miller's loft was. As the man opened the door to push me into the room, I saw Jake and the men escorting him already in the room. He was sitting on the floor with his hands still bound but no longer with a gag in his mouth.

"Jake!" I said when I saw his mouth was free, hoping we might get a chance to talk, if only briefly, before Miller got there.

"No, baby…" He mouthed as he shook his head slightly. I couldn't hear the words but I could read his lips.

"You know… it's taken way longer than I expected but this is almost exactly how I hoped it would happen." Miller was sitting in his chair already, over to the side of the room where I hadn't seen him yet. "Bring her to me, Benton. I wanna see her up close again."

I looked down at Jake as the man escorted me to Miller. I could see he was distraught and probably wanted to bust his ties and kill every man in sight.

"You're almost prettier than I remember." Miller said as Benton pushed me down to kneel on the floor in front of Miller's chair. "What does she mean to you, Miles? You wanna start being honest with me now?"

"What do you want from me, Miller? Whatever you want, I'll get it. You don't need her, just let her go." Jake said it trying to sound calm but I could hear something in his voice that was screaming the complete opposite.

"The time to negotiate is over, Miles… I've given you months to bring me the intel. You refused to do it when I felt lenient, so here we are. Now be a good boy and answer my question."

"You know what she means to me! That should be obvious." Jake said, trying to stay vague.

"You know what I hate more than a liar, Miles?" Miller asked. "A thief!" He said quickly, answering his own question, then looked down, ready to address me now. "You wanna tell me what he is to you since *he* won't answer the question?"

I started to turn around to look at Jake but Miller grabbed my face and pulled me back toward him before I could. "No, no, no… no cheating on the test, Princess… You know the answer. You don't need him to tell you."

"I'm not telling you shit! You can go to hell, you filthy bastard."

Miller smiled like he enjoyed me calling him names. Then he raised his hand, ready to slap me hard across the face when suddenly I heard Jake speak up behind me. "Stop! I love her, okay? I love her…"

Miller lifted his face to look at Jake. "Just as I expected." He said, sounding disgusted. "Now you want to tell me what I told you about the prisoner when I sent you after her?"

I didn't hear anything for a moment, then before long I heard Jake speak up again. "You said she was yours."

"Ohhhh, so you *do* remember? Now you wanna tell me what that makes you?"

Jake hadn't responded yet when Miller suddenly stood up and walked over to him, looking angry. I turned around to see as he began to yell at Jake. "That makes you a thief, Miles, you stole from me!" He yelled at him then kicked him in the side, making Jake wince and moan slightly. "She was my property, and you stole her." Miller continued to scream like a child throwing a tantrum.

"She was never yours," Jake said under his breath as he looked up at me, giving me a look again like he was apologetic that we were even both in this predicament.

When Miller heard that, he smacked Jake hard across the face with the back of his hand. Jake didn't make a sound or act like it hurt but I could tell it must have.

"You wanna know what I do with thieves, Miles?" Miller said as he reached out his hand to one of the men standing behind Jake. "Give me your gun, Banks." He said, now looking over at the agent.

Jake didn't respond again. I didn't know what he was doing, but it didn't seem like anything was going to help us at this point.

The agent took his gun from his holster and gave it to Miller, where he proceeded to rack the slide and hold it up to Jake's face as he continued to yell at him. "This is what I do to thieves, Miles! I discontinue their service—"

"Wait! Stop!" I yelled. I didn't know if Miller would have done it but I didn't want to give him the chance. "I'll tell you, okay? I'll give you the intel. Then you let us go, Miller!" I screamed it so he could hear me over his own rage.

He stopped, surprised and turned to look at me.

"Eva… you can't!" Jake's voice cracked. He probably was still thinking the same way I previously was—about how it would effect everyone, not just ourselves, but I didn't care anymore. I didn't care about everyone. At that moment, I realized what Jake meant to me and what I would do to save him.

"Yes I can, Jake!" I said then looked back up at Miller. "Let him go! I'll give you the intel, then you let me go."

Miller smiled, "Oh really!" He said in a pleasant tone. I knew it was a long shot, but I just wanted to do whatever I could to get him to agree to let Jake go. I would deal with myself after that.

"Eva, baby, you can't do that…" Jake tried to speak up again to talk me out of it. But before he said anything else Miller took the gun and hit him with it across his face, this time making Jake groan.

"Stop it!" I yelled again. I could see it hurt Jake worse this time as blood began to run from his nose. "Don't touch him again, or I won't tell you shit, you freakin' bastard."

Miller continued to smile. I think he enjoyed seeing that he finally had something over me. "Aww, you really do love him… How about we make a deal then, Princess?"

"I already said I'd give you the intel. What else do you want?" I wasn't in the mood to play games with him but I didn't know what else to do to make him release Jake.

"You!" Miller said as he rested the gun on top of Jake's head, taunting me. It wasn't surprising. From everything I remembered about being with him the first time, it didn't surprise me at all. "I kill him and I have my way with you by force again or…" He lifted the gun as he shrugged. "You agree to just be mine again, no fighting me… then I'll let him go."

I didn't know if he would actually hold up his side of the deal in the end but he made a valid point. He was going to have me one way or the other, whether Jake was alive for it or not, so I didn't really have much choice but to agree. Before I got a chance to answer him, Jake spoke up again, "You better kill me first then, because I'll never let you have her back."

Miller looked at him like he was willing to take him up on it. "You hurt him anymore and you don't get me or the intel! Hear me, Miller?" I said, stopping him from proceeding with Jake's delusional plan.

Jake looked up at me like he knew my deal would win and he couldn't bear the thought of it, like he would rather die than see me agree to it.

"So, it's a deal then?" Miller sounded excited as he looked over at me.

I looked away from Jake with a long blink, swallowing hard. I knew what I was agreeing to. I knew what it meant, but even if I couldn't be free, Jake would be. That's all I cared about. I opened my eyes to see Miller staring at me, waiting for a response. I didn't say anything. I just nodded, then looked down.

"Eva, no!" Jake moaned in disbelief. He couldn't help himself. I knew he didn't agree, but I saw no other way.

"Great!" Miller's tone changed instantaneously to now sounding chipper. If I hadn't previously thought he had a mental disorder, I sure did now. He cheerfully handed the gun back to the agent and walked over to his desk then rummaged through the top drawer for a second before pulling out a pen and paper. "Perfect, now give me the code."

He said with a slight change of his tone, apparently switching to his professional personality.

"How do you know what the intel… is?" I couldn't finish the sentence before he gave me a look.

"The power of the serum, my dear…" he didn't say anymore, he just sat there waiting for me to give him the code.

"How do I know you'll hold up your end of the bargain, and you won't hurt Jake after I tell you?" I asked first to make sure.

He used his finger to draw an x across his chest, then a line across his throat before he finally pointed at one of his eyes with a wink.

Cross his heart, hope to die, stick a needle in his eye… I just stared at him blankly. I couldn't help but think to myself, *what the hell have I done? He's insane.*

Seeing that playing charades wasn't satisfactory, he finally spoke up, "My men will hold me to it." He said, as he motioned to them, addressing everyone. "Men… if you see that I have not kept my word with this woman, feel free to incite mutiny… There, happy?" He said now looking back at me.

I nodded. I didn't know if I could believe him or not but I realized you can't make deals with mad men so I just decided to play along hoping it would give Jake or myself more time to think of a way out.

"Great, now give me the code." He said, getting impatient.

I knew it didn't matter if I gave him the right one or not. He wouldn't know the difference until after he freed Jake, so I just rambled off random digits.

"Good, now if this isn't the right code, boys, you see that she's knowingly broken our deal, and I get to shoot Miles."

"Wait… what?" I said suddenly, taken aback by what he had just said. He was smarter than I thought.

"Umm-hmm, just as I thought *Jayde*… or is it Eva… hm? What do I want to call you now that you're mine?" He leaned back in his chair to think about it.

"That wasn't the right code. I'm sorry. I'll give you the right code."

"Good decision." He said, letting his face grow stern as he looked back at the paper and crossed the initial numbers out.

"5493062978… 4," I said them slowly. I didn't want to tell him but I knew I had no choice. As soon as the last number left my lips, even though I just gave them to the devil, I felt relieved. I no longer was the only one that knew them and even though I hated it, I couldn't help but feel a release from the burden that carrying them alone had given me.

"Perfect…" Miller seemed happy, as if he believed me this time. "Banks, Benton, you two take Miles and place him in a holding cell until we can confirm these. Sanchez, you take Princess here down to see the doc." Miller said it so nonchalantly I almost missed it at first, until I thought about it for a second.

"Wait, what?"

It seemed only a few seconds after I caught it so did Jake. "You son of a bitch, that wasn't what you agreed to." He blurted out.

I don't know if it was my imagination but the way Jake was now acting made me think he had a plan, and what Miller just instructed wasn't going to work with that plan.

"I haven't hurt you," Miller stood up from his desk to yell back at Jake. "So, she's mine, just like she agreed. That means if I want to erase her, I can." He finished yelling, then looked at the man standing behind Jake. "Now do what I said, Banks. Take him before I change my mind and everyone is in trouble."

"Wait… You can't do that…" I thought I would take my turn at arguing with him in Jake's absence. I had somewhat of a plan in my head as well, just as I expected Jake to have, and this went totally against mine, too.

"Sanchez," Miller said as he motioned toward me, "take her before she upsets me."

17

SEDUCTION'S EMBRACE

"You can't erase me yet. I could have been lying... you don't know... you should verify it first!" I said whatever I could think of to make him rethink sending me away just yet.

Miller's face instantly turned smug as he walked over to look down at me, where I was still sitting next to his desk. "Stand her up, Sanchez," the way he said it made me regret not taking my out from his presence while I still could. "You're not lying. Wanna know how I know?"

"No," I didn't know what games he was playing, but I hoped if I didn't follow along, then he'd be thrown off.

He smiled like he thought I was enticing him then took a step closer to me and leaned forward with his head over my shoulder. At first, I wasn't sure what he was doing until I heard him take in a deep breath to smell my hair. "Princess..." he creepily whispered next to my ear, "I know you wouldn't lie to me." He brought his hand up and wrapped his fingers around a section of my hair to smell again. "Because if you did... I'll set Agent Miles on fire... then I'll force you to eat the marshmallows we roast over his corpse!"

I didn't say anything; I didn't even move. I squeezed my eyes shut as tightly as I could and tried not to even breathe. I didn't want to

153

remember his smell. It did no good. Memories of the things he'd done to me in the past suddenly started rushing in and it didn't matter how much I thought I knew how to fight; at that moment I was terrified.

"Besides, I know you remember the intel even after you've been erased… Now as for other things…" he took his free hand and set it against my waist, then slowly moved it higher. "Well, let's just say it's more pleasurable for me than it is for you. I like feeling like I get to take something from you for the first time… over and over again. Any chance you remember that too, Princess?"

I still didn't say anything. I gritted my teeth and turned my head away from him as he moved his head in close to me again.

"If you're a good girl, maybe I'll let Miles watch as I enjoy you again before I… set him free."

So many things were going through my mind, I wanted to tell him to go to hell. I wanted to tell him I hoped Jake escaped and came back up here and slaughtered them all. I wanted to cry, but I couldn't. I couldn't do anything but stand there, petrified. It felt like every remnant of Eva vanished and I was now nothing but a weak and vulnerable Kaleah again, standing there all alone, stripped of all hope and dignity.

"Sanchez!" Miller about screamed it as he pulled back from my ear, looking over my shoulder again. "She's all mine this time, hear me?"

"Yes, Sir," the man spoke up, standing not far from me.

"Good! Last time I shared, Robins got too close and thought he needed to rescue her. You're not gonna let that happen again, got it?"

"Yes, Sir," Sanchez sounded almost robotic, like he was so used to taking commands, he couldn't think for himself any longer.

"Good man… I'm leaving her in your charge. I want her erased then brought right back up to me as soon as she's awake again, hear me?" Miller continued barking commands without taking a step back or releasing his hand from me just yet.

"Yes, Sir. I hear you, Sir."

"Good… Because I'd hate to see the same thing happen to you as what happened to Robins…" Miller looked past me toward Sanchez with a smug grin as he finally stepped back then walked toward his chair.

I was so overcome by all the fearful thoughts swirling through my head; I didn't even realize who Miller was actually talking to until I had a second to stand there and think about it. *Sanchez...* I let the name sink in for a moment, then suddenly, I felt his presence directly behind me and a firm tug at my wrists, followed by a jerk.

From memory, I slowly recited the five names in my head of the men I originally intended to kill once I had Eva's memories back. *Campbell, Baker, Robins, Sanchez, and Miller.*

I knew that name sounded familiar. As soon as I realized who he was, all previous feelings of fear escaped, thinking like Eva had returned, and I focused on the thought of a new mission—kill Sanchez, then escape.

As soon as we got to the hall and the door shut behind us, I decided how I would do it. First thing I needed to do was get his head out of the game and the best way to do that was with a distraction; a feminine one.

"I remember you." I said, being vague, though curious about how he would respond.

He stopped pushing me as hard, apparently unable to think about what I said, how to respond, and walk at the same time. Then, before we got to the top of the stairs, he turned me around to look at him. He didn't say anything initially. He just looked at me as if trying to see what I was doing, then he let his eyes travel downward, showing me he really was easily distracted.

"You remember me?" I asked it with a friendly, slightly seductive voice.

"What do you remember?" He asked, falling for my trap. Then he turned to look back at the door to Miller's office, probably realizing where we were wasn't the best place to talk. Before he gave me a chance to respond, he turned me around again to continue down the steps.

I could have taken the conversation so many ways but, like with any maze, I realized there was likely only one way that would work. I had to choose. *Should I play the sympathy card? Should I make him feel guilty for the things he's done to me in the past? Should I play against his manly pride, or is there another way that I can trap him?* It wasn't long before I realized the key to the lock, and it was none of the above. I saw the way he spoke to Miller. I also saw the way he'd just eyed me in the hall.

He didn't have an ego issue because he didn't care that Miller pushed him around, so going for that angle likely would be fruitless. He also wasn't likely to feel guilty or sympathetic toward me either. A man that did the things he'd done wouldn't still be alive and working for Miller if he had a conscience, ergo Robins.

He didn't make it hard to see what he wanted. However, that was probably why Miller thought it was necessary to tell him that he didn't intend to share me this time. Miller would know his men more than anyone else, so if he felt the need to warn Sanchez, then that was my angle. Exactly how I intended to play it, though, I wasn't sure.

"How long do you think I'll be asleep?" I don't know why that was the first thing I thought about asking him, but somewhere inside I trusted Eva and her manipulation tactics so I went along with it.

He didn't respond initially; as if he also thought that was an odd question for me to ask. When he finally answered, he sounded rather pleasant. "I don't know, normally only a couple of hours."

"You were always the nice one. I liked being around you." I figured I would answer his first question about what I remembered. I really just made it all up, though. In reality, I had little memory of him and what memory I did have wasn't pleasant whatsoever.

"So, you do remember me?" He asked. With that, I got the idea I was probably a little wrong about his ego but it wasn't too late to rectify that.

"Mm-hmm… honestly, I think you were my favorite." I hated saying it. The words felt repugnant coming from my mouth. I pushed myself to continue though, since I knew it was the only way and it appeared to be working.

"Really?" He asked like he genuinely believed me and wasn't suspicious that I was making it all up.

I knew I had to be careful. If I went too far, he would see right through it, but just what was too far, I didn't know yet. "Yeah... to be honest I was erased so much I only remember it that one last time. You?"

We were moving slowly down the steps, which I was sure at this point was intentional on his part. "Of course I do... until that freakin' moron, Robins, took you away."

I was almost flabbergasted when I heard him say it. Not only because my tactic was working, but after so many years this man still remembered. At that moment, I couldn't help but believe he probably had no real life outside of working for Miller. That had to be the case if he had held on to such a memory for over five years.

"What was it like? Will you remind me?" I didn't actually want to hear him recount anything. What I wanted was for him to remind himself what he wanted, and that was ultimately to disobey Miller. *That* was the distraction.

He stopped pushing me again almost mid step. Then spun me around as he spoke, "What are you trying to do?"

Shit, I thought. *I went too far.*

"I'm not stupid," he furrowed his brow. Then his eyes slowly raked down me again, probably thinking about exactly what I had intended for him to think.

"I never said you were stupid." I looked at him like I didn't know what he was talking about, then I looked down at his mouth before looking back into his eyes. "I just don't see why Miller can't share me with you. I mean... I won't tell him if you don't." I felt like I wanted to slap myself. I felt disgusted speaking like that until suddenly I saw his face change. Then, like if by magic, I didn't actually feel so bad anymore, not now that I knew it was working.

"I guess you're right. If you're about to be erased, you won't have a chance to tell him anything I've done to you." His eyes widened as he said it. I instantly felt sickened by the idea and the way he was now looking at me, but told myself I had to follow through. *That's the only way out. Just follow through.*

He reached his hand up, about to grab me right then and there when

I moved myself back and down a step. "What? Right here on the steps?" I said as I smiled at him to entice him further. "I thought you said you weren't dumb?"

He squinted to think about it, then reached for my arm and turned me around to continue to walk. "Fine," he pushed me forward until we made it to the bottom floor.

I could see at the end of the hall was a door with a light on. I assumed that was the doctor's office. I had no idea if the doctor would be there or not but I actually hoped in this case he wasn't, not for my plan to work, anyway.

Sanchez opened the door and pushed me in. Just as I had hoped, there was no one in the room. "Sit down in that chair," he said as he turned, I assume to lock the door.

"What, this chair?" I pointed at the only chair that was smack dab in the center of the room.

"Yes, stupid," he said still turned away, not even realizing I had gotten free from my cuffs. Just as I had hoped, he was too distracted to notice and now it was too late.

Before he even had a chance to turn around, I had them wrapped around his throat, pulling as hard as I could. I leveraged my weight to give myself more pulling force by putting my knee into his back. He was larger than me for sure, making it difficult, but not too large. I knew it could take a few minutes before he would be out. I just had to try to hold them there long enough.

Trying to fight me, he moved to the side of the room, probably thinking he could get free by jamming me between him and the wall. At this point, nothing short of divine intervention on his part was going to make me let go, though. This was my way out. I could see my freedom, and I was going to hold on for dear life, literally.

I could tell it was working. Before long, he was losing strength. He started hissing and spitting when finally I had done enough to work him to his knees. I was close, so close I could taste it. The adrenaline surge I was experiencing was invigorating. I had waited five years to kill this bastard, and the joy I was feeling in that moment made it all worth it.

I was hyper-focused, lost in the thrill, when suddenly I felt a sharp jab in the side of my abdomen. I didn't let up but at the same time I was confused about what would have caused it, since Sanchez was almost lifeless in front of me. I looked to my side when I saw motion, then I heard a noise like someone was behind me.

"You can't stop me. He's gonna die! He deserves to die!" I yelled it out, knowing it was probably the doctor. Before I could continue, my arms suddenly became weak, making me loosen the cuffs unintentionally. "No… no, what the hell have you done?" I yelled. At that moment, I realized it might soon be too late. The jab was probably the serum and it could be a matter of moments before I would wake up not remembering any of this even happened.

"Eva?" The man said my name, but his voice wasn't Jake's, or Turner's, or anyone that I recognized that would have been under Miller.

I started to turn to look at him but whatever he stabbed me with was working quickly, making me release the cuffs as my hands fell to the floor.

"Eva? Oh my gosh, what are you doing here?"

I couldn't help but fall backwards, still not knowing who it was or why I recognized their voice when I felt him catch me. "Luca?" His face was upside down but when I paired that with the voice, I finally knew. "What are you…" I was in shock. I couldn't understand how he was there or why, but I realized I was probably about to fall asleep from the serum and wouldn't have much chance to talk to him.

"Eva… oh my gosh," he said again, sounding just as perplexed to see me as I was him. "Holy shit, what were you doing? Here, let me help you." He said as he stood up and helped pull me to sit in the reclining chair that looked like a dentist's chair, centered in the middle of the room.

"Am I… the serum?" I couldn't help but wonder how long I had until I would be asleep.

"Oh, oh… no… no, that wasn't… no… It wasn't the serum, it was a sedative. I didn't know it was you. You aren't going to lose your memory." He said it fast probably so I would have time to talk more before I couldn't. "What are you doing here?" He asked.

"Miller..." It was already getting difficult to make my mouth move. "He... please help... me..."

"Eva..." Luca acted like he was getting the idea that the sedative was beginning to work well. "Crap..." He said as he reached down and brushed the hair from my face. "Ugh... I guess I can still talk to you while it wears off. It shouldn't be long, just relax." He looked around for a moment, then walked over and moved a curtain to the side, revealing a small round chair on wheels. He sat on it and scooted himself over to sit next to me.

I was feeling more than just relaxed, but in other ways I was still very anxious. I tried to look over at Sanchez. I didn't know if I was able to finish him off but he wasn't moving so I was optimistic. If nothing else, I hoped he didn't wake up until after my sedative wore off.

"Eva... I know you can't really tell me what's going on but I want to help." Luca picked up my hand to hold it as he continued to talk to me. "Is it Miles... Did he bring you here?"

I tried to move my head to one side then the other to tell him no, but I couldn't.

"Ugh... don't cry," he said, noticing that I had tears now running from my eyes. "I know we didn't leave off on a good note." He paused, probably wanting to think about what he was going to say before he went on. "But... I just... I'm sorry." He squeezed my hand a little, then brought it up to his forehead as he looked down.

"I never meant to hurt you, I didn't... I should have never hit you, slapped you, taken you... everything... I did things to you that I... If I saw a man treat my Bria like that, I would have done to him what Miles did to me..." He looked back up to me as he said it. "There's no excuse... I just... I wanted you so badly and I didn't know how to treat you. To be honest, you're nothing like my Bria was. You're stronger than she was and well... I didn't know how to handle a strong woman." He looked at me sympathetically, then weakly smiled. I'm sure he was glad I was listening and happy to get it off his chest.

"I don't know why you're here but I can make it up to you... I hope you give me a chance..." He said with another smile as he reached up to stroke my hair. "Oh my gosh... You're still so beautiful... I never thought I'd ever see you again." He started to say something else when suddenly something caught his attention and he quickly glanced over at Sanchez. "Eva..." Luca said softly under his breath still watching for more movement. "Close your eyes, like you've gotten the serum."

18

FORGIVEN

I did what he said and closed my eyes. At first I didn't hear anything, but then after a few moments I heard Luca talking again now over by Sanchez. "Hey, man, are you all right? You took a pretty hard fall."

All I heard that sounded like Sanchez was a bit of grunting. The only thing I could think of was how badly I wished I could have told Luca that Sanchez needed to die. I wanted to open my eyes to see what Luca was doing with him but I knew if I did and Sanchez saw them, it would be harder for Luca to convince him that he had given me the serum already. Also, if Sanchez wasn't dead yet, he needed to think I wasn't a threat anymore. At least until the sedative wore off and I could show him otherwise, since I still intended to kill him.

"Does your head hurt?" Luca's voice sounded close to the floor, probably next to him.

"Ugh… Where is she?" Sanchez huffed, as if waking up from a fog.

"Who, the girl? Don't worry about her. I gave her the serum… She's asleep now."

"Don't worry about her?" Sanchez's voice went up an octave. He sounded mad, and for good reason. His voice was a bit horse as well.

"That li'l bitch about choked the life out of me. What do you mean don't worry about her?"

"She did? Are you certain?" I wasn't sure why that was the direction Luca was taking it, as well as being skeptical of how well it would even work.

"Yes, I'm certain! How did you manage to give her the serum?" Sanchez asked, and just as I thought was now suspicious of what Luca was saying.

"I surprised her from behind... She didn't hear me come in." He seemed to cover for himself pretty well so I hoped that Sanchez believed him.

I didn't hear anything for a moment so I assumed Sanchez was making his way to his feet. I figured it would be a good time for me to test how sedated my body still was with trying to wiggle my pinky finger. It wasn't like normal but I could feel something. That was encouraging, especially not knowing exactly how mad Sanchez was.

"What are you doing?" Luca asked.

"You've done your job, doctor. Now, until Miller needs you again, leave! I'll take care of her from here." Maybe it was because he was still horse but the way Sanchez sounded when he said it frightened me.

Holy shit, what the hell does he plan on doing to me?

"I told you, I gave her the serum already. You don't need that!" I wasn't sure what Sanchez had that Luca was telling him he didn't need, but I was hoping it wasn't more serum.

"And I told *you,* I am done with your services! Now if you don't want to get erased and kicked out on your ass yourself, you'll do what I say, Gypsyin!" Sanchez got louder, yelling at Luca.

"Fine, I'll leave but what do you plan on doing with her?" Luca asked. Everything in me was hoping he was bluffing, and not really planning on leaving this bastard alone with me while I still couldn't move.

"Don't worry about it... I promise she won't remember anything." As soon as the words left his mouth, it was clear he was probably holding the serum. I wanted to open my eyes to confirm it, but knew I shouldn't. I just lay there, hoping Luca could handle it. Hoping this time he wouldn't just sit by while another man intended to do whatever he wanted with me.

"Does Miller know what you're doing with her?" Luca asked.

Sanchez didn't say anything for a moment. I wasn't sure why but I assumed he was giving Luca a dirty look, threatening him with his eyes in case he decided to turn into a snitch. "Miller said I could do whatever I wanted with her, just as long as I return her to him when I'm done. But it isn't any of your business now is it, doctor? So why don't you run along like I told you to? Miller will send for you again the next time we need more serum worked up. I'm sure this won't be the last time she gets erased."

Shit…shit…shit… All I could think about was how screwed I was. Luca, even though he had spirit, wasn't a fighter. I couldn't think of what he could do that had any chance of helping me out of this one.

I didn't hear anything for a moment, expecting to hear Luca reply when suddenly I heard more than that. I heard a commotion like maybe they had begun to tussle with each other. I opened my eyes to see Luca had a knife and was trying to use it against Sanchez but he was holding Luca's arms where he couldn't get it close enough to stab him with it.

"You're not going to do anything… to her… I won't… let… you!" Luca was trying as hard as he could to push the knife closer to Sanchez but it was obviously a struggle for him. Sanchez looked to outweigh him by a decent bit.

"What the hell, doc… Why are you fighting me?" Sanchez didn't sound like he was having as hard of a time as Luca was but he still wasn't able to get the knife away.

I tried to wiggle my fingers again, hoping I had some movement in them. I needed to get up. I needed to help Luca.

As both men came closer to where I was sitting, before I had a chance to make any movements, there was a loud clanging sound. I watched as Sanchez fell backwards over Luca's stool followed by Luca collapsing on top of him. I tried to turn my head to look; it was difficult but I could do it. That was encouraging. I had hoped that more movement would soon follow.

"Luca…" I said faintly, trying to make my mouth work again. He was lying on top of Sanchez. Both men were now practically motionless. I didn't know how they fell or where the knife ended up but I hoped it was inside Sanchez and not Luca.

"Eva…" Luca's voice hitched as he spoke back. "Eva… I'm hurt…"

"Luca?" I said again, trying to see how much range my voice was able to make. "I can't… I can't move yet." I said as I looked back at my hands, still trying to wiggle my fingers. They were getting better, but only a little. I was sure it would take a minute before my arms would actually work, let alone my whole body.

I turned my head back to look at him. I didn't know what had happened or how exactly he got hurt. He was beginning to sit up when I saw what looked like a large gash going across his chest. He was bleeding pretty badly.

"Ah, shit…" He said, looking down at himself.

"Is he dead?" I asked, looking past him at Sanchez. I didn't want another incident to occur where he came back to life yet again.

"I don't know." Luca murmured, not likely concerned about that, since he knew he was in trouble.

"You have to check, Luca. If not, you need to kill him… or he'll kill you!"

No sooner had I said it, then I could see Sanchez's eyelids twitch like he was about to wake again. When I didn't see any obvious abrasions or cuts on him like I did Luca, it was easy to assume he probably just hit his head hard and was only temporarily out from that.

"I can't…" Luca groaned, still looking at his chest, probably wanting to freak out but likely in shock.

"You have to, Luca…" I said, but it didn't seem like he was listening. "Luca!" I said his name louder, trying to snap him out of it and get him to look at me.

"What?" He looked up at me finally.

"If you don't kill him, he's going to kill you, rape me then erase me so Miller can do the same over and over for the rest of my life. So pick up the damn knife and slit his throat!"

He looked at me blankly, blinking a few times, taken aback by what I had yelled at him. Then he looked down, willing to listen and picked it up.

"Good... you can do it... he's a bad guy. He's already raped me before. Kill him... please!" I said again, hoping he could conjure the courage to finish what he'd started.

"Eva... I can't..." He said as he held the knife as if frightened by it suddenly.

"You have to Luca..." I said, beginning to beg. "Please... you have to." I knew what would happen if he didn't. I couldn't let that happen. I looked down at myself again, trying to move my hands and feet as much as I could, trying to wake my body up. Then I looked back at Sanchez to see how much time I probably had before he would be fully awake and aware of his surroundings again.

Luca had set the knife down and was now holding the syringe with the serum in it. He leaned forward, resting his elbow on the ground next to Sanchez, and then quickly jabbed the needle into his abdomen and injected the serum.

"What are you doing?" I asked, not sure why he wouldn't just slit his throat and be done with it.

"I'm not as brave as you, Eva... I'm sorry." He said, sounding like he was growing weak.

"Luca... look at me. Luca?"

"What?" He looked up at me finally but I could tell he wanted to look at his chest again.

I knew he wasn't going to make it. I didn't have to be a doctor to see he was losing too much blood and without emergency intervention he wasn't likely to stay conscious for more than another few minutes. "I forgive you!" I said, hoping to start a conversation that would help him forget the pain and be able to leave this life without regret.

"You do?" He said, as he began to slouch, about to fall over.

"Yes, Luca... I do!" Tears started to cloud my vision, but I quickly blinked them away.

"I really did love you, Eva... I did... I still do..." He said softly —sincerely.

"I know, Luca... I believe you. But you loved Bria more... and...

you're getting ready to go see her now." I couldn't stop my voice from breaking as I said it.

"I am…" he breathed, then closed his eyes like he was trying to envision it. "I miss her so much…"

"I know—" I said, then stopped myself to get my emotions under control before I could say more. "She's gonna be on the other side waiting for you… with my baby…"

His face froze for a second as he gazed off, then suddenly looked up at me again, "I'm sorry…"

"I know you are… Will you and her take care of it for me?" I said softly, trying not to burst into tears.

His eyes began to water as well, then he nodded. "Yes…" he said as he slowly leaned over to let himself fully rest against Sanchez. "We will… I promise."

"Thank you… Luca… You saved my life."

He didn't respond. He just stared at me as he slowly blinked a few more times.

"Will you name her for me?" I said, trying to keep him with me just a little longer.

He smiled, thinking about it. Then I heard him whisper. "Luna…"

"That's beautiful…" I said still looking at him while doing everything I could to wiggle my hands and feet, hoping they could start to work so I could get down and sit with him. "Luca…" I watched as he slowly closed his eyes without opening them again. "Luca!" I said again, hoping he would open them one last time.

I wanted to sit there and scream at him. I wanted to jump down there and shake him, hold him, comfort him. I wanted to do something other than sit there feeling helpless. I turned back to look at my hands; they were moving now but only barely. I sat back in the seat and rested my head against it, letting my eyes close. I could feel what tears had collected in them now begin to run down my cheeks.

He's gone… Dammit, he's gone and I'm alone now. I need to get out of here. I sat there and thought to myself. I had so many emotions I was feeling all at the same time but I needed to stop and push them aside. I felt like I wanted to sit there and sob, but I didn't have time for that now. I could mourn for Luca later. I needed to make a new plan. A plan to find Jake and escape. Or would it be better to find Jake, then we both find Miller and kill him then escape, I wondered. I knew until I was able to move I had nothing better to do than sit there and think.

Miller was relentless. I had to come up with a better plan than my last one because it didn't work as well as I had hoped. I didn't take into account someone other than Sanchez being in the room with us. I knew if that happened again, it might not work out as well for me the second time.

The longer I sat there the more I could feel sensation in my limbs but still only little movement. Then, without any warning, I heard the door open and someone come in. At that moment, I was thankful that I had my eyes closed. I didn't know who it was, but I needed to pretend to be erased. That way, whoever it was didn't feel the need to erase me again.

I tried to lightly lift my eyelids so I could peek through my lashes without the person seeing that I was actually more alert than they realized.

"Holy hell! What happened in here?" The man said as he looked around. I hoped he didn't think I had anything to do with it, since this time I actually didn't.

"Lawson! Get in here! We have a situation!" I couldn't tell from the blurred image of what I was seeing if it was someone I recognized or not but he was dressed in black so it was easy to assume it was another one of Miller's men. I closed my eyes again, so if he looked straight at me, he wouldn't see anything.

"Lawson!" the man screamed again. Then suddenly, a memory hit me like a ton of bricks. *Lawson...* I recognized that name. That was an agent that was with Jake when he came to rescue me from the inn.

I knew better than to trust the men that once swore fealty to Jake but at the same time there was a part of me that hoped this time was different. I hoped he wasn't like Turner and he really was still on Jake's side.

It wasn't long before I heard a second voice. I assumed it was

Lawson that had finally made it into the room. "What the..." He started, sounding perplexed at what he was seeing.

"I know!" the first man agreed. Whatever they were looking at was just as puzzling to him as well.

"What do you think happened?" Lawson asked.

"I don't know but she's obviously still asleep so... I bet whatever happened was after the doc erased her." I could feel myself internally breath a sigh of relief when I realized they assumed what I had hoped, that I'd already been erased.

"What is she doing here?" Lawson asked as if he'd just realized who I was.

"What do you mean? Miller finally found her... He caught Miles, too. Bet that son of a bitch regrets takin' her now!" The first agent said. He sounded like he was closer to me now on the side where Sanchez was laying.

"Oh... ah... yeah, I was just... I mean I know I always heard Miller talk about her but I mean..."

"Yeah, it's different seeing her in real life," the first agent chuckled. "I'm like you. There for a while I started to think Miller was just making shit up. He seemed obsessed, you know... but apparently she is real so... whatever."

"Uh... yeah..." It sounded like Lawson was surprised to see me. I took that as a good sign. Since he wasn't one of the men that caught me and Jake, hopefully we could still rely on him to help us when the time came.

"What do you think happened over here?" It sounded like the first agent was standing over Sanchez. "He doesn't look hurt... Looks like all this blood is comin' from the doc. I don't see a scratch on him, so what do you think is wrong? He's still breathing." He sounded clueless.

"Uh, I don't know." Lawson sounded like he was now standing next to me. I was surprised when I felt what was probably the back of his fingers gently start at my temple and slowly run down my cheek. *Can he feel the trail that my tears left?* Thankfully, I didn't jump or flinch when it surprised me. "I bet you the doc's dead. You're right, looks like all this blood is probably his. She's doesn't seem like she's hurt though, so that's good."

"True… Miller would probably be pretty pissed if she was."

"So, you were there when he found her?" Lawson asked now as he picked up my hand and turned it over to inspect my palm.

"Yeah, man, you should have been there. Miles was freakin' pissed. You could tell if we weren't all pointing our guns at him that he'd have gone banshee on our asses… like for real. Even with my gun out, I was a little concerned. But Miller handled it. He had him tied up and gagged and it went smoothly after that. This one… she's got a mouth on her, though. A dirty little mouth…" He chuckled. "She was doin' all kinds of hollerin'… Cussin' at us with her li'l potty mouth until Benton gave her a good cross to the face. That shut her up real quick. Shame though, her face's so pretty, I hate to see marks on it."

"So, what does Miller plan on doing with her now?" It sounded like Lawson was trying to fill himself in on everything that had happened.

"Oh, I don't know… That's not really any of my business what he does with a Gypsyin. The way I see it, she's his property now, so… it's his prerogative…"

"Right… right…" Lawson started to put my hand down then before he did he ran his finger down the center of my palm. I wasn't prepared for it to tickle me so I didn't stop myself from flinching my arm when he did it. I was instantly concerned when I realized he probably noticed and might figure out I was awake but he didn't say anything. He just gently took it and laid it back against my stomach.

"You have any idea where Andry is? I haven't seen him in a few days." Lawson asked. It sounded like he'd moved to stand at my feet.

"Um, nope…" The first agent's voice was near my head now. "When Miller found out that he was helping Miles he told him to take a few days off. Haven't seen him since… You think if I kick Sanchez maybe he'll wake up? I mean it's weird that he'd be knocked out cold like this."

"Nah… I'd leave him. He'll eventually wake up… or he won't." Lawson said with a slight chuckle. Then I felt him remove one of my shoes and do the same with my sole as he did my palm and run a finger up it, likely checking to see if it tickled. This time I was expecting it though, so I didn't flinch. "I'll take her upstairs to him when she wakes up if Sanchez isn't awake yet. You can clean up the mess."

"Aww, Lawson, you're too kind. For right now though, why don't you stop playing with her feet and come over here and help me sit him up? Then we can decide who gets the shit work…"

19

NOT SO SLEEPING BEAUTY

"Kaleah?" Lawson said, hoping I would respond. After the other agent helped him clean up the blood, he left to take Luca's body away while Lawson stayed to wait for Sanchez to wake up. I think Lawson suspected more than the other guy did though, by the different things he was saying while he waited.

"Kaleah… Can you hear me?" He asked again. I didn't intend to respond to him, though. I was going to keep laying there pretending I was erased as long as I could until I knew I could move on my own again.

When I didn't respond, he didn't say anything for a few moments, then suddenly I heard him now trying to talk to Sanchez. "Hey, buddy… you gonna wake up anytime soon?" His voice was followed by what sounded like a few smacks probably to his face. "I don't know how you can get away with this sleeping on the job stuff, but if I were you, I'd wake up before Miller finds out."

After Sanchez didn't respond, either, it wasn't long until I heard Lawson close to me again. It sounded like he rolled the stool over and was sitting next to me, probably staring. I wasn't sure but some part of me could feel it. "Kaleah…" He whispered as he picked my hand up again. "Did you kill the doctor?" Obviously I didn't respond, but I could tell as the sedative wore off more, it was harder to lie there as perfectly still as I had been when they initially entered the room.

"If you did it, I would understand… But then again… the way you asked for him that time after we came to get ya… Nah, I don't think you'd do it." He started talking to me then ended talking to himself. "What the hell happened in here, Kaleah? Sanchez isn't waking up, the doc is dead, you're pretending to be asleep… I just can't figure it out…" I still didn't move after he said it. He was likely bluffing to see if I would wake up, and until I knew if I could trust him, I wasn't planning on it.

He sat there, holding my hand, slowly dragging his finger starting at my palm, down each of my fingers like he was examining them since he was now bored. "I don't know if you can hear me or not," he said, whispering again, "but you don't have to be afraid of me. I'm not like the other men. I'm gonna help you out of here."

It wasn't long before I heard the door open and close again. "Either of them wake up yet?" It sounded like it was the first agent.

"Nah, man… I think Sanchez got the serum too… That's the only explanation I can think of for why he's still out like she is. Like maybe him and the doc got in a fight and he gave him the serum too, I don't know…"

"All right, well, I went up and told Miller. He's pissed now 'cause he doesn't know where to get another doctor to make more serum for him, but whatever… He wants her up there as soon as we can get her up and walking."

"Ah, I don't know when that's gonna be. She's still pretty out. I mean I've been sittin' here playing with her hand for like the last fifteen minutes and she's not even twitched." Lawson did actually sound like he might be on my side, because I doubt I was that good at playing dead.

"I don't care, smack her… Do what you gotta do to get her to wake up."

I didn't hear Lawson respond, so I assumed he shook his head or something but it wasn't long after that when I felt his hand gently rest on my thigh.

"What's her name again?" Lawson asked finally.

"I don't know... Miller calls her Princess so just call her Gypsyin, I guess."

"Okay... Gypsyin! Wake up..." Lawson said it loudly as he rubbed his warm hand briskly up and down my thigh, then lightly patted it a few times. "Gypsyin... Come on, Gypsyin..."

I tried to wiggle my toes inside my shoe to see how much movement they had. When I felt them move exactly as I had wanted, I tried to slightly adjust my hips next. I hoped it would be a movement the agents wouldn't detect but at the same time, if I was able to move more of my core, it was a good sign that I could move my entire body again and I needed to know what abilities were again under my control.

"You're being too gentle with her, here take her and really shake her." Suddenly, two hands strongly grasped both my shoulders and gave me a good shake just as he'd said I needed. I couldn't keep my eyes closed with that any longer so I opened them finally like I was just awakened from a deep sleep and confused by who he was and where I was.

"There... see? That's all she needed." The agent said as he leaned back, looking at me, proud of himself.

I looked over at Lawson but still didn't say anything. Even if he was on my side, I didn't intend to let him know I wasn't erased just yet. That was all I had at this point and I wasn't about to expose the truth, just for it to be used against me.

"Ka... Gypsyin... Hey..." Lawson said, clearly new to this side of the erasing game and not sure how to address a brand new awake-ee.

I broke eye contact with him and looked around the room for a moment like I would if I had just been erased, then looked back at him. "Where am I?" I asked, making my voice sound shaky and nervous.

"Uh..." Lawson quickly looked at the other agent, unsure what to say.

"You're home... Now get your ass up and I'll go take you to meet your new daddy." I looked at him like I was confused, but also like I thought he was an idiot. I wanted to do more than that when I heard what he said, though. I wanted to stand my ass up and beat his down but I reminded myself that that wasn't my plan.

"Come on, Stevens… that's not called for. Give her a second. Let her adjust, all right?" Lawson quickly spoke up, not agreeing with the other agent's tactics.

"Well, Miller acted like he was in a hurry, so—"

"Dude, Miller's always in a hurry!" Lawson interrupted him. "Just relax. Waiting five more minutes ain't gonna kill him." Then Lawson looked back at me. "How are you feeling? You all right?" He asked, genuinely concerned.

I nodded my head slowly. "I don't remember anything, though," I said softly, keeping up the act.

"Hmm… yeah…" He said, nodding back. "That happens…" Then he let his eyes trail away from mine to think—like he believed me.

"See, she said she was good now, so let's go." Stevens said, trying to get Lawson to follow along. But I was suspicious that Lawson's hesitance was more stalling than it was anything else.

"All right," Lawson said finally. "I'll take her up to Miller. I haven't seen him yet today. You can stay down here with Sanchez. He'll probably wake up soon and need some guidance on where he is now, too."

"Nah, I know she looks like she's been erased but I still don't trust her, Lawson. She's a feisty one. You should have seen her when we picked her up. If she's just acting, she'll kill you before you make it to the second floor."

"What?" I said, acting like all that was new information to me.

"I'll cuff her then, she don't look that dangerous." Lawson said, still trying to convince Stevens that he could handle me by himself.

"No, dude… I'm gonna help you take her up there. I told Miller I would. When we get her there, then we can both come back for him." Stevens said, pointing at Sanchez.

Lawson shrugged, knowing he wasn't going to win the argument then took a hold of my arm to gently help me stand up out of the chair. "Here, can you walk yet?" He asked.

"I don't know… What do you mean I'm feisty and you picked me up… Where was I?" I said continuing to ask questions only a freshly erased Eva would ask.

"Ugh, this is the most irritating part with all these erased Gypsyins. All the stupid questions, constantly." Stevens acted irritated with me.

"Okay, well here. Stand up for me." Lawson didn't say anything in response to him, he just continued to talk to me. I did my best to walk unsteadily to keep up the ruse, but I was pretty sure I had full function back in all my limbs. At least I had that working for me.

The whole charade continued as both men escorted me slowly up the stairs and back into Miller's office. I wasn't nearly as concerned with being there again, especially this time since he suspected I was erased and I knew I wasn't. I wasn't sure where Jake fit into my plan but I was considering just going ahead and killing Miller while I had the chance and then going to find Jake when I was done. If I didn't get stopped by any of his men in the process, that is. I knew that was a risk, but at this point it was one I was not only willing to take but almost forced into.

"Bring her to me." Miller said nonchalantly after the men opened the door and pushed me into the room. "Did you kill my new doctor, Princess?" Miller asked still not looking at me as I walked closer to his desk. The way he mumbled it sounded like he was chewing food.

"Uh… I don't… uh…" I acted shy and bashful like I didn't know what to say and was slightly afraid of him.

"Agh… I'm sure you did." He said as he finally looked up from the paperwork he had been looking through on his desk. "You know how irritating that is? Do you know how hard it is to find a doctor around here anymore?" He paused to wait for my response then quickly went on without it. "I just finished having him trained to make more serum too, dammit. It's not every day my cats drag perfectly good mice in for me, and now you had to go and kill him…" He stopped and looked at me with an irritated expression.

"I don't… I don't remember. I don't think I—"

"Just shut up and get over here." He said, interrupting me then waving me toward him. "Sit down right here by my feet." He said as he pointed to a spot on the floor next to his desk. The same spot I remember where I used to sit in a cage. I looked at the spot, blinking a few times blankly, trying not to let the memories bring about a rage that would break my cover. Then I did as he said and walked over and sat down.

"Lawson, get her cuffs off her. She doesn't need those anymore. She's good and helpless now." Miller said, looking down at me before addressing Stevens. "You and Benton go down and retrieve Miles… What I plan on doing with her next is gonna be fun, and I want him to watch."

Initially, I felt a little terrified by what he said but then I thought about the bright side. This way, after I killed him, he was saving me the trouble of having to go and find Jake myself.

As Stevens and Benton left the room, Lawson bent down next to me and took the cuffs off just as he'd been instructed. He then looked me in the eye with a look like it was my last chance to show him I wasn't erased. I almost took it, thinking he would know if I just winked at him, but then I remembered how Turner had betrayed us, so I stopped myself.

I sat there for what felt like forever, though probably only a few minutes, waiting for them to bring Jake in. I considered standing up and attempting to strangle Miller where he sat but as I looked around the room at the other agents; I realized I wasn't likely going to get far. I needed to wait until the most opportune time. That would be the only way I was getting out of this without Jake or myself getting hurt. Not including Miller and Lawson there were two other agents in the room, neither of which I recognized.

It wasn't long before I heard a commotion in the hall and knew it was probably the men returning with Jake. They all stumbled into the room in a roar with Jake lunging about, trying to fight them to get free from both them and his restraints. At the same time, he was cussing and yelling at them both—until he saw me. Then he almost immediately stilled.

"Eva?" He said, hoping I would look at him with recognition. I wanted to, but I knew better so I just looked over at Miller like I didn't understand who this man was and why he'd be brought in. "Eva… It's me, baby… Oh god, Eva…" He sounded more and more distraught with every second I wouldn't give him some sign that I was still in there. "Miller, I swear you're a dead man. I'm gonna kill you!"

"Silence him," Miller yelled out to the men. Then, before Jake was able to say any more Stevens stuck a knee into Jake's thigh, forcing him to wince and sit down in a chair that sat between the two agents. "Miles, maybe you don't remember but I recall warning you what would happen if you were lying to me."

"You already erased her, man… please just stop…" Jake said it like he was begging because he probably knew that was the only power he had left. I think we both knew Miller wasn't the type to see logically though, so it was more or less futile.

"Lawson, take her to my bedroom." Miller said with a gross grin on his face while he continued to stare at Jake. I think the more Jake acted like he cared the more pleasure Miller felt taunting him.

"You son of a—" Jake started to yell as he tried to lunge forward with both of the men quickly stopping him.

"Oh, Miles… don't worry. You're invited to the show… Why… you even get a front-row seat." Miller said, smirking again like he had grandiose plans. Too bad he wouldn't get to follow through with them though, since I wasn't as erased and docile as he thought I was.

Lawson hesitantly walked back over to me and reached down to help me up. "Let's go." He said, sounding hard like the other agents that were aligned with Miller. I rose to my feet and looked over at Jake. He looked at me now with an expression on his face that I wasn't sure I had ever seen him make before. He looked like a man that was past torment. He looked broken and whipped but at the same time there was a wildness in his eyes like he was ready to dive into death to take back what he knew to be his if the opportunity presented itself.

Lawson walked me past him out into the hall and across to where Miller's room was. He opened a large wooden door into a dimly lit room with not much more than a large bed and a small chair across from it. If I hadn't known any better, I would have suspected he had done to other people what he was now planning on doing to me and Jake.

"Kaleah…" Lawson whispered, "I can't fight them all… I wanna help you but you gotta work with me. Can you fight?"

I wasn't sure if he was being genuine or if he was throwing bait out again to see if I would bite. Then, if I did, he could go back and tell Miller that he knew I wasn't actually erased. If that happened, I could kiss my aspirations of escape goodbye.

"I don't know…" I said, trying to sound like I would if I wasn't Eva.

"Ah shit… ugh… okay…" He said as he set me down on the bed and looked back toward the door.

"What are you gonna do? How can I help?" I figured maybe if I was the one asking the questions I could see just how genuine he was.

"I don't know…" He said quickly still looking at the door like he was thinking while waiting to see it open, when suddenly it did just as we were both expecting it to.

Miller walked in still with a large smirk smeared across his face, likely excited by what he thought he was getting ready to do. "Lie down, Princess." He said as he slowly meandered closer to us then looked back to watch for Jake to be brought in.

I looked up at Lawson who looked back at me but didn't seem to have a good look about him. The way his face read was almost like he was thinking, 'well, shit… you're screwed now… sorry about ya.' It wasn't long before I heard Jake being dragged across the hall by the two agents that were on both sides of him. He was still kicking and fighting the best he could but I could tell he was getting worn out and likely not ready to endure what he thought he was about to endure.

"Sit him in the chair, boys." Miller said, instructing the agents. Lawson hadn't moved away from me yet. I think he probably was on our side and still trying to think of a way out, just as Jake and I both were.

They did as Miller said and sat Jake down, each with a hand on one of his shoulders so he would stay sitting. "Miller!" Jake yelled, trying to get his attention but at this point he was already walking closer to me and Lawson, eyeing me, probably thinking about what exactly he wanted to do.

"I told you to lie down, Princess… You'll learn to listen to me when I tell you something. Now do it!" He said, ignoring everything Jake was screaming at him. I looked back at Lawson who no longer appeared to want to be a part of helping me and moved away from the bed suddenly. I wanted to reach for his gun so then I would have something to kill Miller with but I knew I couldn't. It would reveal my cards too soon. I would just have to try to kill him with my bare hands like I did Kyle at the inn.

I scooted backward toward the middle of the bed and leaned back on my elbows, pretending to comply.

"Stop it! Don't you freakin' touch her!" Jake continued to scream whatever he could. I don't know if he realized everything he was screaming was just fueling Miller's insanity, but he probably didn't feel like he had a choice. I know I would do the same thing if I saw Jake lying helplessly waiting for that savage to do only God knows what to him.

"Lawson, go help the boys restrain him." Miller said calmly while he looked down at me with a sickening evil in his eyes.

I watched as Lawson quickly moved over toward them. Miller put one knee on the bed, then another. As I watched him get closer to me, all I could think about was how I was going to kill him, and how I preferred for it to be before he touched me with his evil, disgusting little hands, not after.

20
A RECKONING

It was almost as if time slowed down while I watched as Miller crawled over toward me. Maybe it was the speed at which my brain was firing or maybe it was something else but it felt like I had a thousand things I was thinking all at once. Did I want to kill him instantly so then I knew for sure that we would be free again? Or did I want to kill him slowly so he could suffer like me and probably so many others he'd hurt? The only problem with doing it slowly though was if one of his men wanted to, they could stop me. That's the last thing I wanted.

It wasn't long before I decided. I tried to map it out in my head so that way I would get it right. I would wait until he was over me, that's when I would grab him, right where it would hurt him most. As an added bonus, his men weren't likely to come check on him when he screamed either, so I could take my time to make sure it really hurt. Then, when I was confident that I had inflicted enough pain to satisfy myself, I would finish him off with a jab in the throat, hopefully breaking his larynx so he could slowly suffocate to death. It would be quick but still painful enough that I'd be satisfied.

I watched as he slowly moved closer and brought his legs over to straddle me. His grin disgusted me. His mustache disgusted me.

Everything about him was revolting. The idea that I was about to avenge myself was the only exhilarating thing I was feeling in that moment. It was short-lived, however, when suddenly from across the room I heard what sounded like more than just Jake making a commotion.

Miller must have noticed it as well, because he took his eyes away from me to turn and see what was going on. Whatever was happening, I couldn't see it myself but I knew I'd lost my chance of inflicting unbelievable pain onto him and now I just needed to work the last of my plan and kill him before it was no longer an option.

I reached down with my left hand to his crotch to grab whatever I could find through his pants. Thankfully, I found exactly what I was looking for and I dug my fingers in as deeply as I could and twisted. It worked. He swung his head around as he started to grimace and wince, wanting to scream but unable to catch his breath to do it. He tried to pull my hand off of him and at the same time lean back to get away from me so when I shot my fist up to punch his throat; he wasn't lined up exactly where I'd pictured and I missed.

He rolled to the side, off of me, about to fall onto the floor but he stopped short, still on the bed. When he moved, I got a brief idea of what the commotion was when I saw what looked like Lawson and Jake both fighting with the other agents in the room. I knew I wouldn't have much time until one of the sides overtook the other so I needed to complete what I intended to do then go help Jake get free.

I quickly sat up and threw my leg over Miller to straddle him this time as I leaned down and put my hands around his throat. It wasn't the quickest way to take him out, but I hoped it would be the most satisfying.

"Call me Princess again, you stupid bastard!" I yelled at him and dug my nails into his neck to help keep my grip in place while watching him struggle to try to break my hands free with no luck. I could tell he was still weakened from the intense pain I had inflicted when I grabbed his crotch or he might have had a bit more strength to fight me off.

"It's Eva, you li'l prick! My name's Eva!" I yelled at him again as he continued to gurgle and choke, gasping for breath. His face was changing colors. Surely it wouldn't be long before he would lose consciousness.

He was trying to wiggle his way close enough to the edge of the bed to fall off and dislodge me from his throat but I wasn't about to let that happen, so I braced one leg against the wall to keep him from being able to move us any closer to the edge of the bed. Then suddenly, I felt a hand pulling at my shoulder, pulling me off of him.

"No!" I yelled at whoever thought it was a good idea to stop me from my mission to rid the earth of that scum.

I shook off the hand and re-positioned my grip on Miller. As I continued to apply forced pressure to his airway, I turned to see who had been pulling at me. It was a different agent that hadn't been in the room. He was trying to get to me to stop me but at the same time someone else was trying to pull and punch him. "Get off me!" I screamed again, then returned my attention to Miller.

"Eva!" someone called my name. It sounded like it came from Jake but I wasn't really listening to what exactly he was saying. I was too focused on taking Miller's life from him the exact way he had done to me several times.

Then, before I heard anyone else scream anything that I was able to comprehend, I heard a gun go off, then another, followed by a third shot. I quickly looked down to make sure I wasn't the target of any of the shots. I knew my adrenaline surge might mask any feeling I had of getting hit, but I didn't initially see anything concerning so I mentally cleared myself to continue what I was doing.

Miller was struggling less now, but if I had learned anything from Sanchez, it's not over until it's over... and even then continue on longer just in case.

"Kaleah!" someone called my name again, but it didn't sound like Jake this time. Then, as I continued to ignore it, I felt another hand at my back again, pulling me. "Let's go... you're hit!" It sounded like Lawson who was saying it.

I wasn't hit. I couldn't have been hit. I already checked myself and didn't see anything. Plus, I needed to finish killing Miller, so I wasn't really having any of it when I hollered back to him. "Don't touch me, I'm killing him… Let me kill him!"

It wasn't more than a few seconds later a large arm swung around my waist and hoisted me off and away from Miller, tearing loose my deathtrap as whoever it was began to drag me backwards. "No!" I screamed, trying to wiggle free. I didn't know who the hell had a hold of me but I wasn't finished. I needed to finish. He wasn't dead yet. "Let me go… I need to finish!"

"He's dead, Eva… You're shot! I need to get you out of here." It sounded like Jake in a haste.

"He's not dead. You don't know that!" I said, still fighting against him to release me.

"More agents are coming, we have to go!" He grunted, refusing to loosening his grip, as he continued to drag me away from Miller and out of the room.

"I'm not shot… I'm fine! I'll kill them too! Now, let me go!" I yelled as I tried to throw my elbows into him, hoping he'd release me.

He didn't, though. He turned me around to look at him as he shook me by my shoulders, trying to make me snap out of it. "Stop it! Hear me? Stop it, right now! You're shot, dammit! Now, stop fighting me so I can get you out of here!"

At that moment, something snapped inside my mind. He shook me again still speaking, trying to break me out of it so I would agree to go with him but I was past that. I couldn't hear him anymore. All I could do was stand there and stare past him down the hall at where we were. Then, as quickly as my hearing began to fade so did my vision. When I realized what must have been happening, I looked down at myself again. *Maybe he's right… Maybe I did get hit.* The first thing that caught my eye was the blood I had on my right hand. *Where'd that come from?*

"Jake?" I said, looking at my hand, wondering where the blood came from since I still didn't feel any pain.

He continued to speak, wrapping his arm around me again to quickly usher me down the hall toward the stairs, but I didn't know what he was saying; all I could think of was the blood. It all happened so fast it felt like a blur. He was next to me. Then there was Lawson that was walking quickly in front of us, opening every door as fast as he could and holding it as we went through.

"Jake…" I said again, hoping he would stop for a second so I could figure out what was going on.

"When we get her to the car, I can drive." A deep voice spoke up from behind us.

"Good… See anyone else coming?" Jake asked as he turned to look back behind us while he continued to quickly walk with me.

"Not yet, but I know Cruze and Dean were both close. I saw them in the stairway when I was coming up to Miller's office." The voice spoke again. This time I recognized it, it was Andry.

When we reached the steps, Jake stopped to look at me again, likely assessing how capable I was of walking down them. He quickly lifted my shirt then dropped it. I didn't say anything but I could tell by the look in his eyes that he was concerned. Meanwhile, I was still clueless where I was actually hit but figured if it was that bad I'd likely feel it soon.

"Here, Boss… I got her!" Andry said, slipping past us to stand on the stairs below, next to Lawson. He then wrapped one arm around my back and pulled me toward him, reaching under my legs with his other arm to carry me.

The men were all silent as they descended the steps with me. They worked and moved in unison like they could read each other's minds. Jake didn't have to bark orders, and yet they each still knew exactly what he wanted and needed of them.

When we made it to the ground floor, Andry continued to carry me. He moved quickly and silently like a giant ninja, or a stealthy mammoth. "Let's take mine!" Andry said in his low monotone voice as he moved closer to a large black SUV.

"Here… put her in the back." Jake said, opening the door.

I watched as Lawson quickly ran around to the front passenger side and got in, then reached over the seat, ready to help Andry position me in the back seat.

They laid me down just inside and shut the door, then Jake came around and got inside the back with me from the other side. "Lie down, baby!" He said, seeing me try to sit up as he moved in closer. "You move around too much and you'll lose too much blood."

"I…" I started to argue with him since I still wasn't sure that I was actually hit. Then I stopped and looked back down at my chest to check again before I did. "Jake… I don't think I'm hit." I said as I inspected my front all the way down to my legs. Then, before he responded, I saw it finally. The lower corner of my shirt at my back looked saturated with a dark crimson liquid.

The same moment my eyes saw it, my mind decided to finally accept it as well. Almost instantly at that moment, I felt it and let out a loud gasp from the onslaught of pain my nerves had just relayed to my brain.

"Eva, baby, try to hold still, all right?" Jake said again as he leaned over and held his hand against my hip to put pressure on it to slow the bleeding. "Andry, where you takin' us? I got a first aid kit back at my house."

"I don't know if that's a good idea, Boss. I got one at mine too. It'd probably be safer to take her there for right now. He wouldn't expect it."

Are you freakin' serious? "Miller wasn't dead, was he, Jake?" I scowled, looking up at him after hearing what Andry had said.

He slowly nodded at Andry in the rearview mirror, agreeing on where to take me, then he looked back down at me. "Eva… I'm sorry." He said softly, with sincerity in his eyes. "I had to get you out of there, baby."

"You said he was dead!" I yelled out as I tried to sit up again to smack at him. "You lied… You said he was dead. I had him, I freakin' had him! He was—"

Jake grabbed me before I could finish and forced me to lie back down against the seat. "Hold your ass still, do you hear me?" He said, matching my tone. He held me like that for a second until I calmed down. "You're shot, baby…" He followed it with a softer, sounding apologetic. "Please… you have to hold still."

"But you said he was dead," I started to cry, looking up at him. "You said, Jake!"

"I know, baby… I'm sorry… I don't know if he is or not, but I know you would be if you continued to fight." He said it softly again as he began to brush my hair away from my face. "I did what I had to do… and that was get you out of there, all right?" I could see in his face now how hard it was for him. "You're gonna be okay now, all right? We're gonna get to Andry's and get you sewn up… You're gonna be okay now." I think he was saying it more for his peace of mind than mine.

"Okay…" I nodded, trying to relax. Then I moved my head up to rest in his lap.

He looked down at me and smiled a forced smile the best he could, then quickly looked up and out the window, probably trying to stop himself from crying as well.

"We'll be there in about ten minutes, Boss. It's not too much farther." Andry said, trying to reassure him.

Lawson turned and looked at me from between the seats. "You did good, Kaleah!" He said with a faint smile, wanting to encourage me as well. "I really thought you were erased."

I smiled back at him, then looked up at Jake again when I saw a different kind of pain in his expression. "What, baby?" I asked, curious what was wrong.

"You wouldn't look at me… when I came in the room…" It wasn't as much a question as I got the idea he was expressing his pain in that moment.

"I'm sorry…" I said as I tried to lift my hand to touch his face.

He nodded, then quickly took my hand and brought it back to my chest. "It's okay, just hold still… We can talk about it later." He said, then looked down at my stomach. "Andry… We're almost there, right?" He asked as he lifted his hand briefly to look at my side.

"Is it bad?" I winced. I knew that the amount of pain doesn't always match the wound so I really wasn't sure how bad it was exactly. I was in a great deal of pain now though, which said something since I generally had a high pain tolerance.

"No, baby, you'll be fine." Jake said but at the same time from the corner of my eye I saw Lawson nodding his head yes until he quit when he heard Jake respond differently.

"Too bad the doctor's dead, or he could have helped," Lawson said like maybe he was trying to make up for his snafu.

"I didn't kill him... He saved me, you know?" I said, looking at him, so he finally knew what happened.

"What are you talking about?" Jake asked, looking at me, then at Lawson.

"Luca," I said willing to tell them both exactly what happened.

"Luca?" Jake looked up at Lawson, confused.

"Ah, yeah... uh..." Lawson stammered. "Well, you see... When we brought him back to Nashville with us... he, uh... he was pretty vocal about being a doctor and all. And when Miller heard, he didn't want his experience going to waste, you know? So, he kept him around and trained him to make more serum for him."

"What? That's not what I told you guys to do with him!" Jake scolded them.

"Ah, yeah, I know. I'm sorry, really. We obviously didn't intend for it to go down like that either, but... We kinda didn't have a choice when Miller decided to keep him around. He would have figured out we were working with you if we tried to buck him, you know?"

Jake nodded like he understood. "That's fair," he said, then looked down at me. "Eva? Are you all right?" He asked now sounding different.

I lay there for a second and thought about what he was asking and how I felt when I realized why he was probably concerned. "Yeah, baby... I'm fine." I said softly, trying to help him feel better, but I knew I was feeling more faint the longer it took to get to where we were going.

"Andry, do you got any water in here?" Jake asked as he looked around under his feet and back toward the seats behind us.

"Uh... nah, Boss, I don't believe so." Andry said still focusing on trying to drive as safely and quickly as he could.

"Kaleah?" Lawson said, continuing to stare at me. "You're looking really pale. You sure you're feeling all right?"

I smiled not knowing how else to help them feel calm. "I'm always pale. Ask him." I said, looking back up at Jake who was now looking a bit pale himself.

He tried to smile back without much luck as he continued to stroke my hair. "Yep… yep… You're all right… She's gonna be all right." He said, looking up at Lawson who looked like he didn't believe him but nodded anyway then slowly turned back around.

"We'll be there in two minutes, Boss!" Andry said with an update, probably trying to help Jake feel better.

"Jake…" I said, trying to get his attention again.

"What, baby?" He asked softly as he looked down at me, then again to my side.

"Look at me, Jake…"

He brought his eyes back to mine with a forced smile, trying his best to not look concerned.

"I love you…" I whispered, feeling more faint.

"Andry, hurry!"

"Eva, baby?"

"Eva?… I love you too, baby!"

21

LOOSE LIPS SINK SHIPS

I heard voices intermittently as I faded in and out of consciousness. It felt like I was being carried by Andry again, but I didn't want to open my eyes so I wasn't certain that it wasn't actually Jake until I heard him speak.

"Where are we going, Andry... in here? Where's a good place for you to lay her?"

"Go to the right." I felt the reverberations from Andry's low voice deep in my chest, making it clear he was carrying me, not Jake. "Just push everything off the table. I'll lay her there, then I'll go get my kit."

"Eva, can you hear me, baby? I'm gonna sew you up now, okay?" I woke up again to Jake's voice talking to me. This time I tried to open my eyes to look at him but still didn't feel like it so I just raised my hand and swatted against the air, giving him the all clear.

"All right... good. Try to lie still for me." I felt the hand resting on my thigh, lift and reposition to my hip.

"Andry, you got any alcohol just in case the pain gets to be too much for her?"

"Ah yeah... Lawson, you wanna go grab it? I got a bottle of whiskey right there in the kitchen to the left of the sink."

"Sure, I'll get her some water too..."

I wanted to open my eyes and look at what all was going on but I knew that's probably why I kept passing out. The idea that I was hit and bleeding was harder for me to handle than probably the wound itself.

"Jake?" I said finally once I had a moment to collect myself before he got started.

"Yeah, baby?" He asked, then went on like he thought he knew what I was inquiring about. "It's okay, I'll let you have some whiskey… If you need it, that's fine. Do you want me to wait?" I felt his hand at my back, probably only a few seconds from beginning.

"What happened?" I asked, not sure how to preface the question.

"Uh… you got shot, baby…" He answered, sounding unsure what I was actually asking about as well.

"Here, Miles…" Lawson said as he got closer.

"I know," I said, responding to what Jake had said. "Is the bullet still in me?" I wanted to know, but I didn't all at the same time, because I was afraid it would make me pass out again if I thought about it too hard.

"No, baby… thank God! Now that I've had a chance to look at it better, it's a clean shot, just a deep graze… So once I get you sewn up you should be all right. You're still bleeding pretty bad, but that's all…"

"Oh… okay." That made sense I thought. "So, I'm not gonna die?" It didn't feel like it was that dire but the way all the men were acting was like it was, so I wanted to make sure.

"Here, open your eyes, baby… Take a drink so I can get started." I felt the hand at my hip move, then an arm was placed under my neck as I opened my eyes to see him standing over me.

"You didn't answer my question." I said as I reached to take the whiskey bottle from Lawson who was standing on the other side of me.

Jake didn't respond at first he just looked at me oddly then Lawson interjected. "Nah… nah, Kaleah… You're not gonna die… you'll be fine. It's just a scratch." He said with a fake smile.

I felt confused. Nothing they were saying was adding up. I lifted the whiskey bottle and took a few large swigs then handed it back to Lawson.

"Is that enough? You think you're good?" Jake asked, still holding me up.

"I don't know," I said as I looked down at Andry who was standing at my feet looking down at my side. I followed the line of where his eyes went to look down at my side as well. The whole bottom half of my shirt on that side was saturated with blood and there was a decent sized pool of it I was laying in, as well.

"Don't look at that, baby. Here, just lay back down." Jake said as he let me down to rest my head against the table again.

I felt a sudden cold chill start at my neck and slowly crawl down my arms. "That doesn't look like a scratch, Lawson." I said, feeling like I was about to pass out again soon.

"Here, I need you to roll over to your side again, baby." I felt Jake lift my hip and push me to roll onto my side so he could get to my wound better. "Tell me if it gets to be too much, okay?"

"Uh, Boss... I think she's..."

I woke up suddenly to a stabbing pain in my back. "Miles!" I yelled out. For a second, I didn't know where I was or what was going on.

"Hey, sweetie... welcome back." I turned my head to see Lawson standing in front of me. I looked down at what I thought was Lawson holding onto my hand tightly, until I realized I was the one clinching my fist around his, not the other way around.

"Lawson?" I asked.

"Yeah, Kaleah... What do you need?"

"Why are you helping me?" I craned my neck to look at his face but I couldn't hold it long before the effort became too much and I had to relax back against the table.

"Uh... because..." He said, confused. "You're Miles' girlfriend. Why wouldn't I?"

"Because," I said softly, thinking he should know. "I'm a Sicari."

As soon as I said it, he suddenly pulled his hand from mine and took a couple of steps back from the table. It was easier to see his face now. He looked surprised and confused. He didn't say anything, but looked up behind me, waiting for Miles to respond.

"Lawson, what are you doing? What's wrong?" Andry asked, likely curious what Lawson's look was about. Then before long, Miles' hand stopped moving like he'd finally caught on to Lawson's demeanor when I heard him address the issue next.

"Lawson? What's wrong? Is Eva all right?" Miles asked as he stood and leaned over me so he could see me better.

"Miles… Uh… Did… Uh, did you hear what she said?" Lawson stammered.

"No, what's wrong?" Miles asked, then looked back down at me, clearly clueless about what Lawson's problem was. "Eva? You all right?"

"She said she's a Sicari…" Lawson spoke louder, wanting to make sure Miles heard him, in case he didn't know.

"Ugh…" Miles nodded at me, then sat back down again to continue his work. "Don't worry about it, Lawson. She's just saying that because she drank the whiskey. She's not a Sicari." He said it so nonchalantly, even I almost believed him.

I looked back over at Lawson's face. He nodded, agreeing to listen to Miles, but was still acting uncertain and a bit skittish about coming back over to me.

"You don't have to be afraid of me." I said, trying to reassure him I wasn't dangerous, or well, not to him anyway.

"But if she's not, why would she say that, Miles?" Lawson asked still keeping his distance.

"Lawson, just leave it alone, man." Andry spoke up now, jumping in on the conversation.

"I'm not trying to make it an issue, I just… I don't get it." Lawson sounded confused.

"I'm a double… kinda… well… not kinda…" I said, trying to clear it up for him until I was beginning to confuse myself. Maybe Miles was right, maybe I just drank too much, I thought. "Miles!" I said loudly so he would hear me and respond.

"What, Ev...a," he asked like he caught something in what I said, but I wasn't sure what. "Baby... I'm almost done. Just try not to talk for a minute, okay? We can talk after I finish."

"What do you mean you're a double? I didn't even know you were an agent..." Lawson said, continuing to talk to me.

"Lawson, man... I told you, just don't listen to anything she says right now, okay?" Miles sounded as if he was beginning to get irritated with the subject.

"I am one." I said, ignoring Miles and continuing on. I figured if Lawson was going to be helping us, he should know the truth.

"Eva! For goodness' sake, could you just stop talking for—" Miles started off sounding more upset but then he stopped suddenly like he figured something out. "Eva?" He said calmly this time.

"What, Miles?" I tried to turn my head to look back at him.

"Give me your hand for a second." He said, reaching up, ready to grab it as soon as I swung it back to him.

"Okay?" I said, thinking maybe he needed me to hold something for him. Then, before I realized what he was doing, he took it and pressed it firmly against my side where my shirt was laying.

"Here, look at that..." He said as he swung my hand back around in front of my face.

"Miles?" I lay there for a second, staring at my bloody hand, wondering what he was doing, when suddenly I wasn't feeling all that well again. I looked up at Lawson, who was now looking back at me, concerned. Then I started to lose control of my eyes as the darkness overtook me again.

"She's fine resting in my bed for right now... I don't know if it's a good idea to stay much longer, though."

"You're right. We need to get her back to New York as soon as possible. That's probably the only place she'll be safe. Why don't you get your vehicle loaded with extra fuel and I'll see what I can find to take that we'll need for the drive there."

"Miles… I'd really like to discuss with you what things she was saying…"

"Lawson, I know you don't understand… It's complicated but I can tell you everything in the car on the way."

"You want me to go with you? I've never even been to New York… Uh, I ah… I mean I can but I ah…"

"You're not safe here anymore now, buddy… I'm sorry. New York is probably the safest place for you for a while too, until we can do something about Miller."

"Miles?" My head felt like it was whirling as I slowly continued to wake up to all the noises and voices around me.

"Hey, baby…" Jake sat on the bed next to me. "How are you feeling?"

"I… um…" I was trying to open my eyes again to look at him but I felt like everything was spinning.

"I got you all cleaned out and sewn up. You should be fine now… I'm gonna go get stuff ready to go. You ready to go back home?"

"Miles…" I said finally getting my eyes to open to look at him. "My tracker?"

He looked over at Lawson who was still standing in the room. "Ugh… Eva…" He said as he turned to look back at me then down as he sighed. "This is why I don't like you drinking alcohol, baby."

Before I got a chance to reply, Lawson did first. "She's being tracked too? By who, the Sicari? Holy shit… what the—"

"Lawson, man… Really, I got it all under control. Everything is fine." Jake said as he stood up from the bed.

"What? You're not concerned they'll come after her? Or us… because we have her?" As upset as he was, Lawson was starting to come to conclusions that were pretty reasonable.

Jake looked at him, then down to the floor as he rested his hands on his thighs, probably thinking of what to say.

"He's right, Miles… They… they won't like… you having me." I didn't intend to fuel Lawson's concern, but it was valid so I thought I'd chime in to agree.

"Eva… please, try not to talk right now…" Jake sounded frustrated. "We need to hurry, and I don't have time for this." He said, looking over at Lawson like he was hoping he'd let it go.

Lawson quickly nodded like he got the idea. "All right, we can talk in the car. What do you need me to do right now?"

Jake looked over at me then hesitated. "Will you just watch her for me? If she needs something, water… whatever, get it for her."

Lawson nodded. "Sure," he said then walked over to sit on the bed by my feet.

"Good… I'll be back in a minute, baby…" Jake stood up quickly, then turned to walk out.

"Do you need anything?" Lawson asked, sounding afraid to talk to me now.

"I'm not gonna hurt you." If that was the case, I hoped to relieve his fear.

"I'm not worried you will." He said, covering for himself then paused like he wanted to ask me something but wasn't sure if he should. "What do you mean when you said you were a double?"

"Miles said I'm shouldn't… I'm not aloud to talk right now…" I said, thinking about how much I'd had to drink and how normal I felt despite what Jake thought. "But… yeah, I'm a double." I smiled, proud of myself. "My dad is Elijah Prescott… I'm a Sicari so I could give my dad intel from them…"

"What?" Lawson's eyes widened as his jaw dropped open. "Elijah Prescott, the First Rank?"

"Uh-huh." I smiled again.

"Are you serious?" He stood up suddenly. "Why didn't Miles mention that?"

"He did… wait no…" I was getting myself confused. I couldn't remember who I'd told and who I hadn't. "Where are you going?"

"He's here—" He stopped what he was saying and looked down at my side. "Kaleah, pull up your shirt." He said, taking a step toward me. "I think you're bleeding again."

"Who's here?" I asked, wondering what he meant as I looked down and pulled my shirt up like he asked. If he answered me, though, I wouldn't have known it because when I saw he was right, my hearing became fuzzy again.

"Lawson?"

"Don't worry... I'll go get Miles." He said quickly, then turned to run out of the room.

I looked down again, even though I knew I shouldn't. "Shit... not on Andry's sheets..."

"Eva, baby..." Jake spoke softly, waking me up as he helped turn me to look at my side.

"Jake... I'm sorry." I said still thinking about Andry's bed and how I felt bad about bleeding all over it.

"For what? You've done nothing wrong, baby. You're fine." He said as he reached over and grabbed my wrist then positioned my palm against my side. "Here, it still looks all right. You just need to keep some pressure on it until—"

Before he could finish, Andry came walking back into the room in a hurry. "I got the fuel loaded, Boss. I'm thinking after we get to a safe area we could find another vehicle to finish the trip, 'cause that thing will chug the gas." He said, looking around, curious why no one else was moving as quickly as him. "What's wrong, Boss?"

"Nothing... She's just bleeding again, but she'll be fine." Jake said like he wanted to believe himself, hoping it really wasn't serious.

"Guys..." Lawson said finally seeing he had a moment to speak to Jake again. "She told me about being a double."

"Lawson!" Jake spun around to look at him while still helping hold pressure on my hand. "I told you we'd discuss it later!"

"I know... but she told me about her father." I could tell Lawson was hesitant to keep going, but he did anyway.

"Eva?" Jake said now turning back to look at me.

"Uh..." I knew he'd asked me to stop talking, and I didn't. I rolled my eyes up and away from him, avoiding eye contact like I didn't know what Lawson was talking about.

"He's here in Nashville!" Lawson pipped up again.

"What?" Jake asked now perking up.

"Yeah… He's not in New York right now. He comes to Nashville at the end of the summer every year for about a month. So if I'm not wrong… he should still be here. We can go—"

"Are you certain?" Jake interrupted him, likely seeing where he was going with it.

"Well, no, but it's—"

"Boss…" Andry interrupted Lawson this time. "Is she really his daughter?" He asked, suddenly having caught on to who they were talking about.

"Yes…" Jake said, as I finally let my eyes connect with his.

"Then Lawson's right… He's here." Andry said, looking relieved.

Jake didn't say anything initially. He just looked at me like he was thinking then looked at Andry. "If we could get to him, would you know how to get there?"

"Yeah, Boss… That's how I know he's here. Last year, I worked at his house. I was the lead agent on guard at the gate."

"Good, then let's go. We're running out of time." Jake quickly stood up. "Can you carry her out to your truck again, Andry?" He asked as he moved over, assuming Andry wouldn't have any issue with the request.

"Sure, Boss," Andry said, stepping forward and looking down at me.

"I'm sorry about the sheets," I said, looking back down at where I'd gotten blood on them.

"You're fine, cupcake, just keep your hand tight on yourself. It'll help the pain." Andry said as he bent down to pick me up.

22

A BROKEN PROMISE

"Here, let me out. I rank the highest so I'll go talk to the guard." Jake said as Andry slowly pulled up to a mansion; probably the previous governor's house.

"I know you're a higher rank, Miles, but if it doesn't go well —" Andry stopped, realizing Jake knew the consequences and didn't need reminded.

"What does he mean, Jake? If what doesn't go well?" I asked, looking over at Jake who was sitting next to me in the back seat.

"We're not allowed to meet with First Ranks without an appointment. We're definitely not allowed to just show up at their house, either." He said, hesitant to get out of the vehicle but still willing.

"Then let me go," I said as I reached for the handle to open the door. I felt much better and capable of walking at that point. "He'll recognize me."

"Eva, no!" Jake shot over across my lap to stop me before I even had a chance to open the door. "You're a Gypsyin, baby. You wouldn't get past the sentries, let alone the gate guard. You can't just waltz up there and expect to have an audience with him, even if he is your dad. I'm sorry."

I felt like I wanted to argue with him but I knew he was probably right. "Oh… okay," I said as I slowly released the handle.

"Don't open it, whatever you do. Hear me?" He said, looking straight at me, warning me.

"Okay?"

"You're obviously not a Coldier agent… You open that door and they see a woman get out, not dressed in uniform… I'm afraid they'd shoot you, baby. So keep it shut. Promise me…"

I was surprised he would ask me to promise but just that he did gave me a better idea of how serious he actually was so I nodded. "Okay… I promise, I won't open it."

"Good!" He said then leaned in and gave me a quick kiss on the forehead before turning to address Andry again. "Andry, I don't know how it'll go down. If it's not how I plan, will you do your best to make sure Eva's safe?"

Hearing him speak like that concerned me. I realized in that moment that I really didn't have a good idea of how things worked in their world and I needed to listen to Jake, even if I didn't feel like it sometimes.

"Of course, Boss." Andry said, looking at him then me in the rear-view mirror.

"I'll make sure she stays in the car, Miles." Lawson spoke up. I really had no idea how he thought he was going to do that though, since I was in the back seat and he was in the front. It didn't matter, though. I made a promise, and I intended to keep it.

"Thanks…" Jake sat back with his hand on the handle and took a deep breath before he quickly opened the door and stepped out.

He got out slowly and raised his hands like he knew multiple men had their guns pointing at him waiting, itching to shoot someone. I watched as he walked across the front of the vehicle and around to the guard shack at the front of the property. Another agent in black stepped out, willing to speak with him.

"What's he saying to them?" I asked, hoping one of the men might have an idea.

"I don't know." Andry answered first with his low monotone voice.

"Probably, don't shoot me... I have the long-lost daughter the First Rank has spent his entire career looking for." Lawson said nonchalantly as he continued to watch along with Andry out the front window.

"He has?" I asked, as I quit watching Jake and looked over at Lawson.

"Uh, yeah!" Lawson said as he briefly turned to look at me then back to watch Jake again.

"So you knew about me?" I was now intrigued. When Jake asked Turner what he knew, he didn't act like he knew much, but Lawson was acting like he knew more.

"Of course!" Lawson said still watching Jake. "As soon as you told me you were his daughter, all the stuff you were saying about being a Sicari all made sense. You're not really a Sicari, they just took you... probably indoctrinated you. So I'm sure that's why you think that. Your father has been searching for you for years."

"Really?" I said softly, staring at him as I spaced out, thinking about what he was saying. "What else do you know about me?" I asked, curious if he knew more than what Jake had already told me about.

"Yeah..." he said quickly, not having to think about it. "Whatever agent brings you back to him, he promised to give them Elite status." He paused, then turned to look at me. "That means whoever brings you in, they get promoted to second rank. So it's kinda a big deal. I can't believe Miles hadn't said anything yet." He turned back to watch Jake after he said it.

"He didn't know..." I said, lifting my hand still pressed against my side to look at it. I could feel it beginning to bleed again.

"It makes sense now. That's probably why Miller called you Princess... I bet he knew who you were."

"And why he wanted me..." I said, thinking out loud. *It was more than just the intel he was after.*

"Why?" Lawson asked like he hadn't connected the dots yet.

"Because he could do whatever he wanted to me, then when he was done he could just erase me, turn me in and become second rank... I guess it'd be a win-win for him." I said, feeling disgusted by the thought. *Being a second rank with the intel would mean… Holy Shit… He'd be unstoppable.*

"Yeah, that sounds accurate." Lawson said still watching Jake. Then I noticed he tensed up like something was wrong.

When I turned to see why, I saw the agent that was previously outside talking to Jake now had Jake laying on the ground and was standing over him. He was holding his gun, pointing it at him while he used his other hand to try to remove his cuffs from his back. I didn't have a chance to think of what I should or shouldn't do, or what I promised I wouldn't do. I did what felt natural and quickly opened my door to jump out and go help him.

As soon as my feet touched the ground, I realized I was breaking my promise when I heard both Andry and Lawson begin to yell at me. At that point, I knew it was too late, and I just needed to proceed with what I intended to do, which was help Jake.

I didn't get far when I felt a large giant's arm wrap around me and Andry's deep voice groan as he attempted to stop me.

"No!" I screamed at him, feeling like I still needed to save Jake from whatever his fate now was, all due to me. "Let me go, Andry!" I tried to wrestle myself away from him with no luck.

Jake and the guard both looked up to see when they heard me. I could tell by Jake's face he was surprised and probably not thrilled. When I hadn't been shot at that point, though, I didn't figure it would hurt to continue what I was doing. It couldn't hurt our position any more than it already had, I didn't guess.

"Jayde, no! Get back in the truck, now!" Jake yelled as he started to push his chest off the pavement to stand up.

"They haven't shot me yet, Andry!" I argued as he pulled me back toward the vehicle to shove me back in.

He didn't say anything, he just folded me like I was paper and made me sit. Then quickly shut the door behind me and stood outside of it.

"What the hell are you thinking?" Lawson didn't waste any time scolding me.

"Jake needs my help!" I said, as I looked at the other back door.

"Oh, no you don't!" Lawson quickly opened his and jumped out to stand outside that one so I couldn't escape.

I sat there for a second thinking about what door I could try to jump through next when I felt my side hurting again. I looked down to see my shirt had a new fresh ring of red higher up than it previously had. I pulled it up to look at my side to see how bad it was again. "Ugh…" It wasn't good. The stitches Jake put in it were now pulled and separated, probably from where Andry had man-handled me. "Andry…" I scooted over to the door he was guarding. "I'm bleeding again!" I yelled, trying to get his attention with no luck.

"Lawson!" I screamed, trying to scoot over to the door he was outside of. "I'm bleeding, Lawson!" He wouldn't turn around either, though. I figured they were probably all pretty upset with me but I didn't care. "Lawson… it's hot in here… I need out!" I tried to say whatever I thought would make him comply. "I'm gonna suffocate!"

"Andry… I'm gonna bleed to death." I yelled, looking over at that door again. Then, when no one would turn I finally leaned over the middle console between the front seats to look at the front doors to see how hard it would be to get out of one of them.

I was about to scream again, hoping they would finally listen since I really didn't feel like climbing over the console but the back door that Andry was guarding opened before I did.

"Andry?" I said, trying to pull myself from between the seats to sit back down.

"Jayde?" It wasn't Andry's voice I heard, or Jake's.

As I leaned back and looked over, it wasn't either man that was standing there looking at me. It was my father. "Jayde?" He said again like he didn't believe he was actually seeing me.

"Dad?" I said softly, not sure I believed that I was seeing him either. Before I got all caught up in the moment though, I realized I didn't know what happened to Jake. "Where's Ja… Miles?"

It looked like he was about to respond when his eyes caught the blood on my shirt and he got sidetracked. "Jayde!" He was instantly concerned. "You're bleeding!"

"I know, Dad… I'm fine." I said, trying to get him to focus again so he would answer me. "Where's Miles?"

He still didn't answer when he turned to look at another man in black standing next to Andry. "Roberts, go call for the doctor. Tell him to meet me in Jayde's room."

"I have a room?" I said, initially shocked, then blinked a few times to snap myself out of it. "Dad!" I said again, trying to get his attention.

"I hear you, Jayde… Settle down… I'm going to take care of you." He was still looking around, probably thinking about what other orders he needed to dish out and to what men.

"No, Dad!" I said more forcefully. "I want Agent Miles!"

He stopped finally and looked at me like he heard then turned to look behind him. "Agent Miles," he said as he took a step to the side.

Behind him stood Jake, patiently waiting to see me. He slowly walked up to the door to look in at me. "Baby?" He said softly. I'm sure he heard me yelling for him, too. Then, before I could answer, he looked down at my shirt like Dad had done and looked concerned just as Dad had been. "You're bleeding more…" He said as he reached in to help me out of the truck.

"Jake…" I said, reaching for him, "It's fine." I didn't know if he would believe me but I hoped so. I felt bad that I didn't listen to him and broke a promise so I didn't want to make him feel worse thinking that I was bleeding badly again too.

"It's not fine, Eva…" He said, helping me out to stand beside the truck.

"Get her inside, men," Dad spoke again from behind Jake. I turned to see multiple men all dressed in black now standing around us.

Jake looked over at Andry who quickly nodded like he could read his mind, then took a few steps toward us between the other agents and reached down to pick me up. "I can walk, Jake." I said, as Andry began to carry me.

"Maybe you can. I don't care. You shouldn't have to. I'd carry you myself if my—" He stopped suddenly, apparently realizing he was about to say something I wouldn't like. "Never mind… Thank you, Andry."

"Jake?" I said, hoping to ask him to continue but my dad began to talk again before I could.

"Fulton, go tell Ms. Mercer to start supper. I'm sure Jayde will need something to eat." He said as he quickly walked in front of Andry to show him the way.

Andry carried me until we made it inside the house, where he slowed down waiting for the men to help direct him. It was grand inside just as it was outside. It almost reminded me of Jake's parents' house, but not quite. It was more grand but less elaborate. I was carried up a large staircase that looked like it had been hand crafted probably over two hundred years ago. Then, when we made it to the second floor, Dad and a few other agents helped guide us to a large room near the center of the house.

As we entered what they considered my room, we were greeted by an elaborate bed adorned by multiple large stuffed animals. The room was painted a pale pink with white lush curtains and a bright pink plush bed spread. It looked like it was designed for a princess—a five-year-old princess—but a princess, nonetheless.

"Lay her down please, Andy." Dad spoke to Andry like he didn't recognize him. Which, with his height and build made me curious, since he was hard to miss.

Andry did what he asked and laid me down, then backed away to the corner of the room where Lawson and Jake were now standing with the other couple of agents that had come in with us.

"I have a doctor coming to take care of you." Dad said as he looked down at me, smiling, happy to see me, then he turned to sit on the bed to talk to me.

I looked around the room in awe, then back at him. "This is my room?" I asked curious why I had my own when I had left before he ever became First Rank or even owned the house.

"Yes…" He said. I'm sure he had so many things he wanted to say but instead he was just happy to sit there and stare at me.

"Are Ellie and Mom here?" I asked, wondering when I would get to see them.

He looked at me a bit confused then away and down. "Um… no.

Ellie is still in New York. And as for your mother..." He sighed, his face suddenly full of pain. "She passed away two years ago in June. I'm sorry, sweetie..." I could tell it was hard for him to tell me.

"What? How?" I didn't understand. It was hard for me to hear. All I could think of was the five years that I could have had with her that I didn't get because I left.

"The Sicari... they—" He stopped and looked down again like he wanted to tell me but couldn't bring himself to do it.

"No... Never mind... I don't wanna know!" I said suddenly hoping he would stop. I'd heard enough.

"Jayde..." he said as if he wanted to address something that was bothering him.

I was about to say, 'what' when an agent walked into the room with a man dressed in gray. They stopped just inside the door and waited like they needed to be addressed before they could proceed any farther.

When Dad saw me looking at something past him, he quickly turned to see, then raised his arm to wave them to come closer.

"Can I have Ja... Agent Miles? I don't like doctors." I asked, realizing that was probably the reason he was still standing to the side as well. He needed waved over like they did.

"Of course..." Dad said, turning around to address all the agents that had come in with us. "Agent Miles," he said, waving him over. When Jake got close enough to hear Dad without raising his voice, he asked Jake to relieve the other agents, then he could come back.

"Thank you," I said, looking at Dad, then back down to my side when I saw the doctor pulling his tools out of his bag at the end of the bed.

"Jayde? What do you remember?" Dad asked while I was still inspecting my side, hoping it really wasn't as bad as I thought it could have been in the truck.

"Not everything, but a lot," I said, without thinking about what that meant to him. I looked up to see how he took it when I saw Jake behind him now walking toward us. "Jake..." I said, hoping he would come around to the other side of the bed and sit next to me. He didn't, though. He stopped at my feet and stood next to the doctor.

"Oh, please…" Dad said, turning to address the doctor. "Take a look at her. Do what you need to do." Then he stood up and took a step back.

The doctor leaned over and pulled my shirt up a little then looked at me before lowering it to walk back to his bag.

"So you did know who I was then when you saw me in New York, at the wedding…" Dad asked, narrowing his eyes on me, probably thinking I had lied to him.

"No," I said initially, then thought back to the way this kind of conversation always went as a child and how he had a hard time believing me. "I really didn't remember you then. I'd been erased with the Sicari's serum… but it's not long lasting like the Coldier's serum is." I said, hoping it would clear it up before he got any of the wrong ideas.

The doctor, seeing we were in another discussion, had walked around to the other side of the bed without me realizing it and crawled across it to get closer to me.

"So you remember me telling you never to come back to Nashville, then?" Dad asked, still sounding upset since here I was, in Nashville.

"I do, but—"

He interrupted me to speak to Jake before I got a chance to explain why I didn't listen to him. "Then why is she back in Nashville, Agent Miles? And why the hell is she bleeding like she's been shot? When I talked to you in New York, you said you would take care of her. This doesn't look like she's taken care of." Dad almost growled, saying he was upset was an understatement.

"Yes, Sir. I understand. I apologize, Sir." Jake nodded, willing to accept all the blame.

"Dad, it's not his fault." I said, trying to defend him then suddenly felt a large stabbing pain in my side, diverting my attention. "Owe!" When I looked down, I saw the doctor beginning to sew me up again.

"Jayde, he had a responsibility to take care of you. And he—"

"I know," I said, interrupting him. "But you're wrong! He did take care of me. Miller is the one who abducted me and brought me back here. He's the reason I got shot. Jake saved me."

"Miller is the very reason I told you never to return to Nashville, Jayde!" Dad acted like he knew something I didn't, when suddenly I realized if Miller was still alive he now had the intel.

"He has the intel…" I said, looking up at Jake, knowing he would understand why it was a problem.

Jake nodded, knowing exactly what I was saying, then looked back at Dad. "Sir, if you don't mind. I need to speak with you… without…" he looked over at the doctor. "In private… Agent to Agent."

Dad looked at the doctor, having gotten the idea. "Of course, follow me." He said, then turned to walk out of the room.

"I'll be right back, baby," Jake said quickly, then turned to follow him.

23

TRUTH BE TOLD

I felt another stick in my side as the doctor continued to sew me up. All I could think about was how nice it would be to have more whiskey and how anxious I felt being with a doctor again, alone. I didn't want to look down to watch since I didn't feel like passing out again so I just leaned my head back against my pillow, closed my eyes, and hoped it would be over soon. Before long, despite what he was doing to my side, I began to feel extremely relaxed.

"Elliceva?" the doctor whispered. He must have felt comfortable talking to me now, since there was no one else left in the room with us.

"Yes?" I said still keeping my eyes shut. I had begun to feel a little woozy too, even with them closed, so I didn't want to open them to speak with him.

"Where's Rennigan?" He asked quietly. He sounded so polite, like a true gentleman.

Rennigan? Oh, right… that's Reagan's exfil name… I sat there and thought about it. "He's dead." I said, remembering what had happened to him. "I didn't kill him, though. Miller killed him. I didn't want him to die. I needed him. He was going to help me."

"Okay… Do the Coldiers have the intel now?" The way he asked was still so calm. I didn't know if it was the sound of his voice or his demeanor when he asked but he made me feel relaxed when he spoke.

"Yes," I said, thinking about Miller and what had happened. "I gave it to Miller, but only because he was going to kill Jake. I didn't want to tell him. I didn't intend to tell them."

"I understand." He said, then I felt him move away from me to reach for his bag at my feet. "Tell me the code and I will tell Parker that you didn't kill Reagan."

I couldn't help but think how considerate that was. He didn't have to do that, but here he was trying to help me out. "Okay," I said, trying to sound as appreciative as possible. "It's 5493062978... 4."

"Perfect." He said softly after a moment like he was writing it down. "Is there anything else that you think I should know?"

"Um..." I stopped to think for a second. "I don't think so."

He didn't say anything else. But I could feel him slowly crawl off the bed, when I opened my eyes finally to ask if he was done. "No, no... you should rest." He said quickly, suggesting I close my eyes again.

"Oh... okay." I said, shutting them.

"Miss Prescott?" I opened my eyes to a man in black standing over me with another gentleman beside him that was dressed similarly to the last doctor.

"Yes?" I said curious what they needed.

"I'm sorry it's taken me so long to get here." The second man said suddenly, setting a bag down at my feet. "I traveled as quickly as I could when I heard Mr. Prescott needed my services."

"Oh, it's okay. Don't worry about it." I said, pulling my shirt up a little to look at my side. "The other doctor already sewed me up." I smiled.

"What other doctor?" The man in black asked, looking suspicious that I wasn't telling the truth.

"The nice man that sewed me up... See?" I said, looking down at my side again, trying to turn so they could see that it wasn't bleeding any longer.

"But… Miss Prescott…" The doctor said, sounding sheepish, "I am the only doctor on duty for the Prescott family right now."

"Oh, I didn't know that." I said as I gently relaxed back against my pillow. "Well, he was very nice… and he sewed me up just fine. See?" I started to pull my shirt up again when the man in black quickly turned to walk out.

"Stay here with her. I'll be back." He said anxiously, now in a rush.

The doctor looked back at him unsure he wanted to stand there and be left alone with me, then he finally looked back at me once the agent had left. "Um…" He sounded nervous, probably unsure what to say. "Did the other doctor give you any medicine… alcohol, perhaps? You act like you're feeling quite relaxed."

"No," I said in a bit of a passive tone. "But that would have been nice of him. It's probably for the best, though, because my fiancé, Agent Miles, doesn't like it when I drink. He says that it makes me have a mouth." I paused to think about what I was saying, since it sounded odd. "Well, I mean I already have a mouth but he says it makes me talk too much." I smiled, feeling satisfied with that explanation.

He hadn't had a chance to reply when my dad, Jake and the other agent came back into the room again all in a haste.

"Eva?" Jake said, getting to me first. "Are you hurt? What did he do to you?"

"No," I said, looking down at my side picking up my shirt to show him. "The first doctor was very nice. He sewed me up and I'm not bleeding anymore. See?"

He didn't say anything for a moment. He just looked at me, perplexed by something I said.

"Jayde, he wasn't a doctor. What happened when he was with you? Where did he go?" Dad stepped up to start asking me questions.

"Oh hey, Dad," I said, happy to see him again. "He really was a nice guy. I didn't know he wasn't the doctor. And I'm sorry, I don't know where he went. I had my eyes closed. He told me to just relax. But he sewed me up like a doctor so I think it's gonna be all right." I looked down at my side again. "Wanna see?" I started to lift my shirt when Jake reached over and rested his palm on my hand to suggest I stop.

"Oh, dear…" My dad's eyes quickly darted around the room as he thought about what to do. "Scott," he said finally looking at the man in black that had come in with them. "You and the other men search the grounds. Find the man pretending to be the doctor and bring him to me."

"I'm afraid it's probably too late," Jake said softly, talking to Dad, then sat on the bed next to my thigh and looked down at me. "Eva… What happened when he was here with you?" He asked it slowly like he thought I was confused and it might help me answer him.

"Nothing… he was very nice." I said, then remembered the conversation we had. "Oh, he also asked me a bunch of questions. But he was so nice. I didn't have any problem telling him the truth." I smiled.

"What questions, baby?" Jake asked calmly.

"Well, um…" I was trying to remember them all and not miss anything since Jake wanted to know and I wanted to be as honest as I could be. "He asked me about Reagan and I told him Miller killed him. And he asked me if the Coldiers had the intel, and I said they do now… you know, since I had to tell Miller. And he asked me to tell him the intel, so I gave him the code. And he—"

"Stop!" Jake said suddenly, then turned to look at my dad. "Something's wrong. She's not acting normal. We need to talk to her alone." It sounded like Jake was suggesting my dad send the other men out.

Dad turned to look at them, but didn't need to say anything. They got the idea from his glance apparently, when they both turned to leave.

"Eva, baby," Jake turned back toward me when he saw that they had left the room. "Who do you think the man was? Did he look familiar to you?"

"Oh, I don't know. Most of the time, I had my eyes shut. He didn't give me any alcohol, so don't worry about that. The last doctor asked me if he gave me medicine but I said nope… No alcohol either 'cause you wouldn't like it if he gave me any. He did mention Parker, though. He said he would tell her I didn't kill Reagan if I gave him the code. He was so nice. I really—"

"Eva…" Jake interrupted me. "I don't know who Parker is. Do you think this man was a Sicari?" He asked, then sort of looked over at my dad timidly. Suddenly, I realized Dad didn't know I was a Sicari yet.

"Oh," I looked up at Dad. "I don't know why I am telling you this but I just feel like I should be honest with you. I'm—"

"Eva, stop!" Jake suddenly put his hand up to my mouth. "Just stop talking for a minute." He said softly, afraid of what I was about to say.

"Miles, you already told me about the intel. You should let her tell me whatever it is that she thinks she still needs to tell me. I'd like for my daughter to not have any secrets from me." Dad didn't sound appreciative of Jake stopping me.

Jake nodded his head slowly to agree but I could tell he didn't like it. "Yes, Sir," he said, lowering his hand from my mouth then giving me a look like I should be careful what I said.

With the look I was afraid of saying something and making him mad so I quickly thought of what else I could say instead. "Uh… I… uh… I'm sad mom's dead…" I said the first thing that came to mind that I felt would still be honest.

"Is that it?" Dad asked, confused.

"Uh…" I paused. "And I'm sorry I ran away from you when I was a kid… you know, when I was sixteen. I thought you were a mean dad, but you weren't." I tried to think of other things to say to add on to it since he was suspicious that I had more. "Oh, oh and… I'm sorry I lied to you that one time when I—"

"Jayde, sweetie…" Dad interrupted me suddenly, "I don't even remember all of those things you've done. You don't have to apologize. I've already forgiven you."

"Oh, okay," I smiled, then looked back at Jake who looked happy that I didn't end up saying what I had started to say.

"I don't understand it," Jake said like he was thinking and not able to figure me out. "If he didn't give you any medication, and you didn't drink anything… What would make you act like this?"

"Like what?" I wasn't sure how the way I was acting was confusing him.

"Uh… this… I don't know how to describe it. You're just not the same. Eva, you're never this uh… open… usually. You know?"

I sat there and thought about it for a moment. "Um… maybe since the man knows Parker, he gave me the truth serum that Reagan said she had."

"The what?" Dad acted shocked by what I said.

"Oh… you guys don't have that stuff?" I asked.

"Eva, baby…" Jake interjected. "No… the Coldiers don't have any other serums except the memory erasing one. What else do you know about it?"

I shrugged, "Nothing, just it's supposed to make you tell the truth." I said, trying to be honest. "Oh, oh, wait, I forgot. Reagan also said it was experimental, and they only gave it to one other guy before and he died afterward. So after that they were going to go back in to tweak it again and hope it worked next time. But they really wanted me to give them the intel, so he said Parker was going to use it on me. I convinced him that I didn't know the intel though, so she never did." I smiled after I said it all like I hoped he was proud of me for remembering.

"What are you talking about? Why would you give the intel to the Sicari?" Dad looked even more confused now.

"Oh… 'cause I was one…" I smiled again. "But Jake said I wasn't one anymore when we were in the car 'cause I was really a Coldier since I was your daughter." Jake acted as if he wanted to put his hand over my mouth again but stopped himself. "But I'm sure I was one since I signed up to be one. But Jake said that you said that I wasn't since I was kidnapped. But I don't actually remember if I was kidnapped or if I signed up to be one… I know how to fight and kill people, though."

Dad didn't say anything he just stared at me with widened eyes. I assumed that meant he wanted to hear more, so I went on. "I've killed a bunch of people, Daddy. Oh… and I had a Sicari that I fell in love with… well I thought I was in love with him but I don't know if I was anymore. Anyway, I ended up killing him when I sent the letter to you to come and get me. Miller got that letter first though, and that's when he came and got me instead." I stopped finally when I saw Jake look over at Dad to see if he had heard enough yet.

"I'm sorry… Am I saying too much again?" I asked, looking at Jake.

"No, baby," he smiled softly at me. "He doesn't want secrets, so…" he shrugged. "I guess I'll let you tell him everything."

"Are you mad, Daddy?" I asked, looking back at him. He looked mad.

"You left to become a Sicari?"

"Um… I think so." After I said it, Jake reached over to take a hold of my hand. Maybe he noticed that Dad didn't look happy, so he was trying to be supportive.

"Why would you do that, Jayde? I can't…" he paused like he was stopping himself from blowing up. "I can't believe this… You're a Sicari?"

"Well… um. I was. But I only did it to try to make you happy."

"What? To try to make me happy? Are you serious? That makes no sense, Jayde. Do you have any idea what things you put your mother and I through? The years of grief we dealt with not knowing what had happened to you? Your sister cried herself to sleep every night for ages when you never came home."

"I just wanted to make you proud of me." I said softly. I didn't like that he was upset with me.

"Proud?" The look on his face was the opposite of what I had wanted to see. "That's the last thing I am of you right now." He turned to walk out, then turned back like he was thinking of something else to say.

"No… really, Daddy… I only did it so I could get intel to bring back to you. I wanted to help you… I only did it for you… Please… I'm being honest!" The more I thought about what he said to me the more upset I became, but I held myself back from crying even though it felt like my heart was being shattered.

Jake squeezed my hand a little then stood up. "Sir, if I may?"

The remnants of grief Dad had been carrying all these years were now written all over his face. "No, I can't... I..." Dad shook his head, clearly done talking to me and not willing to listen to Jake, then turned to walk out.

I didn't know what to say when Jake turned back around and looked down at me, trying to assess how I was taking it. "Eva, baby..." He said like he was about to tell me it would be okay, but he didn't. He just stood there and looked at me then suddenly without warning got his stern face on and turned around to follow after Dad.

"Jake... you can't," I said, trying to remind him that he would get in trouble if he tried to talk to Dad without permission.

"I don't care who he is, he's going to listen to you talk before he decides to judge you like this." He said as he briefly turned before he got to the door.

"No, baby... it's not worth it. You could get in trouble." I said loud enough he could hear me.

He paused for a second, probably considering the consequences. "You're worth it!" He said then turned and walked out.

I sat there for a few moments, looking around my room as I waited for him to return. When I got bored, I decided to finally get up and walk around to look at my room. It was pretty. I was still somewhat shocked that I had my own, too. After a while of doing that, I decided to venture off into the hall to see if I could find Jake and make sure he was okay.

I passed multiple agents who did no more than look at me as they watched me wander around. Most acted like they weren't allowed to speak to me but I figured if I really needed something they probably would. I just didn't have enough gumption to push any of them for it yet.

"Kaleah?" I finally heard a familiar voice as I passed through what looked like a large lounging area into a smaller one. "What are you doing down here? Where's Miles?" Lawson turned the corner behind me and caught me before I turned the next one.

"Oh... hi, Lawson," I said, smiling at him. "Jake went to talk to my dad about me being a Sicari, but he—"

"Wha... shhhh," he quickly stepped toward me and grabbed a hold of my arm as he put his other hand over my mouth, pushing me backward against the wall. "Kaleah?" He whispered as he looked around over his shoulder. "You can't say that out loud here..." He looked back down at me, making sure I understood. When I nodded, he slowly released his hand and took a step back. "I'm sorry..." He said again softly like he thought he probably overstepped his place.

"Eva, you in here?" I heard Jake suddenly behind him.

"Oh, Miles..." Lawson said loudly as if spooked as he turned to look at him. "I didn't realize you were there, man. Kaleah was just looking for you."

"Kaleah..." Jake said, tearing his eyes from Lawson to connect with mine. "Come here, baby." He reached out his hand for mine. I reached past Lawson and took a hold of it, then moved over to stand next to Jake.

Jake didn't say anything for a moment, he just wrapped his arm around me, then stood there looking at Lawson, suspicious about something.

Lawson must have noticed Jake's odd behavior as well, because he started acting a bit nervous. "What, Miles? What's wrong?" He asked rather defensively.

Jake shook his head slightly as he looked away and shrugged. "Ah, nothing, man. I'm sorry. I'm just a bit on edge, you know..." He said as he lifted his hand to run it through his hair. "I've hardly slept any the last two days, plus all the shit that went down with Miller, then Eva getting shot... It's just... the last thing I wanna see when I come find her is you shoving her up against the wall with your hand over her mouth."

Lawson started to say something to defend himself when Jake raised his hand to stop him. "Don't worry about it, man... I know why you did it. She can't help what she says right now." Jake said like he understood and he was excusing him. "But don't ever touch her again, hear me?"

Lawson closed his mouth slowly, then nodded.

"Good… Now, if you don't mind, I'm gonna go take my girl to her room. She needs to get cleaned up and we both need some rest after today."

24

LINGERING QUESTIONS

"How long do you think the serum with last?" Jake asked, shutting the door behind us after we got back to my room.

"I don't know… Reagan never said." I said, looking down at my shirt. Now, not only did it have missing buttons, but it had dried blood all over it. I'm sure I looked like a big mess.

"Here, let me help you take it off…" Jake motioned for me to come closer to him as he walked over and sat on the edge of the bed.

"Did your talk with Dad go well?" I asked as I walked over to him and stood between his legs, raising my arms above my head as I leaned forward so he could remove it for me.

"Well enough… You can put your arms down. I'll just slide it down and you can step out of it."

"Oh, okay." I lowered my arms. "What does 'well enough' mean? I want details…" I said, smiling, hoping he didn't feel so tired that we couldn't talk for a bit before he went to sleep.

He continued to talk as he shimmied my shirt past my shoulders and down my torso until it fell to the floor. "When we spoke in New York, I didn't know he was your father. He asked me to take care of you and of course I said I would, because that was already my plan. But when I talked to him here, I think he was still so upset about

219

everything like you being shot and then him not noticing the first guy wasn't even his doctor that he wasn't all that thrilled when I wanted to speak with him again."

"And he was mad that I'm a Sicari..." I frowned.

He nodded, then slowly brought his hands up to my waist to pull me in closer to him. "He was mad about a lot of things... but that's no excuse to walk out on you like that. I learned that the hard way in New York..."

"So..." I was still curious what they talked about.

"I explained everything, since I realized it wouldn't be as easy for you to at the moment. He knows why you did it now. He knows about Marcus and I told him about what Miller did to you... I pretty well gave him a brief synopsis of the last five years of your life. Or, well, what I know about it, anyway. I'm sure when you're feeling better, you can fill him in on the details."

"And he wasn't mad anymore?"

Jake didn't say anything at first he just looked away then pulled me to where he could rest his cheek against my stomach. "He's your dad... whatever he might still be holding onto... he'll forget about it. Especially when you get to talk to him again as the normal Eva... or, I guess, Jayde."

I knew Jake was being honest with me, but to think that dad was still upset didn't really make me feel that much better. "Oh, okay..." I said probably sounding a little disheartened.

"Here, let me take a look at this." Jake leaned back again, moving me to look at my side where I had been sewn up. "I don't know who the guy was, but it looks like he actually did a good job with the stitches."

"I thought so too..." I said, feeling a bit surprised myself. "They look better than yours." I smiled, so he knew I was teasing him.

"Nah..." He stood up. "Can't be... I'm the best at everything." He grinned as he began to walk around to the other side of the bed. "Are you comfortable here?" He asked, pointing at the bed.

"Yeah, why?" There was a little blood on the top covers where

Andry initially laid me down, but I didn't see any problem with the bed otherwise.

"I just wanna make sure you feel safe. Being here with all the other agents around, nothing should happen to you again, that's all. I wanna make sure you know that." He said as he began to remove his shirt and pants, ready to get into bed.

"Oh…" I hadn't actually thought about it. "Well… yeah, I guess I do feel safe." I removed my pants, then pulled the covers on my side back before getting in to lie down. "Did you discuss with Dad how long we have to stay here… or what he plans on doing about Miller?"

"No, I didn't get a chance before he had other business he had to deal with. But I did tell him all about what Miller did to you and what he was going to do to you again… and he knows what the intel is and that Miller has it. After I get some rest, I can see if he will talk to me again."

"There's so much to tell him…" I said as I rolled to my side then realized I shouldn't when a sharp pain went through it, so I rolled back to my back.

"I know, baby… We'll have time…" By the way Jake was responding, it sounded like he was ready to go to sleep.

"Ok… I'll let you go to sleep now." I said, reaching over so he could grab my hand to hold.

"Thanks… first do you mind if I ask you something?" He grabbed my hand and squeezed it a little.

"No, what?"

"So the way that serum works… uh… you gotta tell the truth, right?"

"Yeah," I said curious to where he was going with it.

"Interesting…"

"What… do you think I'm still keeping secrets from you?" I asked, turning my head to look over at him.

"No… well…" He paused for a moment to think about it. "No, I don't actually, but that doesn't mean there still aren't things you might not have told me. I guess it just feels like it would be a waste for you to have the serum and me to not ask you a bunch of questions while you do." He chuckled.

"Oh… okay, I see." I couldn't blame him. It did seem like a once-in-a-lifetime opportunity. "Well, what do you want to know?"

"Hm," He reached up to scratch his jaw. "Okay, first… How do you feel about my mom?"

"Ha!" I couldn't help but laugh. "I hate her." I said, feeling bad since that was how I felt but compelled to tell him the truth, anyway.

"Yeah…" He sighed, "I guess I kinda already knew that… Okay… Uh… Do you really love me?" He smiled, already knowing the answer to that question as well.

"Yes," I smiled back. "You know I do!"

"Okay… just making sure." He said as he reached up to scratch his cheek while he thought of another. "How many men have you been with… willingly?"

"What? Why would you—"

"It doesn't matter, it's just a question, baby…" He interrupted.

"Two…" I said like I was waiting for the next one.

"Oh, ok… So you really didn't do anything with Luca…" He sounded surprised.

"No, I told you I didn't."

"I know… but I thought maybe you were just saying that so I wouldn't feel so bad," he shrugged. Then continued with the next question almost like rapid fire. "What do you really think about Lane?"

I took a long pause to think about that one before I answered. "Um…"

"Why are you hesitating?"

I smiled. "'Cause I know I gotta tell you the truth, but I don't really want to." I said, laughing slightly. My cheeks felt like they were getting hot.

"Really? Is it that bad?" He moved to rest against his elbow, looking at me, now acting more interested than he was before.

"No… It's just…" I tried to hesitate again, but couldn't. "He's really hot, that's all."

"Ooh," Jake laughed loudly. "That's your problem?" He said then laughed again. "I was afraid you were gonna say you didn't like him."

"No, the opposite actually... I like him a lot." I giggled.

"Oh, really?" He said, then nodded silently as he thought about it. "Like *a lot,* like it's a problem? I mean, do I need to keep him away from you?" He grinned.

"No!" I said like that was a ridiculous suggestion.

"Okay, okay... Just making sure."

"I think you're enjoying this too much..." I couldn't help but state the obvious.

"Nah..." he shook his head then quickly proceeded with another question. "When you first met me, what did you really think about me?"

"Why are you asking me that?" I could think of so many other things that I would ask if I was him and that one hadn't made my list.

He shrugged. "I don't know. I guess knowing you can't slant anything you're saying right now to make me feel better is kinda nice..."

"So you think I normally do that?"

"Yeah... I think it's the agent in you. You say what you think I want to hear or you tell me enough of the truth that you're not lying, but leave out details you know I wouldn't like. Now, why don't you quit stalling and answer the question." He grinned again, thinking he'd caught on to what I was doing.

"Well... hmm... I guess I have to think about that one." I paused and looked up at the ceiling. "I thought you were handsome... and... cold, just really cold more than anything else, honestly."

"Cold?" He acted like he didn't know what I was talking about.

"Yeah... did you forget, you made me sleep in a trunk?" I said, looking back over at him, giving him a long eye.

"Ooh yeahhh..." He said like he did actually forget, then he chuckled. "Sorry about that..."

"No, you're not." I smiled like I was playing, but serious all at the same time.

"Yeah, I know." He chuckled again. "I'm not the one who has to tell the truth, though." He grinned, thinking he was funny.

"You look tired... and bruised." I said, changing the subject.

His grin slowly dissipated as his face became serious again. "Yeah... I am... It's all right though, baby. I'll be fine."

"How badly did he hurt you?" I moved myself over toward him then pulled the covers down to get a better look at his chest.

"Not as bad as you..." He said, intentionally being vague.

"I don't believe you... Do you need a doctor? You were gonna tell Andry why you couldn't carry me, then you stopped."

He pulled the cover back over his chest and reached up to turn my face to look at him. "Baby, if I was hurt bad enough for a doctor, I would let you know... Promise!"

"Okay..." I said with a little smile like that was acceptable.

He stared at me for a second without saying anything else, then he leaned in and kissed me. "Eva?" He said as he leaned back against his pillow. "One more question?"

"Okay?"

"Is it Eva or Kaleah that wants to spend the rest of your life with me?" He asked solemnly.

"I don't understand?" I did but not fully and I wanted him to clarify if I was going to have to be honest.

"Kaleah agreed to marry me... I believe the Kaleah in you is who loves me. But when we were at the cabin and then in the caves... well... Eva knew the truth and knew her past with the Sicari and you still didn't tell me who your father was or what you were really doing in Nashville when you got captured by Miller... You were Kaleah in New York and now you're Eva again... I guess what I'm trying to ask is... Do I have all of you or just the part of you that's in control at the moment?"

"So you wanna know if Eva loves you too?"

"Yes... and if Eva agrees to marry me like Kaleah did?"

"What would you say if the answer was no?"

He furrowed his brows, not expecting that. "I don't know." He looked away like he had to think about it but he didn't really want to. "I guess I would understand."

"Jacob?" I said, getting him to look at me again. "You want the truth?"

"Of course I want the truth… I mean… Ugh, I guess I didn't expect to hear something that I wouldn't like but—"

"I love you…" I interrupted him. "I, Jayde Prescott, love you… and I choose to marry you… Every ounce of who I am as Kaleah, Eva, and Jayde wants you and only you for the rest of my life."

A smile slowly crept up his face and brightened his eyes. "So, you will still marry me?"

"Yes, of course I will." I smiled back. "There's just a few things still stopping us, but after we get those out of the way… Yes!"

He didn't say anything, he just put his hand on the back of my head to pull me toward him for another kiss. "Good," He said, finally releasing it. "I was going to ask your dad, but it didn't feel like the right time." He said, then searched my eyes, probably wanting to make sure that didn't bother me.

"I understand. You'll have time later."

He nodded. "We did discuss you getting a Coldier tag though, so when we go back to New York, you don't have to worry about being a Gypsyin anymore or having to deal with any of the papers again." He smiled, apparently thinking I would be excited about that one.

"What? But I am a Gypsyin?" I wasn't sure why but I didn't want a Coldier tag.

He looked at me, confused. "I know you are but you don't have to be anymore… with the tag we can be married."

"What about the Sicari and my tracker?" I sat up to look down at him.

He didn't say anything for a moment like he didn't know how to answer, but was trying to think of a good one.

"And what about the intel? Both sides have it now, Miles! And it's my fault! There's gonna be another battle! A bigger one than we've probably ever seen before." I said, feeling like I was becoming agitated the more I went on.

"Baby... Calm down." He quickly sat up to wrap his arms around me. "I know there's a lot that we still have to figure out... but we can do it together. You're not alone anymore, Eva!"

I didn't respond. I just nodded my head, then laid it against his shoulder.

"We just need to take baby steps... solve one problem at a time..." He said, still trying to make me feel better. "First, we go back to New York. Then we get you a tag and after that we can start planning the wedding... It'll be fun." I could tell he was trying to sound more optimistic so I wouldn't worry about all the other issues at hand. "Lane's in New York. I'm sure he's eager to see you again."

"But your mom is in New York too, and so is Kat..." I couldn't pull myself from still seeing the pessimistic side of things just yet.

"True..." He said, then paused. "And won't they both be surprised when they see me marrying the First Rank's daughter..."

Finally, something he said made me feel a little better. I lifted my head to look at him again.

He smiled, seeing he'd caught my ear. "I thought you might like that. It's gonna be okay, baby... It's all gonna be okay, I promise!"

I nodded my head, then lay back against my pillow. "Okay... you really shouldn't promise things that you can't control but I'll allow it this time."

He smiled really big, happy that I was beginning to see things his way then leaned down to kiss me again. "We can get married... then go looking for houses... then I can get you pregnant again..." He continued in between kisses.

Hearing him talk about the future made me think more about what all it might really involve. "I guess if there is another battle, I can just fight on the Coldier side since I would have a Coldier tag then." I said, thinking out loud.

He stopped kissing my neck and looked up at me. "You're not gonna be fighting anything... from now on..."

I'm sure the look on my face was sheer confusion. "What? But I'm a fighter... that's what I do... Remember you even said it yourself, I'm good at—"

"When you're my wife, you're done fighting, Eva…" He interrupted me. "I don't care if you're amazing at it, you can be the best freakin' fighter in the world—"

"But—" I tried to interrupt him back.

"Eva, no!" His face was as stern as I'd ever seen it. "I can't lose you again. I can't take a chance at you being taken again, or shot again or—" He stopped, probably not wanting to think about any more of the random things that could happen. "Please, baby… you can't."

I realized in that moment even though the Eva in me did love him; he was asking her to pick between him and the only way of life I really knew. "Miles!" I said, trying to get him to stop and listen. "You're asking me to give up everything that I know… everything that I am!"

"No," He said softly, relaxing back against the bed next to me. "You're wrong… Fighting is only one of the things that Eva is good at. But loving is something that Eva and Kaleah and Jayde are all good at." He stopped to look at me deeply in the eyes. "Baby… I'm not asking you to stop being Eva… I'm asking if you'll choose to be Jayde again. You know, the woman that gave up her life to become something bigger for the sake of the person she loved? If you love me like that… I need you to be there for our future children… for me… for our family."

"Well, what about you then? If there's another battle and you fight in it, our kids might not have a father then either." I said, hoping he could see it went both ways.

He took a deep breath as he briefly looked away. "Okay?…" He said, thinking of what he could say.

"If I can't fight, then you can't either!" I said, thinking he wouldn't agree.

"Fine!" He said it quickly like we were making a deal and I couldn't go back on it.

"That's it?" I was surprised.

"That's it! I wanna be there as much for our kids as I want you there for our kids, so I'll agree. If there's another battle, we both stay out of it. Neither of us will fight for either side… Deal?" I could tell he was talking to the Eva in me when he asked.

"Okay…" I said a little reluctantly.

"Make me a promise." he rested his head against my pillow next to mine with his lips close enough to almost kiss my cheek.

"I promise," I said, knowing what it meant and knowing I'd have to stick to it.

He reached up to turn my head to look at him. "Thank you…" He said softly as he pushed my hair away from my face then kissed me. "Go to sleep now, baby… I'll be right here when you wake up."

Jake and Kaleah's love story continues with book five of the ERASEHER series - Seizing Shattered Promises. CLICK HERE to download now.

A note from Sara...

"The main thing I want my readers to get from my books is that no matter how broken and flawed you are, you are still worthy of unconditional love and no matter how weak you feel, there is still strength inside you." - Sara Nichol Quincy

ABOUT THE AUTHOR

 SARA NICHOL QUINCY is a website designer and novelist born and raised in Indiana. She's a mother, wife, and entrepreneur. The ERASEHER Series reflects her passion for writing romances that are sexy, twisty and edgy. Add in a little dystopian suspense and a touch of crazy and you have yourself an epic love story that only she can tell.

To read more of her personal story and see what other books are in the works, you can visit her website at:

SaraNicholQuincy.com

There you can subscribe to get new release updates and exclusive offers!

Plus… only subscribers get:
- Launch date perks (1st week sales get 20% off!)
- Cover reveals before launch date!
- Exclusive Bonus Chapters that aren't available anywhere else!
- FREE books! (When available)

- ARC Reader offers for new book series and
much more…

Got a question or comment about her work? She'd love to hear from you. Reach her anytime at **Sara@SaraNicholQuincy.Com**

Thank you again for taking your time to read Weaving Whispered Secrets. Please consider leaving an honest review. It would help immensely!

facebook.com/saranicholquincy
twitter.com/SaraNQuincy
instagram.com/saranicholquincy
tiktok.com/@saranicholquincy